Genocide, Blood & Tears

Ryan Mathew Schulz

ISBN: 9798362654603

DEDICATION

This book is dedicated to every single person on this planet doing the best that they can and, to those that have died, doing so.

CONTENTS

Foreword   i

1	Numb	1
2	Dale Cornel	5
3	Dark Smog	15
4	Salts	18
5	The Wanderer – Part One	24
6	The Burden of Sight	31
7	The Wanderer – Part Two	38
8	Strings and Sticks	44
9	Dormant	53
10	Dan Segway	58
11	Buried Glory	65
12	Lavender	72
13	St James's Park	81
14	Meeting Melissa	93
15	Coverage	102
16	Boxed-In	108
17	The Mall	115
18	The Charity	122
19	Once Glistening	132
20	Cover of a Magazine	140
21	Red Dirt	153
22	The Empty Glass	161
23	Blank Spots	168
24	Uprising	176
25	Spilt Milk	188
26	The Echoing Whisper	196
27	On to Windsor	201
28	In Thought	209
29	Dead to Me	214
30	Voided Space	219
31	New World	226
32	The Purple Current	233
33	Mimic	236
34	Blackness	240
35	Begin Again	243
36	Whiteness	248

FOREWORD

Here it is. The final piece of the puzzle and restored peace... or is it? Since publishing my first book (*Glitter*), back in 2015, a lot has happened. A scary lot. Some say not nearly as bad as those before us. Some, say worse, while others see everything in forms of perspective and relative thinking. For me, I see a world that repeats patterns. A world just as bad as the days before. Humans entering the earth, then leaving their filth on it. Promises made, promises broken. Lessons learned, lessons unlearned. Mistakes made to be repeated. Cheaters, abusers, criminals, terrorists. Abused folk, terrorised folk and just trying to get by folk. My tribe, queer as folk, trying to get by all while trying to fit in or, make a stand. Pink triangles may no longer be used to identify such folk, but as we grow and learn to embrace ourselves for who we are, our own proudly built identifiers can be used against us. Tattoos, rainbow love heart print on shirts, painted nails and holding hands on the street with our partner/s.

There's been progress, yes. But, there's still so much further to go. It only takes someone starting with the letter P and ending in the letter N, to stare at the colours yellow and blue, for the world to start walking backward again. Scarily, this final book was written when I was put on furlough, over the duration of the United Kingdom's National Lockdown. Cliche, but oh how I was to find, in writing a book which pays sentiment to certain historical events, that history truly does repeat itself. As sadly, I'm sure others too, will find time and time again. Keep on, readers. Keep on fighting the fight. Making a stand. Trying to fit in. Artistically creating political statements to try and reach further afield. Whatever you can or, feel most comfortable to do, just keep on doing it. The world is going to catch fire around us, no doubt. The best you can do, is stay true to *you*.

In the second book to this series (*Glory*), I gave thanks to individuals in my life, that story very much being a tribute to the industries and communities which I'd found myself in, leading up to the COVID-19 pandemic. I thanked my family, partners, friends and colleagues. For this book, as the third and final part to Michael's tale, I'd like to thank each and every individual person, organisation, charity and movement, passed on and dissolved or, still here with us today, that have strove to make the world a better place. For striving to make positive change, so that those to come after have it just a little bit better. Whichever corner of the world. Whatever cause you've been moving forward. Thank you, from the bottom of my heart. I know I speak for many in saying so. Just some heartfelt words, before a rather intense read. Once you close the final chapter of this book, let the story sit with you. Take it as you will, but do give yourself some time to process it. All I'll say is, explosions start somewhere.

Then, as you place these bound pages back up on the shelf - or more likely exit your digital library - think of ways you too can make the world a better place. Despite what shit it has thrown your way. Is it starting to thank people more often? Is it finally making that apology, to someone you never did, that I can guarantee will lift that weight right off your chest? Or, is it addressing a much larger issue? The longer we turn our backs on things or, settle into behaviors that keep us disconnected, the more likely we turn into… what? That's for you to prevent. Be better than your neighbour. Do better for others. For yourself. Why make life harder for one another if it needn't be? If we each keep shining as best we can, the world will be just a little bit brighter for it. One day, just maybe, the sparkle will outshine the dark smog surrounding us. For now, sit back, forget the world we are living and throw yourself into this dismal one. Maybe, once you finish it, there'll be a rainbow waiting outside your window. Although there's a whole lot of bad in this world, there are certainly good things too. Let's keep them coming. We all have a past. We can only step forward… into the future.

Ryan Mathew Schulz

December 2022

1 NUMB

My eyes spring wide open. I lay still for a moment. *Déjà vu.* The ground feels cold beneath me. Practically frozen. I try to move, but my limbs feel numb. I try to think, but it feels as though my brain is numbed too. I lay confused and unknowing. Ahead of me, straight up from where I lay, the sky spans out in front of me. But it holds an unfamiliarity. An emptiness, as if everything had been drained of it. Not a speck of star, nor a patch of cloud to be seen. I hear the splashing of waves close by. Not large waves like the ones back home on the West Australian beaches. But more a slamming of water against solid concrete. A sad sounding slapping of waves in the dead of the night.

I manage to skew my head as I turn my neck ever so slowly to the left. My cheek rubs against the frozen ground beneath me. It feels like some kind of sludgy substance on a hardened surface. My vision's focus goes in and out, accompanied by a nasty headspin. As my vision begins to clear and steady, I regain focus and look down at my side. I make out a darkened bank of dirt saturated with green moss. I seem to be washed up on a bank beside a concrete wall. Surrounding the bank, splashing up against the wall, are the waves I could hear just a moment ago – even still. Again, concrete walls, d*éjà vu*. But still my mind is numbed to any thoughts past this feeling, my thinking currently reserved to focus on getting up from the moss-covered bank on which I find myself lying.

I look at my arm, sprawled out beside me, focusing on my hand at its end, as I try to move my fingertips, but the cold just feels too much. My limbs, arms and fingers are frozen by it. I try to wet my lips with my tongue – also numbed by the cold – hoping to warm them up and call for help. To warm them enough to form the ability of blowing warm air onto my arm, which just may reach down to my fingertips and allow me sensation enough to push myself up. *A pointless thought really*, I think. But I have to try. I manage to ever so slightly caress my lips with my frozen tongue. I close my mouth to try and moisten it. As I start to move my tongue around, I feel it begin to warm. I swallow and try to blow air out onto my lips in-between caressing them with my tongue. Slowly and surely, I start to feel movement back in my lips.

*

After what felt like a genuine hour, I heard a loud scream echo out into the emptied sky. The scream scared me, and seemed to push some kind of natural reflex onto me, up from the bank on which I now sat. Whether the blowing on my arm had actually begun to work its magic or not, I heard the scream and my body shot straight up. My arms felt like dead weight behind me, but I soon felt the blood rush back into my joints, providing the sensation of pins and needles. The scream continued, although it got fainter and fainter, until I heard nothing but the sound of the sad slapping waves again.

I started to roll my shoulders for relief as the feeling in my arms returned. I wiggled my legs, slowly reeled them into my chest, now able to use my arms to cradle into myself – hopefully providing further warmth. As the feeling returned to my limbs, so did an aching pain in my wrists. I lifted my arms up in front of me to find blackened, crusty, bloody, dried wrists. A flash entered my mind. A memory. Dropping down from the top of Tower Bridge, into the bloody River Thames, as my mind fuzzed and faded to blackness. Before that, how I looked ahead as the dark purple sky became overthrown with vibrant greens, blues and pinks. The Northern Lights were growing out towards me in the night sky. The Dark Realm and Underworld among it, spilling out with creatures that flew towards me and out across London. Darkness filling the world. Bursts of fire and blasts of lightning, taking to the multicoloured sky, and an almost dragon like creature which flew by me with a massive gust of force. Flying into the Shard and coming out the other side. The Shard exploding into shards of glass like miniatures of itself. Around it, around us, the world started to burn.

Us. I remembered letting go of someone's hand as I fell. Before my overwhelmed mind began to fuzz. Before I fell into the depths of the bloody River Thames. I'd let go of the hand that slit these very wrists. Looking at my wrists, I giggled to myself for a moment. I remembered standing in the bathroom mirror as a child ready to do just that to *myself.* I remembered how I'd even looked into exactly how one should slit their wrists for success. Success being measured in *death.* My wrists had been slit the wrong way. Across, rather than upwards. I looked at the dark, blackened crusts of blood across them and giggled again. Perhaps the intention was not to kill me. Although, if it was, she was in for a big surprise. The one that slit my wrists. *Lenroc.* I recalled her name. I looked away from my wrists and down to the sad, slapping water, no longer the monstrous waves of blood I remembered falling into, but the water still seemed to hold a deep red tinge to it. *That shit actually happened, didn't it?*

I looked up at the night sky. The sky which had been drained of anything and everything. The unfamiliarity now made sense. The sky I once knew was no more. I'd awoken in a different world to the one in which my wrists had been slit. I looked over to my right and slowly stood in astonishment... For the very Tower Bridge, which my wrists had been slit above, was no more. At least, not as it had been. Half a tower barely stood, while the other half lay obliviated with its iron railing and demolished roofing poking out from the sad waves of the bloody River Thames. The city behind it had been pulverised. No more fire or exploding shards of glass, just a faint smoke rising and evaporating into the emptied sky.

The defeated City of London, Tower Bridge destroyed, the red bloody water and my crusty dried bloody wrists saw a flash of further memories return to me. Some which made my stomach turn and made me feel like ripping out my gut entirely. I didn't know how long I'd been washed up by the Thames. I didn't know where Lenroc and her army of Dark Enabled and demons and creatures of the Underworld had gotten to. But it was clear that they were finished with London. It was clear that Lenroc was on the move. It was clear that I should be on the move too. If the flashes of memories in my head rang true, I too had done some terrible things, and I needed to clear my head.

Of all the grim and horrific things that entered my mind, a rather vivid image stayed ingrained in my head. Among the flashes of memories, four yellow walls lingered.

2 DALE CORNEL

In the small English country town of Lewes, nestled among the green hills east of Sussex, a young girl sat with four yellow walls on her mind. Insistent with mummy and daddy that her walls be yellow. Mummy and daddy refused. To them, a house doesn't need coloured walls. Not if one hoped to re-sell. The thought of painting their daughter's walls yellow, while they nested and played house and home, having to later re-paint to sell, wasn't even a thought that entered their minds. In fact, when it came to their daughter, they felt resistant in any thought that little Dale Cornel might have.

The resistance came from a place deep in her mother's subconscious. Young Dale's father just went along for the ride. The ride, being Dale's mother and his wife, or otherwise have his head bitten off. There were times he felt for his daughter, wanting to cave so badly and let her paint her walls. But the hold his wife had, over both him and little Dale, was strong. Strong, as the day Dale was born, there had been a movement in the air, so to speak. A movement in the air that seemed to Dale's mother to be rather unsettling. A movement which saw darkness come into the world. A movement that would change the world to come. And Dale's mother was not the only person that felt the movement that day. Members from different walks of life, which would later unite to make up a formation, called *The Collective*, felt it too.

5

A woman reading her book in a Manhattan coffee shop, with the gift of sight, saw her pages burn and turn to black. She dropped the book and clenched her chest while people rushed to her aide. A young man on his daily jog, through a small Polish town's square called Myslenice, collapsed. Pigeons which had gathered flew off and made way for the thud of his body. The young man had an intuitive ability, and the insight he felt as little Dale was born into the world was much too much for his young, fit and healthy body to handle. In London's Greenwich Park, a mother enjoying a picnic on a sunny summer's day, looking over at her children as they played, suddenly had blurry vision and her head felt faint. Her children continued to play as it seemed their mother laid down to rest in the sun. It wasn't until they came back to mummy for a drink that they realised she was out cold, and screamed by her side as strangers gathered by theirs.

Events like this took place all over the world that day. But unlike the children's mother in Greenwich Park, Dale's mother sat up wide awake and alert, as the nurse handed newborn Dale to her. Looking at a pair of eyes which seemed to speak to her. To Dale's mother, Dale's eyes said, *the end is coming – I will see it through*. It was from this day forward that little Dale experienced a continuous resistance from her parents. Her mother always saw to it that Dale's every want or desire was specifically *not* fulfilled. Each Christmas, Dale looked forward to Santa bringing her something from the list she would write every year. Squeezing her eyes tight shut, hoping with every wrapped gift she held in her hands, only to find what she did every other year before the last. Usually, socks or undergarments, which made her feel the same as she did each year before that. That she'd not been on Santa's good list. That she'd been naughty.

It was the year young Dale turned nine that she discovered her ability – being sight enabled. As she sat in front of the Christmas tree, she saw in her mind her mother wrapping a pair of socks, before throwing them carelessly under the tree. As Dale sat, with the present in her hand, she threw it back under the tree. Her mother was appalled and insisted Dale pick it back up. Dale said she didn't need to open it, that Santa wasn't real, and that she knew it was a pair of socks. Not that she'd have needed the ability of sight to have known it.

That Christmas, Dale was sent to her bedroom unfed. Her father stood by her door, hesitant, wanting to hug and comfort her, to tell her everything was okay. But the repercussions of his wife and her reaction would not have been worth it. It would have been Dale's fault, somehow. And Dale would have seen a scolding for it. Her body would have been bruised for it. It started with small smacks on Dale's bum when she'd done something wrong. Which led to almighty whacks, even just if Dale walked into the same room as her mother, who wanted space. Finally, leading to Dale being hit aimlessly, when her mother had a few too many drinks – simply for existing.

The final night Dale spent in the household with colourless walls was the night her father finally made a stand. He couldn't bring himself to turn a blind eye any longer. Unfortunately, he couldn't bring himself to leave his wife either. The night started as Dale's mum called her for dinner, just like any other. Now twelve years old, Dale had learned to not speak unless spoken to. She kept herself small, staying in her room after school until she was called. The three of them sat at the dinner table, with the clanging of cutlery against the crockery heavier than usual on Dale's mother's plate. She seemed to be furious, bottling something up inside of her. Dale and her father sat silently, catching sympathetic eyes from time to time, but quickly deflecting back to the food on their plates at Dale's mother's flinching.

Melody, Dale's mother, asked if Dale had anything she wanted to share.

"Well, do you?" Melody asked, pushing for an answer. A frightened and uncertain feeling ran through Dale's body. It wasn't usual that she would be addressed by her mother at dinner. In fact, the only address Melody would make was once Dale had finished her dinner to have her leave the table.

"I, I, I don't believe so," replied Dale.

"I, I, I, I," Melody mocked Dale. "Speak confidently when asked a question, girl!" Melody shouted across the table. Henry, Dale's father, continued to eat his dinner slowly and quietly between the two of them. As if nothing but a fly had flown across the table. But what flew across the table next was most definitely no fly.

"What in the hell do you call this?!" Melody shouted, as she pulled a pair of knickers from her pocket and threw them at Dale. The knickers landed on Dale's dinner, and she looked down at them with confusion. The knickers were Dale's, but she didn't know why she was looking at them. She knew they were hers, not just because of the smaller sizing, but instantly recognisable by the white cotton generic brand, compared to her mother's, which she folded for her, made of lacy frills and sometimes silk.

When Melody had thrown the knickers, she had startled Henry. He turned and looked down towards Dale's plate, staring at the knickers too. He noticed some small specs of brown dots on the white cotton and knew instantly what Melody was referring to. Dale had gotten her first period, though it wasn't apparent to her. She hadn't even noticed the dots. Not as she stared at the knickers on her plate, and not when she'd taken them off to place them in the washing basket.

Henry's face began to turn red. He looked at his daughter, who was not only speechless, but clueless. Just accepting the behaviour of her mother. Melody sat in silence a moment, waiting for Dale to say something. Dale said nothing. "You expect your own mother to clean these for you, do you? Do you?! Get out a bar of laundry soap and scrub your filthy knickers, girl!" Melody shouted. Henry slammed his fists onto the table which made the cutlery and crockery clatter. Melody looked like she might have seen a ghost, and she turned to acknowledge him, which was something she did rarely in those days.

"That is quite enough," said Henry, calm and controlled as he stared down his wife. Melody gulped, clearing her throat before standing.

"Henry, you can't expect.."

"Expect what, Melody? Our own damn daughter to get her period and have her mother throw her bloody knickers in her face?! No, it's not on. Not anymore!" Henry shouted.

The screams and raised voices of Melody and Henry could have almost lifted the roof off the house. Little Dale ran from the dining room table, covering her ears with her hands as she cried. As she ran, unbeknownst to Dale, in Melody's anger the table had begun to rise. It was Melody's fear and containment of her own ability that had fuelled her fear and containment of Dale. Dale fled the house in tears, overwhelmed by the fight. It was a kind and caring citizen, a neighbour that lived only a few doors down, that noticed little Dale crying on the street corner. The neighbour was very familiar to Dale, as she was mother to one of Dale's peers.

The neighbour's household was one of comfort and warmth to Dale. A place where, when she visited for sleepovers or play dates, she could be herself. She could speak her mind. She could speak. So, to have been approached by her neighbour, Mrs. Douglas, in a moment of despair, was welcomed more than Mrs. Douglas knew. That said, the woman did have her suspicions of how Dale was treated at home. It was in the rapid change of Dale's nature – from when her mother was around, to when she was not. It was in the way Dale held herself: insecure, hunched and arms folded in the presence of Melody. How, when Melody left Dale, her shoulders seemed to relax back into a natural state. Her arms opened up to the people around her, to the world, no longer closed off. The tension simply fled.

As warm and inviting as Mrs. Douglas may have seemed, she had always been a more conservative woman. Mrs. Douglas indeed held her suspicions, even catching sight of bruising on the back of Dale's little legs, as she played with her daughter on their living room floor. Mrs. Douglas, however, merely turned a blind eye to such things. To her mind, it was none of her business. *Could have been a fall,* she told herself. *Could have been a fall,* on multiple occasions.

9

The night Dale ran from her family home was a night Dale dreaded what awaited her should she return. Walking back through that door, was something that frightened little Dale beyond belief. As such, when Mrs. Douglas approached Dale on that street corner - in a matching sky blue tracksuit with headband – Dale let out an overwhelming cry to her neighbour. A cry for help. A cry for change. A cry that said, *I don't want to go back to that life.* A cry for a better life. But also, a cry for a girl, whose parents had not chased after her when she'd fled the house. It was a cry not even a conservative woman like Mrs. Douglas could turn a blind eye to.

*

The years that followed saw Dale's life in foster care begin. Her father might have been strong enough to make a stand the night Dale fled, but he wasn't strong enough to make a stand for himself, entrapped in his unhappy marriage. A father who wasn't strong enough for the fight to take custody of his very own daughter. As a young woman, Dale later learned that her father had become a drunk. A drunk whom, by the time Dale learned that Melody had taken her very own life, was too far gone for recovery. The last time Dale saw him was at Melody's funeral. An event that Dale very much had to build the courage to attend, and although she'd managed to build such courage, she lingered back by the trees at the service. Dale watched as her father stood by the coffin, watching his wife being lowered into the ground. He blubbered and sobbed. But Dale knew it wasn't for his wife. The tears he expelled were for himself and the life that he'd thrown away.

At the end of the service, Dale decided to confront Henry. She watched him as he stared down at the coffin in the ground, while people around him offered their condolences and slowly departed one by one. Dale watched as the only two left standing were himself, and her, in the distance. Immersed in his own grief, of whatever loss he was mourning, it seemed his vision did not span further than that coffin, his stare isolated to it. With the guests from the service gone, it was clear to Dale that in Henry's weakness, tied to Melody, he hadn't a friend left in the world. Dale slowly stepped out from the trees in the distance and walked towards him, her arms folded and closed off like when she was a little girl.

"You sad, sad man!" Henry's engrossed stare broke instantly. He looked up to see his little girl, now a grown woman, looking at him with angst. He looked on at the only thing in his life he'd made a stand for. Equally, the only thing in his life he wished he'd fought for.

"Dale..." he began.

"No!" Dale shouted at him as she began to cry. "You don't get to speak to me! You don't get to say a word!"

"Dale, I..."

"No!"

They both stood still in silence. Henry wanted nothing more than to reach out and grab hold of Dale and bring her into his arms. But he knew better. He knew her rightful angst. "Dad. God, if I can even call you that. Do you know what living in that house was like? Do you know what foster care was like? How I can't even make my mind up about what was worse - living in a house where I was physically and mentally abused every day by a woman that hated me, or growing up in homes with strangers that sexually abused me?! But then, by that stage I'd pretty much lost all feeling of anything in the world and can't say I felt ever present. Then, that's no damn justification. Answer me this. Should a girl even be put in that position? Shouldn't someone have stepped in before things got there?" Dale started to sob. "No, actually don't. I don't want to hear your bullshit." Dale left. Henry stood alone. She made her parting, and he knew he hadn't a leg to stand on. That was the last time either of the two saw one another again. Dale was nineteen years old. She'd learned that she was the only person she could rely on in this world. She wasn't about to let someone who already failed her, back in.

Learning that she could only ever rely on herself wasn't the only thing Dale learned over the years. She'd also taken to her gift of sight. The gift which, as Lenroc, she harnessed alongside a full set of abilities. As a child, she'd picked up on her gift after a few instances, knowing things she potentially shouldn't have, or knowing things she really had no way of knowing - by seeing them or being able to read minds. Knowing that it was her first foster father's birthday, when he'd not cared to acknowledge it. Knowing, the first night that he entered her room while she lay anxious under the covers, as she saw glimpses of his intentions. It didn't stop there though, and her time in foster care saw her abilities grow.

The first home Dale moved on from was because the wife had caught her husband touching Dale's leg late one night. The two were watching television, as he raised his hand a little too high up Dale's skirt. The reaction from his wife was one Dale had wished her own father took, the first time Melody had beat her. The wife gathered Dale, without so much as hearing the words that her husband spat out of his mouth. In the car and straight to the police station they went. Dale, of course, was young, innocent and naïve in the house of two grown strangers. She wasn't about to cause a fuss - especially not after the pattern her own mother had set - and so her foster mum's attention was strange to Dale. Strange, but unfamiliarly welcomed.

The next foster home was one Dale rather enjoyed. For a while. A husband and wife who seemed picture perfect to any outside eye. That is, until Dale grew and began to mature, developing into a woman. It was then that her foster dad's eye thought *Dale* was rather picture perfect. Dale knew it was wrong. It was no longer just her own feeling, but reassured and imprinted by the actions of her last foster mum. That the actions of her previous foster dad and new one alike were wrong. Even so, Dale still couldn't break the pattern that Melody had set within her. Which was, of course, to keep quiet and do as the adults told her.

As Dale expressed to Henry at Melody's funeral, the years that passed by had seen Dale form a loss of feeling, where, when such nasty things took place, her subconscious mind left her body. When her foster dad entered the room and took off his belt, she entered an automatic response, blanking her mind. The sooner she took what she was giving, the sooner it was over. What's worse, as Dale's sight developed it became harder to escape such things, as images of what was coming her way entered her mind, vivid and realistic.

One afternoon, on her sixteenth birthday, enough was enough. While Dale sat at the picture-perfect table, with a picture-perfect cake, from her picture-perfect foster parents, what entered her mind was too much to handle. It was the words the night before that Dale found most disturbing - before her mind had even begun to run a reel of vivid images inside her head. The words that came out of her foster dad's mouth, as he walked towards her bed. The words being, *now that you're sixteen.*

As Dale sat at that picture-perfect table, in front of that picture-perfect cake, she felt dread, fear and sickness all at once. The motions riddled her body. As her foster parents stood on the other side of the table, Dale looked up from the cake and locked eyes with her foster dad. Her blood pressure rose and the vessels in her eyes just about burst. What happened next was not so much intentional, as it was her body and mind's natural response to protecting Dale. Her foster dad stopped singing happy birthday and stood with a vacant expression for a moment. A moment that was long enough for his wife to take notice, as she stopped singing herself and looked at him.

"Honey. Honey, are you okay?" He didn't respond, and instead marched towards the cake. Marching, as his mind clearly tried to resist what had taken control - Dale. Dale rather enjoyed seeing the dread and fear of what was happening in his eyes. Once he reached the cake, he took his hand and grabbed hold of the knife which was placed beside it. His body doing so, but a fatal look in his eyes remained, suggesting his mind was reluctant. "Honey, Dale hasn't blown out the candles yet. Honey, what are you doing?"

He lifted the knife up to his throat, while his eyes bulged with panic and locked with Dale. Dale's own eyes, bulging with a satisfied suggestiveness that said, *you had this coming and you know it.* His wife ran to him and pulled at his arms, but he was too strong. Physically strong, at least, for his will was weak. His resistance was no match next to Dale's control. Dale's squeezed her eyes shut tight. As her eyelids closed, her foster dad pulled the knife across his throat, as blood began to gush out over the cake, with spurts of blood taking to Dale's face. It was the last spurt of anything he would get to have, ever again.

3 DARK SMOG

I managed to stand myself up on the bank upon which I had awoken. I stared down at my feet, attempting to lift off from the green sludge in which I stood. But it was no use. I was too weak. To my right was a set of concrete steps, joined to the concrete wall which the sad waves of the bloody River Thames had been slapping up against. I took them. Each step I took, I could practically feel my muscles scream at me to rest. But I had to make a start, and so, I persisted. I pushed through the pain.

Reaching the top of the steps, I looked out ahead of me, and there stood the historical castle that was the Tower of London. Her Majesty's Royal Palace and Fortress by what was once Tower Bridge. The home of the Crown Jewels of England and a structure which had seen several phases and centuries of expansion.

The Tower of London stood untouched. Standing tall among its surroundings of destruction. Not only that, but it glowed a deep purple, as if it held some kind of aura. My mind cast back quickly to the story which Margret had told. The story of the Dark Enabled times. When the illuminating towers that rose from the earth's own rock took to the land. The story was told to me when I'd stood with the Collective in the space of white nothingness.

My mind came back to where I stood now. Two thoughts entered it. *One*, that if the Tower of London now glowed an illuminating purple, much like the towers I envisioned in the story of the Dark Enabled times, then the Tower of London was likely acting as some sort of Dark Enabled base. While my body was weak and recovering, it probably wasn't a place I wanted to investigate at this very second. *Two*, thinking back to the portal at Buckingham Palace that had taken me to the Collective as I entered the white nothingness, I wondered if Buckingham Palace itself still stood. If perhaps the British Monarchy were part of this fight. Fighting against Lenroc and the Dark Enabled, and, if Buckingham Palace did indeed still stand, if the royal family may be home, planning their fight.

These two thoughts in mind, I cautiously walked on, leaving the Tower of London and the defeat that was Tower Bridge behind. It would be quite a walk, but if I managed to follow the River Thames back around to Westminster Bridge, I would remember my way to Buckingham Palace from there. It was a walk I'd once been rather fond of. It was a walk I recall once proudly taking Jade on. Showing off the city that was London in all its glory. *Jade*, I thought. My stomach turned. My knees gave way and I fell to the ground. My mind flashed back to her flowing blue hair. Her glistening eyes... Eyes of deceit. The eyes of a succubus. Of the demon that toyed with my heart. The demon which had pulled me away from Pree and Rubis. *Pree Possessing* and *Miss Rubis Rouge*.

I laid down on the frozen cold ground. It wasn't just my knees that had given way. My whole body fell into some kind of state. Not overwhelmed. This state was worse. Stronger. Whatever state this was, it had me question my thoughts to walk on and fight this fight. A fight I had so selfishly given up on as I handed Lenroc the enchanted knife. *What was the point of a fight without anything to fight for? What would I be fighting, should I make my way to Buckingham Palace? Would Pree and Rubis even still be alive? If not, what was left?* I'd held my reservations about them already – about polyamory. But that was before all this carnage. It seemed an apocalypse did a lot to a person's perspective. I could feel the love I felt for them deep within me. An urge to see them again. Hold them again. Kiss them again. The ground rumbled as I laid upon it. I felt the rumblings of whatever havoc was taking place in the world around me, questioning so many things and looking back on my life.

As I looked ahead, with my right cheek flat on the pavement, I closed my eyes and a small smile took to my face. Thinking back on the life that I'd made for myself in this once glorious city. The life that I'd made, along with the wonderful characters that filled it. I remembered the colourful characters of Café De Paris. The banter between Ava Royal and Bonnie Fire, The Café Girls. I remembered the feeling I felt when Lenroc – Dale – had first taken me to the show. How I'd known what I wanted my future to hold. The desire to be part of the glamour and sparkle. The exhilarating feeling that took hold of me, the first moment I ran from that balcony, flying around the golden mezzanine that framed the splendour of Café De Paris. How Pree always referred to the space as the most glamorous bunker in London, paying tribute to the days it was able to stay open during the Second World War, being twenty feet underground, promoted by its manager as the 'safest and gaiest restaurant in town.'

Café De Paris, I thought. My eyes sprung back open. If there was any chance Pree and Rubis were alive I was sure they would be there. They had to be. How could they not? The thought of Pree's pompous step and pink puff of hair. Rubis' soft yet striking demure. I was suddenly filled with determination and got back up off of the ground. A detour was due. It was one I knew just as well as the path to Buckingham Palace. A path that filled my body with hope and feeling again. A fire was lit under my arse, figuratively of course, and off I set amongst a dark smog, covering the glory that was once London.

4 SALTS

Dale fled from the final household where she would live under the roof and care of adults. Running with spurts of blood on her face. The spurts that had come from the neck of her first kill and, although she didn't know it back then, it was the first kill of many to come. But at sixteen years old, all she knew was that she wasn't going to let anyone touch her *like that* again. No matter *what* her actions were deemed. It wasn't even a distinctive choice for Dale. It was a reactive and instinctive action. Choice didn't even come into it.

Fleeing once more with the clothes on her back, this time with headphones around her neck, Dale ran to the nearest train station. With a lack of care for where the train she got on went, she let it take her and her blood splattered face and headphones away. As she fled, she had done so fuelled by adrenaline. Adrenaline which came from her relief of escape. Her relief on *its* end. But also, adrenaline which came from disbelief, trying to comprehend what had just happened. As she took her seat on the train, one might have thought she would have burst out into tears. But the lack of feeling that Dale had adopted over the years saw her escape her body and mind, as the train ran along its rickety tracks.

In absent mind, Dale felt a rather strange sensation take over her body as she sat on that train, which riddled her. It wasn't shock, revolt or anything to do with what she'd just underwent. It was a sensation similar to that of the ones experienced around the world the day she herself had been born. It was an overpowering and forceful sensation. One that she felt connected to her someone. Destiny, of a kind. One that spiked an urgent sense of protection within her. She didn't yet know it, but the sensation she felt was the birth of young Michael entering the world. Her ability, and overwhelmed state fuelled with adrenaline, engaged her subconscious to send a form of cloaking out to the minds her own birth had disturbed. To hide the essence she sensed from them. Keeping it hidden. Keeping it for herself. Then, as her body used up its final ounce of energy, she passed out against the train window.

*

Dale woke to find a cleaner lightly shaking her shoulder. 'Miss. Miss, excuse me miss,' the cleaner said, and asked if she was okay, not just spotting Dale asleep, but also the dried blood on her face. Dale apologised and said that she was fine – leaving the confused cleaner on the train. She entered a station which held large, eroded columns that held up two arched rows of transparent roofing. The evening filter of sun that was left for the day shone through it. She made her way out of the station, while her brain tried to register a familiar scent in the air. People stared at the blood on Dale's face, something they had done earlier that afternoon, although she hadn't taken any notice, being filled with adrenaline and on mission getaway. As she reached the outside of the station, she entered an open space and the start of one long road, which led to the answer of the scent in the air. Ahead, now knowingly and agreeably breathing in that scent with a smile on her face, was the seaside. Not just any seaside, but a place her father once took her for a weekend trip, before he'd become whipped and conditioned by Melody. It was the only real place where Dale held nothing but fond memories of just the two of them. She had arrived in the seaside town called Brighton.

As Dale began to walk the long road, not knowing where the path might lead her - other than the Brighton seafront - she looked around at the cream-coloured buildings with peeling paint and iron rusted railings. Pride flags hung and flowed in the air from windows; Brighton was so well known for its vibrancy and pride. Same-sex couples walked hand in hand, both as if going about their ordinary daily business, or here clearly for a visit to the beach with towels draped over their shoulders. Equally, parents walked linked with children in-between them - same-sex or not. Some children were piggy backed. A memory which also sat fondly in Dale's mind. Continuing to walk, Dale passed by the centre clock tower, sparking another memory, this one not so fond. After a nice day out at the seaside, Henry had taken Dale off of his shoulders and placed her back on the pavement. He'd needed to take a call from Melody, caving to her demand to get back home, as they had been gone all day.

Dale tossed the memory aside, it now tarnishing the good ones, focusing on what was right in front of her. The sea. Getting closer and closer, with every step she took, it was as if the sea was calling for her to come and wash her past away. Start fresh. Once she reached the end of the long road, she came to a T-junction and crossed the interconnecting road. Reaching a seemingly never-ending path, which ran along the interconnecting road, Brighton's famous turquoise fencing lined the pebbled beach below. Rather than walk the path, Dale bypassed the fencing and walked down some side steps. Dale looked out over to her left where Brighton's pier and funfair sat, in the foreground, built up on top of the sea by thick planks of wood.

Making her way to the sea water which washed over the pebbles on which she walked, Dale's focus turned away from the pier and to the open sea in front of her, breathing the salty air into her lungs with each step she took. People continued to look at the bloody faced girl walking onto the beach. One family even started to pack up their things and move away. Dale, however, took no notice, continuing to walk towards the sea. Her feet started to get wet as she stepped deeper and deeper into the water. She walked until the water hit her waist, then stopped. Looking out onto the open water, dusk had started to set and she felt sure this was a new beginning.

The tears that one thought Dale might have experienced when she'd sat on the train began to fall here. The salts of her body joined the salts of the sea. She started to cry and began to breathe heavily. She reached down into the water with her hands and began to splash and rub her face. Every splash began to wash away the dried blood. She began to rub harder; she felt dirty, and she wanted to be clean. She cried and she rubbed, the salt of the sea rubbing against the salts expelled on her face. She rubbed and rubbed until she heard the sound of a voice project out from behind her.

'Is everything alright?'

Dale stopped rubbing her face and half stopped crying.

'I'm coming out to you! I'm just coming to see that everything's alright, okay? Don't be alarmed!'

Dale turned around to see the origins of the voice that was approaching. It sounded like a kind voice. A concerned voice. As she turned she saw a boy with jet-black hair and eyes which looked as though they were made up of the sea water itself: a clear green which glistened as he approached. Dale's tears started to dry, instinctively going into a defensive mode, no longer trusting people. Her instincts knew the darker side of a person. Picture-perfect wasn't so.

"I'm fine," she said. The water hit just below the boy's waist as he reached her, being slightly taller than Dale. He caught sight of the little blood that remained on her face. He bent down, dabbing his hand in the water to bring up towards her face. The girl with pre-existing patterns that remained inside Dale let him. The boy held the side of Dale's cheek with his fingers, as his thumb wiped the rest of the blood away.

Dale looked down at the water, avoiding eye contact, like she'd all too well become accustomed to. But something deep inside said, *It's okay, Dale.* Rattled, she couldn't quite focus enough to read his mind. But her instincts said, *He's okay.*

"You don't look like a girl that's fine," said the boy. Dale looked up at him and into his glistening sea eyes. She wanted to speak but the girl who was used to keeping quiet crept back inside. "It's okay, you're safe. Nobody out here is going to hurt you," he said. Dale quickly took to his kind and caring way of speaking, accompanied by the glistening of his eyes. "Talk to me. Are you alright?"

"I... I think I'm going to be," she replied. The boy smiled. He continued to rub her face despite the fact that the blood had washed away.

"How about we grab a bite to eat? My treat."

"I... I don't even know you."

"I get that. But honestly, I was just finishing up with some friends over there. I was only heading home. I don't mind taking a moment to catch your breath with you. I'll even just come to see you sit down with a glass of water and be on my way. If that's what you want."

"Okay. Okay, that would be nice."

The boy took her to a rooftop bar which overlooked the never-ending path and turquoise fence, insistent with the staff that greeted them that they should be in the open air. He asked that a glass of water be brought over straight away. Dale sat down and looked up at the boy who had washed away the last of the blood from her face.

"Okay, well you're in good hands. I hope you'll…"

"You can stay," said Dale, taking a breath. "Actually. I - I'd like you to stay," she finished. The boy smiled and pulled out the seat on the other side of the table.

"I can do that," he said, as he took his seat. The waiter brought over the glass of water that had been ordered. The boy asked for an orange juice and gestured to Dale if she would like anything else.

"Oh, yeah. A juice sounds nice."

"Some sugar isn't too bad an idea for you. Maybe even some salt after those tears? Fancy some chips? Burger and fries?"

"Okay, sure. Just chips are fine though." Dale formed a shy grin at his clear attempt to lighten the mood.

After ordering a large serving of chips, the boy went about apologising for his manners and introduced himself. His name was Derek. He extended his hand, and as Dale shook it, she introduced herself too.

"So, I'm not going to prod. But if you did want to talk about why a girl with blood on her face walked into the sea, I'm happy to hear it," said Derek.

"If you don't mind, I think I'd rather not."

"Most perfectly fine," said Derek, with a smile.

"Can I ask *you* a question?"

"Certainly."

"Why did you come to me?"

"Why did I come to you?"

"Yeah. Like, why did you feel the need to come over?"

"Well, you were clearly in distress. Okay, now that sounds like I wanted to be your knight in shining armour. I just saw someone that might need some help. Why wouldn't I help if I could?"

Derek's answer baffled Dale. A complete stranger, that saw another stranger, and just thought they might be able to help. Derek's reasoning felt as genuine as the voice he spoke with. A person just helping another. Dale was sitting on a rooftop bar full of other people after all - it wasn't like he was being nice to work his way into her pants. It wasn't even a date; he had offered to see her down on her seat and make his departure. He was excusing himself when she told him he could stay.

21

The way Derek spoke to Dale, more and more made her feel at ease. He explained that it was his belief that we were all put on this earth to help one another, questioning why someone would turn their back on someone else in clear need of help. He also seemed to hold a natural smile that was plastered to his face. A smile that charmed. A smile she felt she wanted to melt into as she adopted a glazed stare while he spoke, but quickly snapped out of it as Derek asked her what her story was.

"My story?"

"Yes. Your story. Where are you from? What school do you go to? What's the plan?"

"The plan?"

"Yeah, the almighty plan for Dale's life! What do you want to be? What do you want to do?" Derek continued to ask more questions. It rather shook Dale. Where she was from and where she went to school would trail back to answers. Answers answers the life she'd led up to this point. She wanted to forget that life. She wanted to move away from it.

"I've moved around a lot," she said, deflecting. "I just got here today, actually. I don't know what I'm doing to be honest. How about we just say I've run away to join the circus?" Dale said in a mirrored jest to Derek's way.

"The circus, hey? Well, I don't think I got word that the circus had come to town, but does this circus include accommodation?" Derek asked, seeing through the lines of Dale's story. Dale started to hunch into the way she used to around her mother, then folded her arms as she curled into herself.

"No. No it doesn't."

"Fear not. I've got a mate who manages the Brighton Hostel. I'm sure he'd be able to hook you up with something semi-permanent until you find a more fixed arrangement," he said. Dale honestly couldn't believe what she was hearing. Derek seemed too good to be true. Dale gulped for a moment as a thought entered her mind.

"I don't have any money," she said shamefully.

"It's not a problem. The gent owes me a big favour. Honestly, wait right there. I'm pretty sure he was staying on with the people I just left," he explained.

Just like that, it may have seemed too good to be true, but too good was better than anything else at that moment. Derek brought his friend up to the rooftop bar to meet Dale, and before she knew it, she was fitting her sheets to a bed in the Brighton Hostel. Derek's mate asked her not to share with anyone that this was an in-kind arrangement, as it wouldn't look good. He also asked if she minded volunteering at the front desk, when he needed some help, saying that would do for payment just fine.

Soon enough, Dale had proven herself an indispensable asset, and Derek's friend managed to arrange for her hire. Not as a receptionist, he didn't like to refer to the front desk as reception, so he joked and called her their maître d'. As a cash job, after school hours, she didn't have an official title per se. Dale didn't actually attend school once she settled in Brighton, although she told the boys that she did. She'd started to live a double life. But she managed to do it well and kept them convinced. The truth was that she'd started working at a coffee shop to save some funds, just on the outskirts of Brighton. Somewhere she felt sure the people in her circles wouldn't find out. Keeping busy kept her mind occupied. Keeping busy meant she didn't think. Working kept her busy. School had seen Dale's mind wander into thoughts. Disgusting thoughts. Heartbreaking thoughts. Thoughts of her foster dads. Thoughts of her mother Melody. Why her father had never helped. Why her father had never tried to find her.

There were still times Dale's mind drifted off into such thoughts. But, as things she started to value entered her life, she managed to close the thoughts down quicker than she once could. Although one image had imprinted on Dale's mind. An image that was ingrained in it. The image of her second foster dad's bloody throat, when she opened her eyes, sat in front of her birthday cake. It came to her at quiet times, when she might be wiping down a table in the coffee shop. While she sat on the toilet. While she lay awake in bed. Still, life went on. She learned to live with thoughts for a time. She had no other choice.

A year or so after Dale had supposedly *graduated*, telling the boys she didn't want to make a big deal about it, she stuck to a story that she'd mostly kept to herself, saying that she only really had friends outside of school. Friends she'd made through the hostel. Next to Derek, of course. Derek whom she'd started dating. Derek's kind and genuine care continued into their relationship. Their first kiss was the first time Dale fell into a real natural state of comfort and ease. Letting the wall she'd built around her come down. Not fleeing from her shell of a body. Her mind still drifted at times, as she lay beside Derek, awake in bed, beginning to spend some nights at his parent's house. But at least, on those nights, she wasn't alone. At least those nights she had someone to hold as she burst into tears. Derek, waking to comfort her, then holding *her* in *his* arms. Never questioning her. Just holding her.

Dale and Derek had kissed - and many a time at that - but on this particular night they lay on his bed while watching the late night movie on the box in his room and Derek had started to make *the moves*. Dale had embraced him for just a moment, so wanting to let the boy that had made her feel ease and comfort know it, but she was triggered by his touch on her inner thigh. She shied away and asked that he stop. He did, instantly, along with reassurance that it was okay. Derek told Dale that they had all the time in the world. He told her that when she was ready, he would be. He assured her that there was no rush, and that was exactly what Dale needed in a boyfriend.

5 THE WANDERED - PART ONE

Determined to make my way to Café De Paris, London's most glamorous bunker, I'd started to head through the ruins of the city that Lenroc and her creatures of darkness had taken the liberty of creating, sifting through their trail of destruction. The smog was thick, the air was cold, and the path that I followed along the River Thames to Westminster Bridge was covered in dead bodies. Although, not as many as one might have thought; they seemed to pop up here and there amongst the rubble. Perhaps most of the people were underneath that very rubble. Further back, closer to where I'd awoken by Tower Bridge, I managed to take some extra layers of clothing off of a few bodies that were relatively intact. I had snagged myself a few extra shirts, a couple of sweaters and a nice big scarf and coat.

It was an interesting thing, pulling clothing off of a dead body. I mean, I'd murdered people in cold blood. Stuck a knife into their guts and hacked at their chests. I'd fucking exploded the bodies of my ex-boyfriend Victor and his side-piece *Buttocks Boy* with the god-damned tightening and clenching of my fists. Blood, guts and bone splattering everywhere. The difference was that I knew their story. Their actions and impact on my life lead to those moments. Whether they'd deserved what they got or not. I wasn't in any state of mind for sympathy right now. The fact of the matter was, when I pulled the clothing off from these dead bodies, I felt a kind of sorrow. I didn't know their story. I doubted they even had time to contemplate their deaths. It was probably so sudden. Unless it wasn't. Unless they ran for their life, as determined to get back to their loved ones as I was to Pree and Rubis. I just didn't know, and that made it sadder somehow.

I looked down at each body as I tore or yanked at their clothing. The coat, a shabby woollen piece from an elderly woman who was probably someone's grandmother. The cashmere-like scarf unravelled off of some young man in a business suit. Maybe an intern with his whole career ahead. His whole life ahead. The shirts and sweaters from likely working mums and dads, their children at home with a sitter, maybe at school in the daytime. Who knew when all this had taken place? When everyone was slaughtered like farm animals. Yet, they were honestly so few and far between, it was odd to not be walking over a sea of corpses. Nice that I wasn't, but odd. Still, the dead bodies I did come across didn't hit me as hard as the odd few bodies of dead children I walked by. Innocents, yet to make a mistake in the world. Their chance to choose right or wrong was taken away from them. Some were huddled or laid next to who, I assume, were the adult figures in their lives. Some laid dead all on their own, separated from whoever they were with.

What hit me the hardest was something I saw poking out from a pile of rubble as I made my way past London Bridge, the bridge that had split as I took off from it into the air moments before my encounter with Lenroc. It was a small child's wrist and open hand. A miniature red telephone box was resting on top of the inside of the child's fingers. A child who must have been visiting this once wondrous, historical city, filled with exciting tourist attractions and tacky rip-off souvenirs, with a souvenir that they had clearly clung on to tightly, not wanting to let it go, even throughout whatever carnage came their way. Their little red telephone box from London. An item they could take back to whatever side of the world they came from. Show their classmates at 'show and tell.' The joy that miniature telephone box must have brought to that child when they saw it. Probably pleading with their parents to buy it for them. It wouldn't have been cheap this central to London either. Their parents had probably rolled their eyes and tried to keep walking on from whatever pop-up shop set themselves up by the bridge, which, after standing still for a moment in solidarity and catching my breath, is exactly what I did. I walked on. What's done is done. There was no changing that. The longer I stood and pondered over what a child's final moments might have been, the longer I risked missing Pree and Rubis, had they made their way inside Café De Paris. The longer I stood and pondered, the greater chance that they'd move on, with the debris caused by the destruction of the underworld now settled. Making their way through the smog, just like I was.

As I wandered around the River Thames, making out what I could, surrounded by the darkened smog, I wasn't sure where I had gotten to. I just about fell down into the bloody River Thames, through a huge destroyed gap in the path, which looked as if a bomb had hit it. I luckily caught myself and swung my fall off to the side of it. Fallen close to the edge, I gasped and looked down to find rubble and debris falling in my place. The bloody water, having made its way into the gap, slapped up against it with its sad waves. I quickly became startled by a scream.

In my startlement, I rolled away from the gap in the path, looking all around me, below the dark smog. It was as if the smog had made way for the rats to run along what was left of the pavement, scavenging through the remains of Old London Town. I saw nothing. No-one.

"Hello!" I shouted. "Is anyone there?!" No response. Then, after a moment of continued silence, another scream projected into the air. This time for longer. Followed by a cry for help.

'For fuck's sake, is anyone alive out there?!' It screamed. The voice sounded male. Deep in tone. A voice that carried out from wherever it was. Unlike mine, which he clearly hadn't heard.

The voice continued to shout out for help in the far distance. It didn't seem they were in immediate danger or faced with a threat. It was more a lost voice seeking other living folk. I shouted out again, but it was no use. I couldn't throw my voice far enough for them to hear. I stood from where I'd fallen, brushing the muck off my shaggy woollen coat. I wrapped the coat up around me tightly, pulling the sash that came with it strong around my waist. If it had a good wash it might have been multi-coloured. The old lady who'd worn it had been a vibrant character, that was for sure. Perfectly fitting for a queer boy walking the streets in an apocalypse. I began listening out for the voice. I started to move towards where I thought it was coming from.

I consciously tried to remember my steps as I walked away from the River Thames, hopping over broken pavement, heaped piles of cobblestone, and twisting and turning my way around buildings towards the deep screaming voice. I called out in response as I got closer to the voice. Feeling a little disorientated, I just about walked into walls with the smog seemingly thicker between the buildings. Finally, I received a reply.

"Hello! Where are you?! Please come and help me!"

"Sir, stay where you are! I'm trying to get to you!" I shouted.

"Oh, don't worry! I'm not going anywhere, matey!"

"Can you count out loud? Or sing something for me?!"

"Count out loud or fucking sing? What is this? Fucking kindergarten?!"

"Kindergarten? I wouldn't be talking to a fellow Australian, would I?"

"Ha! Mate! You would! Newcastle, New South Wales! You?"

"Perth! West Australia!" I said, chuckling a little to myself. Fancy the two Australians in the dark smog finding one another.

"Perth boy! Got family in Perth!"

"Do you? Whereabouts?" I shouted, trying to continue to find my way through the ruins and my disorientation.

As the voice in the distance continued to talk, he spoke fondly of his extended family in a suburb called Jandakot. They held a parcel of land that he would take his sons to when he visited, to ride horses. I tried to engage and focus on his story, but I started to feel as if I were in a vivid dream. It felt as though I was trying to escape from a maze with dead ends at every turn. Or the kind of dream you have when you're under a bedsheet, and you keep trying to pull it away, but the bedsheet is endless.

"You still with me, mate?"

"Ah, yeah! I just can't seem to pinpoint your voice…"

"Greg, mate! The name's Greg!"

"I just can't seem to pinpoint your voice, Greg! I don't know. Really could use those numbers or a song right about now!" I joked. "I honestly have no idea where I am!"

"Well, how about you start with telling me who you are?"

"Sorry! Michael! It's Michael!"

"What you doing in London, Michael?"

"Ah! It's a bit of a long story!" I said comically, rather sure that telling a stranger I was transported to Brixton Prison, after massacring drag queens in a nightclub, wasn't the best idea. Nor that I was part and parcel of the destruction around us. The golden child of a prophecy. *The dark enabled will break the boundaries of earth and the underworld by the spilled blood of a torn lover.* Yeah, not the best idea.

"What about home then? Miss anything in Perth?"

Greg's question startled me a moment. I didn't react with an instant answer. I'd been so wrapped up in my new created world in London and these damn abilities that I hadn't really taken the time to reflect on it. I mean, my family was dead. The visit from the police, to inform me of their accident, was what set off my little rampage. But I took a moment to think. The dark smog helped to clear my mind. There *was* something I missed. *Someone.*

"Yeah! My best mate! Andrew! I haven't ever found a pal like him again!" I shouted.

"School friend?"

"Yeah! How'd you figure?"

"Can't replace them! All that history! All the firsts!"

I thought about what Greg was saying. He was damn right. The friends I'd made here were great. But they weren't Andrew. I remembered how he used to get his brother to grab us alcohol, in high school, at Lumiere. How he joked when we sat at the dinner table with my parents and, when we told them we were studying 'Oliver' and he said *Yeah, we like playing the old Londonas* in his shifty attempt at a cockney accent. Oh, if he only knew. Who knew what he thought of me or if he knew what I'd done, if my rampage had made its way to the papers? Or, if this carnage had potentially taken to the globe? If he was still alive? My thoughts quickly escaped me as Greg shouted out asking if I was still with him.

"Yep! Still here!"

"Hit a sore spot didn't I? Sorry about that, matey!"

"Hey! It's alright! I just… I guess I didn't realise how much I missed him! You know?"

"I know!" Greg shouted, but softening in tone.

"What were you doing when all this went down, Greg? What did you see?" I asked, curious if he might have some insight for me, from when I hit the bloody River Thames, to when I awoke on the bank beside it.

"Oh, I was just wandering, Michael! I'm a wanderer! First time here and was on my way to see St. Paul's Cathedral! Well, I can tell you now I'm looking straight at it matey and she's a beauty! Can't say I saw a thing. I completely blacked out and here I woke! What happened?! Damn terrorist attack it was, wasn't it? Typically, the one time I check out London it's a target!"

"Ah! That's a bit of a long story too! When I find you I'm sure we can talk about it!" I answered. *If I can find you*, I thought. It wouldn't be too bad an idea to have some company. To have someone to keep me going.

"Well, you just keep a-comin'! I'm honestly not going anywhere!"

"Yes! What are you doing hanging out around a cathedral?"

"Umm… I wouldn't say I'm hanging out! After I blacked out, I woke up under a nice thick sheet of glass! Need a crane to pull this thing off of my legs

I reckon! Or at least get the junk off of the top of it! I remember hearing a loud ruckus, that's for sure, but just damn well thought a freak storm was blowin' in!"

It all suddenly made sense. The guy, Greg. He was stuck. Calling out for help. In need of assistance to help clear his legs free. Probably some industrial sheet of glass off one of the scrapers. I was surprised it hadn't smashed out over him. Sliced him up. I had to find him. The two Aussies *had* to meet. I couldn't leave him stranded.

6 THE BURDEN OF SIGHT

Two years had passed by. At just eighteen years old, Dale had set up a life of sorts with Derek. A year older than Dale and, having entered the workforce full-time, Derek was able to provide for Dale and leased a studio apartment not far from the very part of the seaside that they met. However the life the two of them had setup started to become rocky. In their first year, Dale had begun to sleep over at Derek's parents' house rather regularly. The comfort she felt in his presence built and Derek's parents became rather fond of Dale. They thought she was a sweet girl, well-mannered and thoughtful. However, when the sleepovers became more regular, they felt a little smothered by his parents. So, their own apartment felt like the right step.

Slowly and surely, towards the beginning of their second year together as the two of them set up house and home, the continued kind and caring comfort which Derek portrayed saw Dale draw closer to him. She began to trust in him, completely, and her trust in him saw her visions drift away, spawned previously on anxious and nervous energy. When she was with him, she didn't hold one thought or image in the world. Her mind and body didn't escape so much as they did relish his hold and immerse herself in his presence. She basked in the feelings she'd adopted around him, and with her sight being something very much associated with her past, her ability was something she didn't actively try to pursue. She'd let it drift like a note in a bottle thrown into the ocean. Still out there, but out of sight.

A few months after Dale and Derek had settled into their new apartment, Dale felt ready for further intimacy. Ready to show Derek the full extent of her comfort and ease in him. But most importantly, she felt ready herself. Dale *wanted* Derek. She wanted him to touch her. She wanted him to feel her. She wanted him inside of her. It had been a touchy subject the first night that they moved in: Derek had poured them both some wine to toast their new apartment, followed by *the moves*. Dale had toasted, but she had again shied away from his touch. She wasn't ready, and Derek persisted with his kind, caring and understanding nature. It was a nature which Dale had fallen in love with but she knew that on that particular night, her shying away had hurt Derek, whether he showed his frustration or not. She could understand his frustration, especially considering she'd never enlightened him to her past. But a few months later, the boxes were unpacked, the curtains hung, the cushions placed on the couch... And Dale was ready.

It was Dale's night off from maître'd at Brighton Hostel, and she had gone about setting up a romantic atmosphere for when Derek came home. She'd lit candles and chilled champagne. Not yet eighteen, she'd arranged for a mature aged friend from the hostel to fetch it. Dale wore a red dress with a slit up the side, which, when she'd tried it on at the store, her knee peeked out from, and she poked her tongue out at herself sillily. It wasn't her usual style. But she knew Derek would appreciate it. She'd seen his eyes innocently wander, when they were out and about, towards women in such garments before, until loyally quickly retracting it.

The lights were dim, with the candlelight flickering and casting shadows. As Derek opened the door he found Dale by the bottle of chilling champagne, waiting for him. Dale approached him as he stood speechless at the door. Dinner was in the oven with the roasting smell wafting through the apartment. But Dale couldn't wait until dinner; she decided she was ready. She was ready *now*. Once she reached Derek by the door, she tugged with both hands at his collar and told him she was sorry it had taken her so long.

"Sorry *what* has taken you so long? To cook? What is that? It smells good!" Dale laughed. Yes, she didn't cook and this was a first. She wanted the night to be special.

"No, silly. I'm ready. For you. To touch me," said Dale. She said no more. Dale grabbed Derek's tie with her right hand and held the back of his head with her left, starting to kiss him. Derek closed the door behind him with his foot as he wrapped his arms around Dale. She pulled him by his tie towards the bed, conveniently beside the candlelit table. But before she pulled him down onto it, she spoke as she broke their kiss, speaking softly. "Please be gentle with me. Please take it slow."

"Of course," he whispered back. "If it gets too much, just tell me, okay?"

"Okay," agreed Dale. She began to kiss him again, as she let go of his tie, letting *him* take control. He held her from her back and gently guided her further towards the bed. After a few moments, passionately kissing and caressing each other, he turned Dale around to carefully unzip her dress. He commented on how lovely it was. He liked it.

"Lovely? Come on, what were your thoughts when you saw me in it?" Derek started to slowly pull the dress from her shoulders and took a nervous breath.

"That you were damn sexy," Derek murmured.

"Just *damn* sexy?" Dale asked, as she began to press herself up against his crotch, as her arse cheeks felt how firm she was making him.

"*Fucking* sexy. Fucking sexy as hell," he added. With her arse pressed firmly against him, now even firmer against her, Derek pulled the dress beneath her breasts and started to caress them with his hands. He kissed the back of her neck. Dale pulled his hands off of her and turned around to face him. She laid down on the bed, now looking up at him, as she asked him to take off her dress. "With pleasure," answered Derek.

The dress came off, revealing Dale's bare skin, which flickered in the candlelight. Derek knelt down and began to kiss her legs, slowly opening them to kiss her inner thighs, while his hands glided their way up and around her waist. He pulled her further forward. Dale let go entirely. She felt his every kiss, touch and grasp with pleasure. She had never felt so much pleasure. She had never allowed herself to feel such pleasure. Next, off came Derek's clothing, by her control. He'd made his way up from kissing her thigh, her stomach, her breasts, her neck, and back to her lips, when Dale pushed him over onto the bed. She began unbuttoning his shirt. Once unbuttoned she pulled his torso up by it, now sat on top of his lap, and then tore off his shirt. A force entered her body as she pushed his now bare chest and back down onto the bed. She unbuttoned his belt and ripped it off, throwing it to the side, followed by his shoes and then trousers.

Dale knelt down in front of Derek, seeing a man who not only stood tall in his pair of underpants, but a young man who had made a young woman feel good. A man that she loved. His skin also flickered in the candlelight. She wanted to make this man feel good. As good as he'd made her feel. So, she stood, and took off her own undergarments, standing bare naked in front of him as he looked up at her.

"I love you Dale," he said. The words ran over her like warm shower water. Her body craved him. She started to kiss his thighs as he had begun with her, making her way up to where she stopped, to pull down his underpants and, revealing his firm dick as it pulsated for her in the candlelight.

Dale's instincts took hold, and she crawled herself up to where she wrapped her mouth around him, rolling her tongue around his dick's tip, and sliding it up and down to the base of his balls. The sounds he made reassured Dale that she was making him feel good. And in turn, it made her feel good, and even felt something she hadn't experienced before. She felt herself moisten, inside. She felt wet, for him. Dale crawled on top of Derek, mounting him as she grabbed hold of his dick and started to jerk it, shortly before positioning it to slowly slide herself onto it. Her body started to move with his as he began to thrust in and out of her. Her arms gave, as she fell onto Derek's chest, with what she felt, feeling so fucking good, that all her strength seemed to vanish.

Derek grabbed Dale and rolled her around as he started to kiss her again. Dale remembered wanting to melt into his smile the first day they'd met, and this night she felt as though she did, but it was as if she melted into his entire body. Derek moved and laid Dale's head onto a pillow. He pulled her legs up around him, as if he could not get close enough. He held himself over the top of her as he continued to thrust in and out of her. Their bodily fluids mixed and slid between them. He felt so good inside her. Dale didn't want him to stop. He didn't want to stop. Though he did for a moment, as he slowly pulled out from her. But he wasn't finished; he started to roll his tongue down her neck and chest towards her nipples. As he rolled his tongue around her nipples, he'd started to roll his fingers around places that Dale felt had come to life for the very first time.

Derek wanted Dale's first time, with him, to last. They rolled in bed and turned on every angle, every touch feeling was better than the last. Every feeling lasting, every moment intensifying. The final moment, before Derek came, asking Dale if she had come. She grabbed him while she spoke.

"Fuck me, Derek. I think I've come a thousand times." He began to fuck her, hard. Although as he came, a flash of images entered Dale's mind. Not images she had seen before or images she expected. For whatever reason, in the final moments of their intimacy, Dale saw flashes of Derek coming inside other women, as he came inside her.

Dale squeezed her eyes shut and pushed Derek off of her as he let out an almighty groan. Flashing images of other women's bodies came into Dale's mind like flipping quickly through a scrapbook. She curled up on the edge of the bed and tried to breathe, not quite understanding what she was seeing, or why. She hadn't opened up to Derek about many things. Her ability of sight was certainly one of them. She didn't know what to say. How to explain to him what had just happened. She didn't quite know what had just happened herself. She wondered if it was just a reel of past girlfriends. Her common-sense said, no. Her images were vivid. The two of them had been together for just over a year at that point, and the images that entered her mind were most definitely not of a younger Derek – not of the boy that she met but the man that she loved. She felt sure that, in that moment, Derek had been unfaithful. Unfaithful with many women.

That particular night, Dale let it go. She put her sight to the side. When Derek questioned what happened in that final moment, she merely told him that she didn't think she was quite as ready as she had thought. The truth was that she *wasn't*, not for what just happened. Not jolted by the images which had triggered her before, but taken by surprise with a set of new ones. As usual, Derek didn't push. He accepted her answer and went to snuggle in behind her. Dale told him she needed some space. Again, he accepted, but told her what an incredible night it had been. Dale told him dinner was in the oven and to help himself. She wasn't hungry anymore.

*

While Derek ate dinner alone, at the candlelit table, he did so in a rather awkward silence. Dale stayed curled on the edge of her side of the bed. She held her eyes shut tight and tried to pace her breathing. The thought that the boyfriend, who she'd once thought was everything she needed, had been messing around behind her back, was a little too much to bear. Try as she might, she could no longer hold in her tears, and they began to fall onto her pillow. Derek stopped eating and came to be by her side.

Dale didn't feel ready to talk with him. At least, not about her sight. But she did feel perhaps it was time to open up about her childhood. She thought perhaps if she did that, the hurt he felt when she shied away, and the frustration he must have held in himself, would all fall into place, the place not being personal. The place becoming one of understanding. Dale thought she just might be able to turn a blind eye – if she opened up about all and considered moving forward. As she hoped he might too. But even if his own past stayed unspoken, unfaithful or not, Derek was still the best thing that had ever happened to her. She didn't want to lose that. It was time to invest.

7 THE WANDERED - PART TWO

I had almost given up at times, trying to fight my way through the smog to Greg's voice. Giving up on the idea of the two Aussies making their way through the torn down city. But I persisted. We'd engaged. In a way, we'd bonded. In a way, we'd gotten to know each other. Two strangers' voices getting to know one another through the dark smog of the Dark Enabled's return - unbeknownst to him. And in my persistence, the smog thinned, as I made my way out from a street lined with standing builds. I walked out to a large open space with the big dome and point of St. Paul's Cathedral set in all its former glory. Untouched. Untarnished. It had been a while since I'd taken in the beauty of the gorgeous grandeur of the old cathedral. I stood in awe for a moment as the smog passed around it like a moving haze.

Snapping myself out of it, I shouted for Greg.

"Greg! Where are you?"

"Michael! Michael I can see you! Over here! Over here!" I turned in an instant at the sound of his voice. In the open space, it came directly my way, no longer filtered by twisting streets. There he was. The other Aussie in the smog. He was wedged up against a car, in a heap of rubble that covered the sheet of glass jammed on top of his legs. Positioned perfectly to sit and admire St. Paul's Cathedral. The very thing he had *wandered* over to see. I ran his way, my arms flailing beside me in the big shaggy coat, and I knelt down beside him. I smiled.

"Hey!"

"Ah, Michael. You're not a poof, are ya?"

I couldn't quite believe my ears. All that time spent talking over the smog getting to know one another and the fucker had the nerve. The typical hetero-normative Australian response to someone prancing – even when that poof was coming to rescue them, apparently. He'd asked me if I missed anything about Perth as we had gotten to know each other when he hit a chord about Andrew. Well, the likes of Greg was something I definitely *did not* miss about Perth – the backward, narrow minded state of most of the population. I'd become so immersed in London life I truly had forgotten it existed. *Hashtag, not-all-of-Perth.* I stayed knelt beside him, wedged in between the car and the sheet of glass piled with rubble, feeling just about strong enough to maybe have attempted to use my abilities, to lift the pile off of his legs. But I definitely wasn't about to now.

"What gave it away? My campy run to rescue you or my fluffy coloured coat?" I laughed. "It's not even mine!"

Greg looked at me, uncertainly. He shrugged my questions away as if it didn't matter, just glad he had said what he did so I knew he didn't agree with it. I looked at him in awkward silence.

"Sorry. I didn't mean anything by it. I just.."

"Just need to check yourself? You're damn right. And I'm bisexual, I'll have you know. Well, I might be pan, I haven't figured that bit out yet," I said, talking my thoughts out to myself too.

"It's all beyond me. God made woman and man and that is that, I say."

"Well, I didn't ask you what you had to say about it now, did I, Greg? What makes you think I want your two-bob's worth? The world is moving forward, Greg, and you better damn well catch up, or get left behind." Greg held a look of shame, perhaps letting go of some masculine fragility he had held that he usually felt the needed to prove his masculinity. Probably used to making snarky comments around his mates. Realising his mates weren't around, just being two Aussies in some smog, one of which *was* a so-called poof.

We both stayed still for a moment in the silence. But it was his turn to speak. Redeem himself, if he wanted my help. I kept silent. Greg looked in deep thought for a moment. I wanted to prod, but I also wanted him to break down his own fragile wall.

"Can I tell you something?" He sounded as if he was about to open up with some massive confession. Maybe he was a *poof* too.

"Sure. It's not like I'm going to walk and leave you here. Although I can't lie, the thought *did* cross my mind!"

"That's fair. I deserve that."

"What's on your mind?" I asked. Greg looked up through the smog as his eyes became glassy. He was a big man. A bearded man. The kind you might find wearing a grotty singlet, sat on the couch, with a stubby and beer in hand after a hard day's work. But, *stone me crows*, as this type of gent would say, he just about looked as if he was going to cry. He took a deep breath.

"I think one of my sons might be gay."

"Okay. Well, if that's what you're about to cry about I'm definitely jumping up and leaving you here."

"No, no. It's not that. I think I've always known, you know? Building myself to accept it. Come to terms with it. Heck, stick up for him if a mate of mine made a comment about it," he explained, as he closed his eyes and breathed heavily, as if he had more to say.

"Well, that sounds pretty positive to me, what's so bad about that?" I asked.

"Ah, jeez Michael. Look you got me all worked up."

"Hey, it's okay. It's just us here. Who am I going to tell?" I tried to lift the mood jokingly. Greg laughed for a moment, breaking his brink of falling into tears.

"I wasn't a good dad, Michael. I was a bit of a drunk. Washed away in the drink every night. My wife got custody. It's why I travel so much. Why I wander. Wander the world. Trying to fill the void, I guess. Or at least have stories to bring back home to the boys. Be the dad that shows them the world through his eyes. Keep them close."

"I'm sorry about that. But it sounds like you're on the right path now," I tried to reassure him.

"That's just it, mate. When I wasn't such a good dad, I noticed the one I told ya about playing with a doll. Got it from a friend's house, I think. I took it right off him and threw it in the bin. But laying here now... Well... I'd buy every fucking doll in the world for him." His eyes started to tear. The tears rolled out onto his face. Then he started to laugh. "Look what you damn well done. You've turned me into a bloody pussy," he said.

"Hey. None of that. I won't have degrading words around here, thank you very much." He cracked a smirk and apologised. "I mean it. That's a horrible word, Greg. As is *poof*. There's so much attached to them." He listened. It was pretty amazing how quickly the guy broke down his wall too. It just took being rescued by a queer. I did wonder, had we been at a pub over in Australia, if we'd be having the same conversation. Most likely not. But just maybe, should he get back home, I might have been his turning point. Played a part in his change. Moved his way of thinking forward. He seemed genuine at heart. He was just another man caught up in society's impressions, set up by the Hollywood American dream and Christianity's marriage values. I had faith from what I'd witnessed that he was on his way to leading a better life. He'd clearly already pondered on his son, and sat in the smog. I hadn't been part of that.

Greg leaned his head back on the car behind him. I looked at the rubble piled over him and the sheet of industrial glass. I wondered, indeed, if I'd built up enough strength to move it all with my mind.

"So, what's next?" Greg asked.

41

"Well. I'm going to blow your mind even further a moment," I said, thinking about how to word what I was about to do. But there was no time like the present and I had to make tracks to Café De Paris. I'd wasted enough time trying to find my way to Greg. So, I just came out with it. "You might not believe me. But I'm not only a bisexual come pan questioning man. I also have the ability to move things with my mind."

Greg looked up at me and let out a real big man belly laugh. As he did, there was no time for further explanation. I stood up from where I was knelt and shot out my hands in front of me. The sleeves of my big woollen coat dangled below my wrists. I focused my mind and closed my eyes as Greg began to speak.

"Come on, mate. Enough with the funny business. Let's move some of this stuff off of me."

"Shut your trap. That's exactly what I'm trying to do."

I felt a rumble below my feet. I felt my knees begin to quiver. As I slowly opened my eyes I looked out between my arms and now shaking hands. The rubble piled over Greg started to shake. It not only shook but began to clear off the sheet of glass that lay on his legs. He looked up at me with confusion and amazement. His big belly laugh returned, this time into an excitable one.

"What are you doing?! This is crazy! Mate, you're doing it!"

"Just a little more," I said, as I started to feel my strength weaken. My hands started to shake more and my knees felt as if they were about to collapse. I closed my eyes again to focus on my strength, hoping to not just shift the rubble but slide the sheet of glass from his legs too.

With my eyes tight shut, my legs gave under me, and I fell flat on my arse. I'd used up all the strength I had built up. I opened my eyes and looked over at Greg. Slowly pushing myself back up, I rubbed my butt cheeks which I was sure would shortly see bruising.

"Mate. That was incredible. I've never seen anything like it!" Greg looked around at the rubble which had cleared clean off the glass. I, however, approached Greg, not so much looking at the rubble I'd managed to clear, but through the glass at his legs, into which one of the sheds was now wedged. Sliced in between his foot and his left leg. His left foot slanted and cut open, not trapped by the glass, just about detached from it. My eyes traced his legs back up to his body, stopping at his waist.

Through the glass, before camouflaged as part of the rubble, a piece of street signage stuck out from it. It had pierced clean through. I blinked with shock, as I realised what the sign had also pierced through. *Greg.* An area of vital organs, too. I had no doubt the sign was currently keeping such organs in place. He was not getting up from this place.

I looked up at Greg with not one word to say. Not knowing what to say. His big man belly laugh had stopped. He started down at himself and looked ghostly.

"Greg. Greg, I…"

"No. No, it's okay. I think you've done all you can do. That's it. If emergency services come along maybe I'll get out of here. If they don't, well maybe that's me done, Michael. I'm glad, if it is, that I got to share the story of my boy with you." My own eyes started to fill with tears.

"Well, now look at what you've done. You've turned me into a.. Well, a blubbering mess," I said, as I felt this bond flee. As I felt the moment of two Aussies in the smog about to come to an end. Glad that I was the one that found him. The one other Aussie in the smog – another wanderer.

8 STRINGS AND STICKS

Dale had opened up to Derek, still not about her sight, but very much about her abusive past. As ever, he held her while she spilled her tears, comforting her with his kind and caring ways. Despite his deceit. Dale felt a huge weight lift from her chest, feeling that the investment she put into him by delving into her past might have seen a change in his ways. She thought it might have seen him stop messing around in the background, now, with a better understanding. In a way, she'd hoped he might have, in turn, opened up to her, about his frustrations over the course of their relationship which had led to his deceit. He did not.

Dale still wasn't about to lose the best thing that had come into her life, and so she held onto the hope that now she had further invested in him, he would in her. Just maybe he would bring up his own history in his own time. But that wasn't for her to prompt, still having hidden the last part of herself. Dale wanted to let a natural progression take its course. She didn't want to be the girlfriend that had to pin her boyfriend down for forced information. She wanted Derek to open up in his own time. Willingly.

Two years on from the day that they had met, Dale turned eighteen years old. The months that led to her eighteenth birthday saw sorrow and disappointment hit their small studio apartment. Joined by tension and raised voices, then the very night of her eighteenth birthday saw heated jealousy take hold. Jealousy which took hold on both sides. The months of sorrow hit, as the flashes of Derek with other girls had become a regular pattern within Dale's mind. The pattern saw Dale begin to shy away from Derek again when he made an advance. This, Dale felt sure, resulted in a continued pattern of his ways, resulting deeper and deeper in Dale's distrust and lack of respect for him, which in turn Dale felt sure had begun to activate her sight more frequently.

Dale gave in to her visions. Her sight. She started feeding off of them. Honing in and assessing them. Trying to figure out if they were visions of what had been or what was yet to be. Clinging on to the hope that she'd once held in Derek opening up to her about his own history. His current activity. One night, coming home after a late night shift at the hostel, Dale walked into their flat, opening the door to a vision that felt as if it smacked her right in the face. Dale felt nauseous as she dropped to the floor with a flicker of images entering her mind: *Derek passing a drink to a woman by their bed; Derek throwing his glass aside as he takes the woman in his arms and starts to ravish her.*

Derek ran to Dale's side on the floor. He went to touch her.

"Don't fucking touch me!" Derek flinched and stood back, unprepared for such a reaction.

"Dale. Babe. What's wrong?"

"Don't you fucking dare." She'd had enough. She couldn't wait any longer. *Our fucking bed?* Dale looked over at the bed and its messed up covers. To the side of the room, where Derek had clearly tried to clear up his smashed glass, but a shard of his thrown glass remained. Dale started to cry. Derek shut the door behind him and walked around to kneel and face her. "Just tell me. Just come out and god-damn tell me."

The studio flat sat quiet for a few seconds as Dale sensed the wheels turning in Derek's mind.

"What am I supposed to tell you?" Dale laughed in his face.

"Derek. The fucking bed. I made it this morning."

"Sorry babe. It was a big day. I needed a nap."

"I call fucking bullshit! Just own it. Fucking come out and say it!"

"Say what?!"

"That you fucked someone in our bed! That you've been fucking other people our entire relationship. That you just couldn't wait for me to be ready like you said you would!"

Confronted by Dale, Derek didn't find ways to hide or justify his actions. He knew why he'd done what he did, and so did Dale, but it didn't excuse it. He'd hurt her. He'd lied to her. He'd deceived her. His pathetic excuse of not being able to wait for his girlfriend before whipping out his cock again was not going to fly. It was a hard night, for them both, with many deep words exchanged. Dale further shied away from Derek for some time after, even in the absence of any advances. But the two of them worked through it. That is, until the night that he'd come home with a flicker of new images for Dale to digest. This was when the tension began.

Dale found herself caught in a repetitious cycle. Not wanting to let the best thing that had happened in her life go – despite the best thing that happened not being able to show her mutual respect. Dale's faith in Derek dwindled, as did her energy, her ability to care. She saw a man hating himself for the times he screwed around on her. But equally, she saw the images of a man making the same mistakes over and over. Though with dwindling faith and a lack of energy, Dale soon stopped addressing what she saw, accepting it for a life she felt was as good as she would get. Somehow finding it in her to feel sorry for Derek and help him through his mistakes rather than abandon him. A subtle trait not known to her, but one definitely set from her own experience with her father.

Unbeknownst to either Dale or Derek, Derek's own ways were also set onto him by childhood experiences. The urge to be noticed, wanted and loved, growing up in a household with preoccupied parents whose only attention seemed to be addressed with the presence of others from outside their household. Clients, friends or equally preoccupied extended family who walked in with no notice for young little Derek. *Annoying Derek*, as his aunty used to say.

The feeling of not being wanted, which Dale's own triggers had distilled inside him from the days his own mother and father would brush him aside like crumbs of toast on the kitchen counter, too focused on their work, as business-minded folk.

Alhough the tension leading up to Dale's eighteenth birthday grew, so did the feeling inside Dale that said *don't abandon this boy, he's been good to you, and he'll be good still.* Alongside the tension and repeated mistakes, Derek tried as he might to make it up to Dale each time. Flowers, roses, chocolates and pleas on his knees. Torn between his love for her and his set traits of the need to be seen and embraced. Dale's eighteenth birthday was one he wanted to make a fuss over, and one he wanted to highlight to her his genuine love, regardless of his mistakes.

In the time Derek and Dale had been together, they'd learned much about one another: one thing that Derek had learned of Dale was her absolute love for music. Although she hadn't divulged the events which led to her need for escapism through headphones, she'd certainly addressed her love of flying away from earth with the tunes made by strings and sticks. Indie rock was a particular favourite of hers.

Derek wanted Dale's love for such sounds which made the human body move in rhythm, for her first night as a legal aged adult, to take her out to the Brighton Musicians Bar. He wanted to watch her eyes fixate on a live band as her body swayed with drink in hand. He wanted to see her get lost in a room where the strings and sticks bounced off the walls. Although the thought seemed perfect, backed up even more so when Derek pulled out the tickets to show her as Dale smiled ecstatically and wrapped her arms around him, Derek never could have foretold that it would be the night to change their lives - sending them on their separate ways. Derek never could have foretold that it was the night that Dale would meet a man named Dan.

Walking into the Brighton Musicians Bar sent pulsing adrenaline through Dale's veins. It kicked in even more as she stood outside in the line holding Derek's hand, hearing the beats and bass rumble through the brick walls. As Dale walked inside her eyes filled with the gleam of chasing colours from the cans pointing at the stage. The stage flashed colours as the band played. The band filled the stage with movement and sound. The sound made by the band filled the room with life. The room filled with people, stood as they moved with that life. People walked in front, behind and to the side of Dale and Derek. Some headed for their mates with drinks in their hands while others headed for the bar with their wallets.

Dale looked over at the bar which ran along the side of the venue, the stage front and centre and a set of pool tables at the back. Glasses clinked and voices mashed with volume.

"What do you think? Good place to spend your eighteenth?" Derek asked.

"I love it!" Derek placed his arm around Dale's waist as he began to guide her over to the bar.

"Let's get a drink, shall we?" Derek shouted over the crowd as they walked through it. They squeezed through groups of people bobbing in one spot.

"Sure! I'll have a rum and cola I think!"

Once they reached the bar, Derek insisted Dale turn and watch the band while he got their drinks. She did. Right at the moment she turned to face the stage, the lead singer of the band stepped forward and into a spotlight. The coloured lights from the cans faded. *This one's for some very special people in my life,* he said. *They couldn't be here tonight, but it goes out to them.* He began to sing, and he started to play the guitar which hung from a strap around his shoulders. It seemed the band bowed out for this one. He was going solo.

The energy of the room changed. Not negatively, it just changed. The energy had gone from buzzing and banging to admiration and respect. Derek turned around to be back with Dale as he handed her the rum and cola. She took it from him, with her eyes transfixed on the man that stood under the spotlight. The words he sang spoke of sharing, love, attentiveness, and one showing another a life that couldn't be imagined. Derek looked at Dale, her eyes glued to the stage, and smiled as he put his arm around her. His hold broke Dale's focus for just a second, as she looked at his hand now clutching her shoulder, but quickly looked back to the stage. The song soon came to an end. *That was 'Three Peas in a Pod' and I've been Dan Segway,* said the lead as he waved goodnight to the crowd. His solo had finished the band's set as another group took to the stage, the existing group packing off.

Dale watched as Dan Segway left the spotlight, which had shone a warm light on his chocolate brown hair, him stepping off of the stage into the crowd. People patted his back with smiles and girls flirted around him.

"Dale... Dale, did you hear me?" Derek asked. Dale hadn't heard a word he'd said in her mesmerisation. The words to the song had moved her, but so had the way Dan held his guitar, with the attentiveness of which he'd sung, as described about the care of the people in the song.

"Sorry, sorry. I - I need to go to the bathroom. Do you mind?" Dale asked, handing him her drink.

Dale made her way to the back of the room by the pool tables and stood in a line for the ladies' bathroom, with Dan still imprinted on her mind. The way his song had made her feel still vibrated through her body. Dale looked around the room, absorbed in the atmosphere, moved in a way she'd never been moved before. The new band began to play and a new set of energy took to the room. Dale looked around at the people enjoying themselves, and then as she turned back toward the pool tables, there was Dan, standing at the back of the bar's end.

Dale froze a moment. She looked away and down to the ground. A lady behind her asked if she was in line. Dale said she wasn't. Her brain had stopped functioning. Quickly realising she *had* been in the line, the line had already adjusted and moved around her. Dale started to move around awkwardly, letting the people which had hopped onto the back of the line behind her in front.

"You alright, miss?" Dan asked. Dale looked up. Dan Segway had walked right up to her. He was looking directly at her. She looked directly at him. "You look a little lost. Like you might have misplaced something." Dale giggled, and thought she must have looked like a right git. *Of course, this is how I meet Dan Segway*, she thought.

That was that. The conversation, no matter how awkward it had started, had begun. Dale praised Dan on his performance. She looked into his hazel eyes as he spoke back with gratitude. His eyes made her feel the way his music had. They spoke a short while and Dan rather suggestively had Dale take out the brick of a phone he spotted wedged into her jeans. Not many people had them, but the hostel had invested in one for her so she could be on call. He gently took it from her, with the green screen lighting his face as he dialled in his number. He joked about it as he tried to navigate his way to do so. Dale said she didn't even really know how to use it herself, she just answered it if it rang. He handed the phone back to her.

"If you're ever lost in this place again, flick me a message and I'll come find you. Lead of the band's got one too," he insisted. The green light from the phone lit her smile as she told him that she would. "Well go on then, call me so I've got yours," said Dan. "Who knows - maybe I'll need you to come find me sometime," he finished.

Dan watched her with his hazel eyes as she did – he felt the buzz on his hip with his phone clipped to his belt as he smiled.

"My name's Dale, by the way. You know, so you can save the number under my name," but the light from her screen quickly vanished as she dropped it at the unexpected feel of the clutch of a hand on her shoulder. The hand that had caused her so much grief. The hand that she held hope for. Derek's hand.

"Babe, there you are. I've been waiting at the bar for you. I finished both our drinks," laughed Derek.

The feeling Dale got when Derek had clutched her sunk her stomach. It was an odd feeling. A feeling that questioned why he was there. A feeling that said, *no, go away, this is my moment.* Dan bent down and picked up Dale's phone and handed it back to her.

"Got to be careful with those things, they're damn expensive. And, sorry, I didn't realise I was keeping her from someone. Please, excuse me," said Dan.

"It was nice to meet you," said Dale.

"It was nice to meet you too, Dale." Dan smiled her way, followed with a nod to Derek, and walked off. Derek let go of Dale's shoulder and turned to her.

"Thanks Dale. Thanks for leaving me hanging on the night of your eighteenth birthday while you get chatted up by a musician."

"Derek, I was just waiting to go to the bathroom and he started talking to me. What was I supposed to do?"

"Oh yeah, 'cause there's such a long line," said Derek, gesturing towards the bathroom door. Time had slipped through Dale's fingers while she was talking to Dan. The line she'd been in was no more. She'd sunk into Dan's hazel eyes and let the world around her dissolve.

"I'm sorry Derek," said Dale.

"No. You know what, I'm done tonight. If that's how the start of your birthday's going to be, I'll see you at home. Have fun!"

It was a reaction Dale hadn't yet experienced from Derek and triggered the abandonment of her father within her. It didn't even cross Dale's mind that his attitude was unfounded. She reached out to grab Derek's arm as she screamed his name.

"Derek, stay!" She felt something vibrate through her body. Derek turned around and looked at Dale as his facial expression blanked over.

"Okay Dale," he said. Dale felt a strange sensation come over her. Although she suspected it, she didn't quite know it for certain, but she had indeed in that moment taken control of Derek's mind.

"Come on. Derek. It's my birthday. Dance with me." Derek stood in the Brighton Musicians Bar, surrounded by people and clanging glasses, among the music bouncing from the walls, completely blanked in his ability to do or say anything at his own will, entirely at Dale's disposal.

Dale took Derek's hand and led the two of them back through the crowd of people to where Dale began to dance with him. Derek, however, stood still. Unable to move, his mind blanked by the overpower of Dale's want for him to stay. Dale nestled her head into his chest and closed her eyes as she swayed with him to the sounds of the music, escaping the world that she lived in with the sounds of strings and sticks.

9 DORMANT

I walked on, leaving Greg, the other Aussie in the smog, behind me. As I walked, I felt my chest clench tight. I wiped tears which had started to fall from my eyes. As I tried to find my way back through the twists and turns, in the thickened smog, I felt a moment of overwhelming emotion. I fell to the ground feeling just about ready to give up and started to cry. I sat still for a while as my tears fell onto the rubble covered ground below me. Then, I heard a scream. But it wasn't Greg. It sounded as though it was the scream I'd heard when I woke up on the bank by the bloody River Thames. The one that had faded.

My tears dried. I straightened my slumped posture and listened out. The scream took to the air, again. Then, again. This time, more lasting. Louder. It sounded closer and closer. I heard a loud bang and crash. It frightened me. It didn't sound far at all. The scream continued and just about sounded as if it was coming straight for me. Then as if it was right in front of my face, as I saw a girl with long bright red hair emerge from the smog, falling down in front of me. She looked up and directly into my eyes. Her eyes were full of fright. What felt like a paused moment when our eyes locked was quickly broken as a figure in a large black coat and hood plunged down out from the smog, grabbing the redhead's legs.

The black hooded figure pulled the red head back with it into the thickened smog. I stood instantly as I felt a wind of urgency take to the air –

tossing my thoughts of giving up aside. The urgency felt like it filled my body with an emergency instinctive strength. Standing tall, I clapped my hands together, engaging the energy of emergency strength. The smog ahead of me parted down the street on which I stood. The wind of urgency was now in my control, blowing the smog from my sight and out down the street.

Ahead of me now within my line of sight, the black hooded figure stopped in its tracks, dropping the redhead's ankles from its grip. It looked up and around it, seemingly confused by the vanishing smog, and turned around to find me standing with my hands clapped together. I didn't know the story. I didn't know the events that had led the two figures here. But I wasn't about to stand for a girl being dragged by her ankle and seemingly frightened for her life. I released my hands, clenching my left fist, while my right hand formed its fingers as if a baseball had been placed in my palm, and just like baseball I proceeded to bring my right hand under and then over me, although in place of a ball being released like an overarm throw, with my hand back in front of me, I clenched it with aim at the black hooded figure and pulled my fist back towards me.

The black hooded figure flew towards me in an instant and stopped, suspended above the ground directly in front of me. His flight my way saw his hood fall from his head, revealing nothing but a pathetic, aged, frail man. I wondered how such a man could have held the strength to drag the frightened redhead behind him down the street at such a rapid pace. No matter; it was not how you treated a lady, and I told him so before joining my left hand with my right. As my hands joined, I tore them away from each other, like I imagined Moses might have done when he parted the Red Sea. I didn't part the sea, so much as I tore the figure in front of me into two.

Oh, the pleasure I felt as, for a split second, I saw the frail man's eyes fill with the fear he had instilled into the redhead, just before his body had split into two. Both sides slammed against the buildings either side of the street and slid down to the ground. I started to make my way towards the redhead as the smog crept back into the street. She had begun to scream again and crawled her way up against the wall of the building on my right.

"What are you?! What are you?! What are you?!"

I bent down beside her, realising that a man torn in half while suspended in the air would have been a horrific sight. Despite my own desensitisation to it.

"It's okay. I mean you no harm. He wasn't a good guy. What's your name?" I asked, and paused for a moment seeing the fright still in her eyes. "If you want me to stay you can answer. If you don't, I'll leave you be." The redhead caught her breath and looked up at me, then looked over at the two halves of the black hooded figure's body. She then looked back at me.

"I'm... Precious," she replied. I smiled. I was glad she answered me. I stood up and extended my hand.

"Pleasure, Precious. I'm Michael." Precious took my hand, and I helped her back up on her feet. As she stood she'd started to brush herself down. She was wrapped in a brown trench coat, her red hair resting vibrantly on it. She pulled something out from inside the coat. It was a fuzzy dark brown beret. She held it in one hand while she pulled her fingers through her hair with the other. Then she proceeded to pull the beret onto her head.

"Thanks for your help, Michael. I mean that. Thank you. But what the fuck was that?!"

"Shall we walk and talk?" Precious laughed, not so much friendly as almost psychotically.

"Sure! Sure, Michael! Let's walk and talk about how you ripped a man in two!" Precious said sarcastically. "Where to?"

I explained how I was heading towards Café De Paris, to see if some people I knew were there. That it was classed as London's most glamorous bunker. She thought it was a good destination if ever there was one. The two of us began to make our way back through the smog and returned to the path alongside the bloody River Thames.

"So, you don't seem overly shocked about what I just did, I have to say…"

"I've just spent the last day hiding and being chased by a man that bashed down walls with his fists and smashed his way through windows by walking through them. Before that, I swear I saw a fucking dragon flying in the sky, and before that… Well, before that I was in Leicester Square with some friends when the sky filled with a fuck load of fluorescent colours and everyone in the square – including my friends – was zapped from it. The whole area emptied of everyone in it. Except me. So, yeah, seeing a man ripped in two… Not the most shocking to me right now," explained Precious. "I was more thankful that you didn't come and do it to me."

I couldn't quite believe my ears. *The dragon - yes, I'd seen something quite similar before I'd fallen into the bloody waters of the River Thames. The fluorescent colours in the sky - absolutely. I was witness to it all myself. But Leicester Square? Everyone vanishing apart from this girl - why?* I asked if Precious had seen anything else leading up to that moment. But she pulled me up on the fact that I hadn't answered her question yet. I hadn't explained what I'd just done or who I was. She said that if we were going to start an apocalyptic adventure together, she wanted to know exactly who she was adventuring with and if I knew anything else about what was going on. That, and why I was wearing a shaggy wool coat. She laughed.

Precious' personality intrigued me. It did seem a little careless as she skipped along the path by the Thames - oblivious to the destruction around her. But at the same time, her presence felt encouraging. A new spark of energy that told my mind, that had been so ready to give up, to carry on. I explained to Precious about my ability. She was fascinated. But again, strangely not surprised. Lord knows how long I'd been passed out on that bank. Precious had clearly seen a lot. I, of course, left out the gritty details of the events that had led me to London, but I did tell her that I held a past I wasn't so proud of, and that London was a fresh start for me. She then proceeded to walk up close to me and grabbed hold of my hands. She held them as she spoke to me. She said that we all have a past. She said that I needed to let it go. That what I did in the present, here and now, is what matters.

I looked at Precious as she spoke. She seemed to speak from experience. I knew there was more to this girl, and I was looking forward to getting to know a bit more about her. I was glad to have the company. The new spark of energy. Somehow, she made all the heaviness in the world right now seem lighter. As if she was here to help carry it. Like an extra pair of hands on a big grocery shop. Appreciated. As we walked I went on to tell Precious about my abilities. I was vague on detail, but shared that there had been someone very close to me who betrayed me. Misguided me. As well as a circle of others close to them. Jade being the hardest hitting. Precious took in every moment. Not questioning one thing. Just listening and taking in what I had to say, and grabbing hold of my hand while we walked to let me know that she was there. That I wasn't alone anymore. The girl was welcomed, and refreshing.

10 DAN SEGWAY

Eighteen years old and into her third year with Derek, Dale's hope for him changing his ways started to fade. One night, the guy stepped into their flat virtually in tears, clearly having carried the guilt home with him, as he spoke the words *Dale, I fucked up again*. Having relied so heavily on Derek the last few years of her life – since escaping foster care – their circle of friends were *his* friends. She'd never gotten close to anyone at work – never wanting to get close enough to someone that might pry into her past. Dale didn't have anyone she could turn to, or speak to, as Derek had always been the one she would open up to when she needed to. Except, this time it was *him* about whom she needed to open up.

The words *I fucked up again* hit Dale like a brick in the face and she was all out of energy to say one word back. She let the brick hit her and drop without reaction. She made her way to the bathroom and splashed her face, then walked out of the door. Derek, feeling he had no place to stop Dale, let her. She made her way to the Brighton Musicians' Bar. Being a weeknight, it was a quiet night, which actually suited Dale just fine. In her state, she felt the only thing that could soothe her soul would be the sounds of those strings and sticks, which was welcomed without the loud crowds of people and clanging glasses.

Dale pulled a stool up to the side of the bar. She ordered herself a rum and cola as she listened to the band on stage. The room was set for the quiet night that it was, with tall tables and stools scattered around the room. Some held couples, one held a table of one and some were empty, but Dale felt more comfortable up by the bar. She wanted to admire the sounds the band made from afar. The tunes this night felt much more mellow. It was certainly a sombre night in comparison to the night of Dale's eighteenth birthday.

Stirring her drink with the straw which the bartender had thrown into it, Dale listened to the ice cubes clunk against each other in her glass, and then caught a fright as someone pulled up a stool. Dale looked at the person who had placed themselves in front of her. Hazel eyes. It was Dan.

"Well, hi there Dee! Can I call you Dee?" Dan asked. Dale smiled. She hadn't been given a nickname before.

"Hi, Dan. Dee works." She couldn't seem to get the smile off her face. She hadn't come back to this bar just for the music. Deep down she'd hoped by chance something like this might have happened. That she'd run into Dan. Someone she could talk to. But she hadn't quite thought it would have happened like it did. Dan, pulling *his* stool up to *her*.

"It's so good to see you back. Where's your fella?" Dan asked. All of a sudden it wasn't so hard to get rid of her smile. Dan looked at the way she had curled into herself and quickly and intuitively responded. "Ah, you know what? Think it's good for a lady to get out for some self-lovin'! What brings you back? Here to check out Lounge Night?"

"Lounge Night?"

"Dee! Dee, Dee, Dee, Dee, where have you been? Lounge Night! The one night in here you can sit and enjoy the vibes without a drink getting spilled on you. Great night for a date if I do say so myself. But then, I'm biased; I just love this place."

"Yeah, the vibes are nice and chilled tonight," said Dale as she nodded. "So, are you?"

"Am I?"

"On a date tonight?" Dan laughed.

"No such luck. I was standing up this evening, so I thought I'd have a drink with myself over there." He pointed to the table where Dale had seen the table of one – not knowing it was him from the back of his head. "Join me?" Dan asked.

"Sure. Okay, yeah," answered Dale, appearing to be convincing herself to do so. Dan smiled and extended his hand to her.

Dale didn't so much mind the change of seating anymore. If she was honest with herself, she'd sat by the bar in hope of seeing him walk through the door. She was with him now. She didn't mind where they sat. The table had a small tealight candle in the middle of it which lit a warm covering of light over Dan's face as he took his seat beside her. He gestured up to the stage and looked back at Dale.

"Love these guys. The Table Turners." Dale looked up at the stage and started bobbing her head to the beat. There was no singer. The people on stage just played as a four-piece ensemble.

Dan looked at Dale as she bobbed her head. He cracked a slight smirk to himself. He liked that she liked them. Also, further intuitively, he liked that she looked as though she was enjoying herself. He had clocked that it wasn't a great night for her. Whatever the reasoning.

Dan leaned in closer to her and spoke as he continued to watch the stage.

"So, you're new around here, aren't you? BMB is a kind of local hangout. I've not seen you around before the night we met."

"BMB?"

"Brighton Musicians Bar," he explained as he laughed.

"Oh. Sorry. Not with it tonight. Yeah, the night you met me was my eighteenth birthday."

"Was it now? Well happy birthday! I hope you had a nice night!" Dale smiled, then tried to change the topic.

"So, what about you? You end up having a good night?"

"Yeah, it ended up being a big one actually. Trace made it down in the end. Her shift finished early."

"Trace?"

"Trace, one of the three in the pod. My song. My girlfriend. Well, one of them."

Dale sat a little confused for a moment. She thought back on when Dan had said he was stood up. Then to the song he'd sung. Then to what he'd just said. *My girlfriend. Well, one of them.*

"I'm sorry. I'm a little confused. Your girlfriend? Weren't you out for a date tonight? Was Trace who stood you up?" Dale asked. Dan laughed.

"No, no. I go on dates sometimes. I've got my core-cule, but I'm a free spirit. I like to meet new people and investigate sparks when they pop up."

"Sorry, you're going to have to spell this out for me. I'm really confused," laughed Dale.

"Ah, new to the concept of polyamory, hey? Not surprised. It's only a fairly recent term. Hit the dictionary in ninety-two I believe. Although, the term polyfidelity, considered a subset of polyamory, was coined in the seventies when I'm guessing you were born!" The pair laughed.

"Polyamory?"

"Yeah, multiple people in non-monogamous relationships. Me, I've got my primary partner, Trace. She's my high school sweetheart actually. We were monogamous for a while. But I guess we both kind of grew as two individuals wanting to explore other things. Rather than go our separate ways, we decided to explore side by side. Not together - we hold our own relationships outside of ours - but side by side for sure. It's actually the darndest thing when your partner comes home from a date and tells you all the juicy goss. It's like hearing your best mate talk about a date they went on – but it's your partner," Dan tried to explain.

"Right, so who's the third pea?" Dale asked.

"Ah, Melissa. Dear, dear, Melissa. Melissa is my secondary, you would say. My second partner in line to Trace. My two peas!"

Dale didn't comprehend absolutely everything Dan spoke about. But she didn't want to pin him down about it all either. By the way he spoke about polyamory, he clearly loved it. It worked for him. The way he spoke about his girlfriends was with such pride, such love and respect. That's all Dale needed to know. Right now, a man with beautiful hazel eyes sat beside her, and she wanted to get to know him. This beautiful and honest man named Dan. *Honest* being the word that began to reel her interest in him even more.

The night Dan pulled his stool up to Dale was the start of something more to come. At first it was most definitely friends. Dale wouldn't have let it go beyond anything else, whether Dan had been interested or not. What made him an even better friend was that he himself had the option to pursue her, and yet, friends they stayed. Dale's fascination with Dan grew and grew as the weeks and then months passed by. Dale became quite the little regular at *BMB*. Before shifts. After shifts. But never with Derek. It became her new place of escape. A place she came to forget the world outside. A place she came to forget Derek.

Derek did begin to question her regular nights out. Despite the fact that she always came home. Although she fast squished his entitlement to question her - not having any. So, Dale, now with her place of escape, continued life happier than it had been. Dan became quite the pal. The two of them got on like a house on fire. She'd even befriended Trace. But she felt closest to Dan. Mel, she was yet to meet, as Dan's relationship with her was long distance. Mel lived in Wales, in the city of Cardiff.

When Dan had a few drinks, he would talk about life, in a way that made so much sense to Dale. His way of speaking was passionate and fulfilling. Dale envied it at times. But she was glad that it was so for him. She soon came to think that Dan was just everything. When she looked into his eyes, she saw the world. A world that perhaps she thought she might want to live in. A world she was curious about. A world with *him* in it. The closer the two of them became as their friendship flourished, the more questions Dale started to ask about Dan's life and polyamory. Not what polyamory was or how it worked - logistically she'd wrapped her head around it - but Dale wanted to know Dan's feelings on it.

To Dale's ears, he made it sound like a magical fairy tale world. He talked about how polyamory allowed you to form connections with multiple people. Explore flames that arose around you. As opposed to monogamy, where you're expected to defuse a flame or turn your back on it if it appears. He prided his life on it. He thought it was a beautiful thing. To be able to form a connection with someone and see where it might lead. It sounded wholesome to Dale. Honest. Real. Refreshing.

One night, Dale pried as to how Dan pictured his future, and potentially without making it obvious, she thought about how she might fit into it. Before too long, Dale felt the connection had become more than a friendship. Regardless of Dan remaining gentlemanly and not making an advance. Before too long, without realising it, Dale was head over heels in love with the guy. When he spoke, he made Dale feel like there was an honest and consenting way to live life. A life that Derek hadn't been able to give her – she wasn't sure that he could.

Dale plucked up the courage one night to bring the topic of conversation up with Derek. To see if polyamory is something he might have considered. If so, maybe she'd be able to have Dan as a secondary. If so, maybe he could help with Derek's troubles in the honesty department. She also thought that, just maybe, if Derek had the freedom and consent to do so, then his honesty would follow. In actual fact, it probably would have served and fed Derek's desire to be seen and loved in a much less toxic form. However, the thought was outrageous to him. Funnily enough, he couldn't stand the thought of Dale with another man. He'd come around to the thought of Dale getting with another girl if she wanted. The thought of Dale and another girl even turned him on. He'd even suggested it be something they try together one night – another girl in the bedroom with them. But Dale wasn't interested in another girl. She was interested in Dan.

Dan had become a real escape for Dale, and the thought of taking that relationship somewhere romantic really appealed to her. The appeal grew inside her like a warm loaf of bread rising in the oven with the baked aroma making you hunger for it. The thought of kissing Dan made Dale feel like she might float out from the earth's atmosphere and into the greater universe around it. The more Dan and Dale's friendship grew, the more Dale wanted him, although she kept that to herself.

The more their friendship grew, and the closer Dale and Dan became, and the further and further Dale drifted from Derek. Although Derek had once been the boy that picked Dale up and helped stand her on her two feet, she was now standing tall. It was Derek who was the only reason she sometimes found herself about to topple again. Six months into their third year together, and six months of friendship with hazel eyes Dan, Dale knew her worth when Derek expelled the words *Dale, I fucked up again*, one last time.

Dale had been doing the dishes in the sink when Derek walked in and told her. Whether it was because, in Dale's mind, she had already moved on, or that she knew she had someone that would catch her fall, she simply washed the last dish in silence and placed it on the drying rack. Her mind didn't react. She took no power over Derek. She simply dried her hands with the tea-towel, turned to face him, and told him she was done, before walking out of the door. As she walked down the road she dialled the number Dan had put into her phone. When Dan answered, she spoke the words: *I've left him.*

11 BURIED GLORY

Precious walked by my side as we navigated our way through the remains of Old London Town. Her vibrant red hair blew in the wind. It added some colour and vivacity to the darkened smog around us. She started to skip off to the right down a side street.

"What are you doing?!" I shouted out to her. She laughed and turned as she carried on skipping away.

"Come join me and find out!" I looked back at the bloody River Thames and then to Precious skipping away. I exhaled, knowing this little detour of hers – whatever it was for – would only further delay us. But her personality was just so infectious; I couldn't help but follow. I picked up my feet and jogged down the street to join her.

Catching up with her, Precious looked my way and smiled, as she grabbed my hand. She pulled it, trying to get me to pick up the pace.

"Where are we going?" I asked, shuffling quickly as she pulled me forward.

"We can't have you seen at Café De Paris in a woollen shaggy coat now, can we?"

"What now?" I was confused. Precious laughed and continued to tug me along.

"Just keep up, mister," she said. I let go of her hand as we started to weave our way through a line of jammed cars, some crashed up against another, some which had made a clear attempt to swerve but had crashed up against buildings, perhaps after looking up at the coloured lights that took to the sky. But, as I glanced inside them, they were each empty. Bodies seemed to be scarce. For a city like London, the bodies were far too few. It didn't quite equate to me. It hadn't before. But now… Empty cars. Something wasn't right. Nevertheless, Precious marched on, and so did I behind her.

Precious turned left onto the street ahead. She called out for me to come her way. As I jogged up to join her, not one, or two, nor five or six, but a street of what must have been ten or so red double decker buses toppled over and fell on each other stretched out before us in a line of other vehicles and black cabs.

"Far. Fucking. Out," I murmured to myself under my breath. Precious continued to skip down the street, beginning to twirl around in a circle with her arms out in the air. She laughed as she spun. This girl seemed way too ecstatic for someone who had seen what she'd seen. I looked out around the toppled buses. I knew this street. A memory of Pree and their pompous step came rushing into my mind. Delivering me to Dale. Parting with me after the first night we'd spent together. Precious had brought me to the Strand, the road that led on to Trafalgar Square. Where the lions had jumped from their stone blocks. Where the enchanted knife had been hidden and protected, which Dale, Lenroc, now had in their possession. Because of me. It was the road that led further onto the Mall, the long grand stretch towards Buckingham Palace. To the portal.

I stood still as I felt a rush of memories and emotions take over my body. It was also the road that I had walked as I stormed London in an almighty rage. Before I lost myself. Knowing that I was just that. Lost.

"Yo! Mikey! Get!" She broke my stance, I looked all around having lost sight of her. Then, to the right of the street I saw her standing within the frame of a storefront broken window, waving a broken mannequin's detached arm at me. I laughed. This girl might have been an oddball, but she certainly knew how to keep spirits high. I made my way over to her as she jumped down from the storefront and further into the store, her red hair lighting up the darkness.

I stepped up into the storefront. I brushed away shards of broken glass with my feet, then jumped down from it into the store. We had entered a clothing store. Precious wanted to dress me for the occasion. She really had something against my warm woollen coat. Or maybe she just wanted my reunion to be a picturesque one. Precious ran up to me in her oblivious world of joy – oh, to be inside that head of hers! – with some clothing draped over her arm.

"And what do we have here?" I asked.

"Now, now. No time for questions, only directions: just get this woollen eyesore of a thing off!"

As the woollen eyesore fell to my feet, Precious started to dress me. As she dressed me, she did so in a whimsical way. She hummed to herself and smiled in-between as she caught my stare. Because boy, did I stare. I stared into this vibrant, fun ball of energy's crystal eyes of a deep ocean blue. Precious had lived *some* life. Whatever life that was, it prepared her to push on, keep positive and make the most of all. Even an apocalyptic world. I found it hard to think anyone had pushed these ways upon her. As I stared into those eyes, I thought perhaps she'd led a life that saw her have to push them upon herself.

Precious clapped her hands together and spun on the spot, throwing a hand in the air with a click of her fingers.

"That's me done then?"

"That's you done? That's you done, did you say? I just snapped my fingers hun-tay, you ain't done, you are good to go!" Precious replied, in a very insightful queer cultured manner. It made me like the girl even more. Made me smirk even more. She patted me down. The clothing was covered with a dusty powder. The kind before you mix in the water to make cement. The kind that might cover a city when the Dark Enabled take to it. Precious grabbed my hand

and ran with me to the back of the store where it was lined with mirrors. I looked ahead.

Looking at myself in the mirror, I saw a speck of the old me. The me before I had become lost. A smirk on my face. Not of sinister intention or dark clouded judgment, but a smirk of endearment. Precious was starting to rub off on me. Make me feel good. I stood in fine fitted clothing, a silk tie, a sweater vest, a jacket and long thick dress-coat wrapped in a scarf. I almost looked as if I were off to the opera. *If this was what one gets to wear in an apocalyptic world, maybe it isn't going to be so bad.* I looked over at Precious, having absorbed some of her positive energy, and thanked her.

"What dress size are you?" I asked.

I had Precious take a seat while I browsed the cement powdered store for a garment she could slip into herself. In the corner of the room I noticed a dark red come maroon shimmery fabric. I walked to it and picked it up, dusting it off and looking at its size. I smiled. A red dress for the redhead. As a former drag queen, I could appreciate the cut. It was going to frame her shoulders perfectly. I walked back over and handed it to her. She smiled. She excused herself, making her way to a dressing room. I walked around the store with my hands in my new jacket's pockets while I waited for her. I walked back towards the storefront and looked out at the red double decker buses lined on the street. I wondered what was to come.

"Tens, tens, tens across the board darling!" Precious shouted. I turned to see her walking up to me, waving one hand high in the air, while the other held her dress up. It shaped her beautifully. Perfectly. Although, it hung off the shoulders.

"Oh, I'm sorry, allow me!" I ran to her as she turned to me to zip her up. I dragged the zip up slowly. It pulled in tight around her shoulders. Her shoulders were perfect too. As was her neck. I brushed her hair aside and out of the way of the zipper as it reached the top. My hand paused for a moment, as I let her hair go and I rested my hand on her left shoulder.

Precious turned around to face me after pausing a moment herself. I was sure that we'd both felt an interconnecting energy pass between us. She looked up at me.

"Do I look pretty?" A pause, again. I looked her up and down and stepped away, breaking the interconnecting energy between us, as Rubis popped into my mind. The ruby dress springing the first time I'd seen her enter Café De Paris.

"You do. You look astonishing."

"Shall we?"

"We shall," I replied, as I grabbed her brown coat and held it up for her. She turned, and placed her arms into it. As she buttoned her coat and wrapped herself in her scarf, I did the same. I felt, had I stayed in close proximity to Precious a few seconds more, something spontaneous and heated might have just occurred. In the middle of the buried glory that was London. In the middle of the emptied and cement powdered streets. I felt sure of it. But it wasn't the time or place. Rubis had come to mind, as had Pree not a few moments before. It was *their* time. It was time to venture on to Café De Paris. Or at least, to start there.

I extended my hand, and as Precious took it, we both walked back up and over the storefront's shattered window and returned to the Strand. I guided Precious back towards the River Thames; I wasn't about to walk towards Trafalgar Square. Precious had just snapped me out of my sorrow. I wasn't ready to face such a place. We started to weave our way back through the cars as we walked back down the street Precious had turned.

As we reached its end, we both jumped in fright as a long drawn out *squaaaaaark* took to the sky, a large gust of wind taking to the air with it. Flying over the bloody River Thames was the creature with wings both Precious and I had once witnessed separately. Its wings flapped and sprawled out large across the sky. In a matter of seconds it had passed us and become a mere figure in the distance as it flew back towards the Tower of London. Precious clung on to me tight in her fright. Holding me close, we both watched it as it flew away. Neither of us spoke a word; we just watched. Precious took back hold of my hand and we continued to walk on in the opposite direction.

While Precious and I walked along the river, she asked about the people I was hoping to find at Café De Paris. She wanted to know who we were going to meet and what they meant to me. She gripped my hand firmly as she said she wanted to know more about me too. I felt comfortable. She felt sincere. Genuine. Her queer references also made me feel like she was a person I could open up to freely. So, I did. As we walked on to Café De Paris, I told her we were off to meet Pree Possessing and Miss Rubis Rouge, two beautiful people who had opened my life up to a brand new world. The world of cabaret, and the world of polyamory. How Rubis had opened my eyes to it. How I had in fact opened Pree's eyes to it. As I spoke their names, and thought back on our experiences together, I felt hopeful. Perhaps I had given up on them too soon. Perhaps I hadn't made as much of an effort in keeping in touch as I could. Relationships were work. Polyamorous relationships were probably *a lot* of work. I hadn't put that work in. Jade had clouded my judgment and pulled me away. I cared for Pree and Rubis greatly. Speaking of them to Precious confirmed that. It was time to invest. They'd shown me nothing but open loving arms when they invited me into their world. It was my turn to reciprocate.

Precious spoke highly about her thoughts on polyamorous relationships. She felt they made sense. Weren't possessive. In her experience she said she felt many monogamous relationships were toxic, fuelled and possessing.

"It's just not in our nature to be monogamous. Hollywood's vintage family values distilled it into our society, as did the church through marriage. Along with a bunch of other horrifying vintage values of which we're thankfully ridding the world."

"I couldn't agree with you more." Precious threw me another smile and squeezed my hand.

"I can't wait to meet them."

"Well, you're not Pree's type. But I'm pretty sure when Rubis sees you in that dress her mind is going to go goo-goo ga-ga!"

We turned the tight curve of the River Thames, flashes of when I'd flown over the top of the London Eye ran into my mind, as I'd blown it down with the metal wheel and its pods crashing into the water below me. There on our left, straight ahead, was the very London Eye, indeed fallen into the bloody River Thames.

"Fuck."

"Fuck indeed," I said, not elaborating on what I'd done. I wanted to. Something in me told me that I could open up to Precious. That she'd take hold of my hands and listen. But something in me also said, once again, that it wasn't the time or place. I'd have my moment with Precious. But that moment wasn't yet.

I stopped walking and stood still as she pulled on my arm. She laughed.

"What are you doing, silly? We're going to Café De Paris, aren't we? It's up this way!"

"Precious. Please. Not that way." I pleaded subtly, knowing that the street she wanted to turn onto led up to Trafalgar Square.

"Okay. Okay, we can go another way," she said, empathetically.

"If we make our way down to Westminster, and through St James's Park, we can come back up and around through Piccadilly Circus."

"It's quite the detour. But sure, we can do that," said Precious, smiling at me with reassurance. God, she really was good. Just the companion I needed for this journey. We walked on. Hand in hand.

12 LAVENDER

Dale arrived on Dan's doorstep, collapsing in his arms, in a pool of tears. She found herself falling into his comforting grasp. Which, although was a very physical fall, as he held her in tears on his couch, she also very much metaphorically fell into his comforting grasp, which led onto falling into his magical world of polyamory. The world she'd seen through his eyes that she admired and respected. The world of integrity within which she thought she'd feel some comfort. After having tried so hard in a relationship full of lies and deception.

When Dale had arrived at Dan's house, his primary-partner Tracey had already left for work, working as an *actual* maître'd at one of Brighton's finest establishments. Dan had been having a night in with his guitar when Dale called, while he worked on a new solo for his set. Although, with his good friend in distress on the other end of the phone, his new addition to the set could wait. The two of them lay snug on the couch, Dale curled up into his chest, as she spilled out her emotions and feelings to do with Derek and his final straw. Just being there, on that couch with Dan, almost felt like it had healed her. It also felt right. It felt as if it was where she was meant to be. The days of deceit behind her, in the arms of a man she'd fallen in love with, albeit without his knowledge.

Dan, himself, sat there looking down at Dale with his own unshared realisation of love. A love that had grown over time through building a bond and a friendship. A love that had grown over time through seeing this individual open her mind to new and diverse people. A love that had grown over time in the back of his mind. A love that wasn't an option at the time. At first, he was certainly attracted to her when he approached. But as it unfolded that she was a taken, monogamous woman, he'd closed his mind off to anything other than friendship. That is, until this very moment.

As Dan held Dale in his arms, in a new found realisation of his love, he tried to resist asking her for a kiss. He didn't want it to be seen as taking advantage of her in her vulnerable state. Also, he wasn't sure he was willing to risk his bond and friendship with her. He'd dated former friends, which ultimately turned awkward. Sour, even. But, as he continued to stare down at her while she spoke, he felt his realised feelings for her were profound. Unique. He couldn't resist.

"Dale..." Dan interjected.

"Yes?"

"Can I kiss you?" In the blink of an eye, the answer needn't be given. Dale's eyes had widened with his words, being pure delight to her ears, and she leaned up to kiss *him*. She pulled back.

"You don't know how long I've been waiting to do that," said Dale. Dan smiled. He held her face and they started to kiss again.

"Is it weird how right this feels?" Dan asked. Dale very much agreed and took hold of the back of his neck, continuing to kiss him.

It was an extraordinary feeling to Dale. To be in someone's arms, kissing, in complete and utter comfort. Although she'd felt comfort to some extent, when she kissed Derek, she always felt on edge, that he might have made *his moves*. Kissing Dan felt new. Kissing Dan felt like the good forces in the world had overpowered evil in triumph. That no evil in the world could ever hurt her again. That there were good people in the world and she was with one. Dale pulled back from Dan's kiss.

"Take me to your room?"

Dan was taken back. But it was a surprise even to Dale. That she would be the one to suggest it. That she would feel comfortable enough, on first kiss, to be with someone. But he wasn't just anyone. He was Dan. In a way, she felt like Dan had made her comfortable some time ago. She had been ready to take that step with Dan for a while. It was just that she was never in the position to be able to take that step with him. That night, stepping out of Derek's life, she was.

Dan didn't even question it. The feeling in the room, the air, and between them, was too strong to push back. The only option between the two of them was to get closer. To be closer. Be as close as they could. To have him touch her. For his bare skin to rub against hers. For her to feel him inside her. For him to *be* inside her.

Having made their way to Dan's room, the pair of them took their time in undressing; taking in each other's features; Dan caressing Dale's neck and shoulders with his hands; Dale caressing his chest with hers; Dan massaging her breasts before taking his tongue to each of her nipples; Dale rubbing his thighs before softly stroking each of his freed balls; Dan running his hands down Dale's curves and onto her back – pulling her in to kiss her; their hands feeling their way around each other's bodies, soaking one another up; inhaling one another's scents and beginning to make love as Dan pushed his way inside of her.

It was the first time Dale had felt any satisfaction in sex. It was more than satisfaction: she felt liberated. It was the first time she'd felt someone's touch without a trigger or hesitation in her mind. What Dale felt with Dan that night was pure ecstasy. As Dan and Dale lay on his bed stroking each other's bodies, after having made sweet, intense and passionate love, they talked of each other's feelings: Dan of his subtle attraction towards her and emerged, profound feelings, which he'd come to realise as he held her on the couch; Dale of her deep respect and admiration for him and the life that he led.

From that night forward Dale well and truly fell into Dan's arms and into his life. She found it new and exciting to be introduced as his girlfriend at his gigs and social affairs. They became inseparable. They started going on date nights multiple times a week with a habit of sleepovers. Dan mostly stayed over at Dale's new flat-share, as opposed to her staying at his and Tracey's place. Tracey and Dan only had a one-bedroom apartment. The offer was there, and Dale did stay at theirs on the odd occasion. But with Tracey working nights, she looked forward to crashing at home in the early hours of the morning, to collapse on her and Dan's comfortable bed. Even so, Tracey had offered to take the couch some nights, while Dan and Dale had the bedroom. But it made Dale feel a little off. Not quite right. She couldn't put her finger on it, but she just couldn't get used to the arrangement.

Dale just preferred when Dan stayed with her. When she didn't have to share him with someone else in the morning. At hers, he felt like *hers*. At hers, it felt like there was nobody else in the picture. Like she felt secure he would stay, having the insecurities that she did with her preset ways, telling her he may leave her. *He may not need her forever,* they said. *Look what else he's got. Look who else he's got. Look at the life he has with Tracey. He has Melissa too.*

Although Melissa had already been in Dan's life, the more and more time Dan and Dale spent together, the less and less he and Melissa spent together. And Dale started to develop a new trigger. Melissa. It would go off when Dan talked about her. It was as if Dale had convinced herself she was secondary to Tracey. She questioned who Melissa, this third pea in the pod that lived in Wales, even *was* to Dan. All of a sudden Dale felt herself closing off from the guy with which she'd come to be able to enter an honest and open life. Things seemed to be manageable for a while. But as Dan realised he'd been showing Dale all his attention, he knew he needed to pick things back up with Melissa. Truth was, he'd only started seeing Melissa just before Dale and he had met. But when he started seeing Dale, his line of sight had become centred around her. Although, subconsciously, Dale's insecurities had made sure of that.

Dale had gotten used to being the girl on Dan's arm while Tracey was at work. She'd gotten used to being front and centre in his life. Their relationship had started passionately and intensely, jumping out of Derek's arms and into Dan's, that the mere thought of Melissa coming back, and more prominently at that, worked Dale up something fierce. She felt Melissa could take hold of Dan's life as front and centre. That she could be the girl he'd choose to have on his arm in place of hers one night. She couldn't even begin to comprehend the idea of the two of them on his arm.

In Dale's newly formed, closed off way, she bit her tongue as Dan started seeing Melissa more frequently. Dale sat back at her flat-share in her room like an anxious mess. She wondered what they were doing. She saw images of them flashing into her mind, not knowing how to differentiate which were just imaginary concoctions of her insecurities, and which might have been her ability growing stronger, seeing exactly what the pair were up to. She wondered if Dan was going to take Melissa home, or the days he travelled to Wales, if he was staying at hers. She wondered if Dan exchanged the same words to Melissa that he spoke to her, not understanding Dan's outlook that each relationship was its own. Not being able to separate herself as an individual, in his circle of individuals, that each formed their own bonds in their own ways.

The nights that Dale and Dan did spend together became nights Dale would spend trying to avoid any mention of Melissa's name. For if the name was brought up, an awful shudder would take to Dale's body, quivering at the thought of Dan with her. It slowly caused tension for Dale as jealousy crept in. As a knock-on effect, it caused tension for Dan, not wanting to say the wrong thing, Dale coming to tell him that she didn't want to hear anything about people outside of their relationship. Dale asked Dan if, when he was with her, could they just talk about things related to them? It killed her a little, because Dale saw that she'd begun to cripple the guy. This man, who used to talk about polyamory and his partners so openly and freely, had begun to tiptoe around Dale's feelings and anxieties, aware of how she had started to feel.

The calendar rolled on and, before she knew it, the anxiety-festered months blinded time, as her birthday approached. A day that had never been pleasant for Dale. She feared that her nineteenth birthday might be just the same. Another joyless birthday in the bank. This year, it could be a birthday fuelled with insecurities and bitten tongue. Secretly, Dan had arranged with the Brighton Musicians Bar to hold a themed night - a Prom. He'd put in a lot of preparation and pulled a few strings to make it happen. Things may have been tense, but he still felt the strong, passionate love for Dale that he did the day she fell into his arms. He organised the event knowing Dale supposedly didn't have friends at Brighton High and never went to her own Prom, not knowing she had never gone to Brighton High at all.

Dale walked to her door unenthusiastically when she heard the doorbell ring, so she was rather taken by overwhelming surprise when she opened it: Dan in a tuxedo and top hat, with a lavender bow-tie and matching vest.

"A very happy birthday to you, m'lady," said Dan, as he took Dale's hand and kissed it as he bowed. He held two boxes in his hand. One he said was for him to hold for a minute, and the other, he said Dale needed to take to her room. He said she would understand why when she opened it, and that he would wait in the common area. Dale smiled, let him inside, and did as he suggested. As she entered her room and closed the door behind her, she put the box on her bed and opened it. Inside was a silk lavender slip that he'd taken the liberty of getting in her size. Her heart just about burst with over-fluttering.

Dale undressed as an exciting buzz took to her, with enthusiasm rushing in, and she slipped on the lavender silk. She looked in the mirror at herself and began to buzz even more. Though her hair had been down, in her unenthused state, as enthusiasm rushed in she proceeded to do it up, feeling it looked more fitting off of her face. She walked out to Dan who stood talking to one of her flatmates, and he turned and practically lost his breath when catching sight of her.

"I'll, ah, leave you two to it," said the flatmate as they walked off. Dale smiled and gushed as she approached Dan.

"What are we doing tonight Dan?" It was a conflicting moment for Dale, when he told her. A Prom, being an event you take *the one.* Her being *one of.* But it was *her* birthday and Dan was *her* boyfriend whether or not he was others' too. So, she chose to relish in the gesture.

Dale looked down at her dress, then back up at Dan in his tuxedo, with matching lavender silks. He opened the box he had kept with him, which held a lavender corsage, and he took Dale's hand as he slipped it onto her wrist. This night was a moment Dale felt she would remember. It was a birthday she thought she just might enjoy for once in her life. Not having to control her boyfriend's mind to dance with her in fear of him leaving her. Not having to have someone slice their own throat with the insight of their intentions. Not having to be told her birthday was just another day, the same as every other, by her very own mother. She felt a lump in her throat form and swallowed it with pride, as the thought that she wasn't *the one* crossed her mind. As she thought of Melissa. Dale didn't want to let herself spoil the night ahead. What they had was special. She felt Dan wanted her to know that.

The night had been magical. Dale felt as though she was whisked away into a fairytale. She didn't even recognise the bar as they walked into it, dressed in streamers and decorative panels hung across the ceiling. A smile had come back onto her face. One that wasn't forced. If she was honest with herself, she had questioned if this life was for her, but it was no use as she was in love with Dan and the thought of leaving him didn't seem like a possibility to her. So, she stayed. Regardless of the anxieties and insecurities that started to fester.

The night was full of laughs. Tears too, as Dale divulged a little more about her life to Dan. About her abusive mother. The abusive foster fathers. She had truly let down her guard and let the magic of the night take over. The two of them chatted between themselves, but later also with mutual friends, who let on that they knew of Dan's plans and told Dale she had a keeper. She smiled. She knew. He *was* a keeper. Then Dan excused himself as the music mellowed and he asked Dale to dance. She of course accepted.

As Dan and Dale took to the dance floor, she placed her head on his chest, closing her eyes and taking in the night's affairs which warmed her whole heart. Although she didn't want to mention Tracey or Melissa by name, she felt in that moment she ought to bring them up, in her appreciation. She looked up at Dan.

"Thank you, Dan. Thank you for not inviting *them*. Thank you for making tonight about me." Dan smiled. The moment was as conflicting for him as it had been for when Dale was told he was taking her to a Prom. But he too swallowed his pride, and smiled her way.

"You're welcome." As they swayed on the dancefloor, Dan's mind sparked at the thought of his two other partners. Without a second thought in his eased state, he went to joke about what Tracey and Melissa had said, when he told them he had organised a Prom for Dale. He laughed. "Tracey and Melissa said...' but that was all he spat out before quickly shutting himself up.

Dale shuddered. She felt pin prick spikes take over her body. The faces of Tracey and Melissa entered her mind. Images of Dan's bare skin next to theirs. Dale lost it. She pushed Dan away from her.

"You couldn't do it, could you?! You couldn't just let me have this one night! You couldn't just let me pretend! As if it was just the two of us for one single night!"

"Dale..." Dan reached out to her. People around them stared. "Dale, I didn't..."

"No! You know what? You just say what you want. If I can't handle it, I'm just going to have to deal with that. But tonight is over. Happy birthday to me. Will you take me home please?"

The night that had started with unenthusiasm for Dale, ended as such. The night that started with Dan tiptoeing his way off of the patch of eggshells, saw him thrown back on them. Although Dale stated that it was now up to her to deal with whatever words came out of Dan's mouth, it was too late. Dan had become conditioned to the anxiety-fuelled relationship their intensity had formed. Both stuck in a relationship that, to the outside eye, was not meant to be. Stuck in a deep, toxic, bubbling love.

*

A few weeks passed by, with tension rising to a new level on both sides. Dale felt it was time to settle the dust. If she wanted to live the open and honest relationship she'd envisioned, when she spoke to Dan back while she was still with Derek, then there was a person she needed to make peace with. Not Tracey, she'd always tolerated Tracey. Even if the girl still played on her insecurities. She wanted to meet Melissa. Almost a year had gone by and she still hadn't met her. Dan had suggested it in the early days. But Dale rejected the suggestion quicker than she could close her eyes. She couldn't meet her *with* Dan though – that was further rumbling toxicity she wasn't ready to deal with. Dale was going to arrange to meet up with Melissa alone.

13 ST JAMES'S PARK

Hand in hand, Precious and I approached what was left of Westminster. What I had left of it before I saw it crack and crumble in the blink of an eye. I tried to steer the conversation away from the shock of such defeated sites, while also steering us towards St James's Park.

"So, Leicester Square. When your friends vanished. Before we met. Were you on your way anywhere in particular?" Precious let a few seconds of silence pass before answering me.

"I wasn't, no," she answered sombrely. "To be honest with you, I didn't know what to do. I didn't know where to go. Blood isn't thicker than water, to me. I'm another one of the many Londoners that built their own family here. I was walking with them in Leicester Square."

"Shit. I'm sorry."

"No, don't be. I guess with them gone, it was a moment of unknown for me. I didn't know where to go. It wasn't a matter of not knowing who to turn to – I had no one to turn to. They'd just been zapped from thin air right around me," explained Precious. She started to cry.

I imagined Precious walking the emptied streets of London. Alone. The impression she'd given me was of a strong, independent woman. This just may have been the first moment she had with someone to express her feelings.

We stopped walking. I held her in my arms as she cried into my chest. I placed my hand at the back of her head and held her close. I could sympathise, in a way, as I thought back to the police on my doorstep. Although blood, my family had too once vanished. In their own way. It *felt* as though they had been zapped from thin air. In the world one moment and gone the next. But this moment wasn't about me.

"Precious, I can't even imagine. I'm so sorry."

"They were just... Gone."

Oh, how I felt her words. I shed a small tear quietly to myself and rested my chin on top of her head. I closed my eyes as I held her. The one moment that led to this whole dire world. When I closed the door on the police. When I felt I had nothing else to live for as I took a knife to the drag queens of *Para-dice, etc.* When I felt alone. I didn't want Precious to feel like she had nothing left to live for. I didn't want her to feel alone. I held her tight, so she knew someone was with her. There for her. Just as I used to as a child, when Mum cried by the front door after Dad had been sent away with the army.

Precious let out a big sigh and stepped out from my hold, as she wiped her tears from her face. "Well, that's quite enough of that!"

"Are you okay?"

"I'm not. But I will be."

I looked on at her, wiping her tears, straightening herself and ruffling her fingers through her hair. She was certainly one that had pulled through a few events in her lifetime. Miss Independent. Looking at her I wondered if she'd seen some dark days herself. Maybe not as dark as someone pushed to the edge, with a plague of the brain, slicing and dicing their way through sequins and contour. But dark days of her own kind.

"Shall we?" I asked, as I extended my hand to her. She held her shoulders back and shook off her tears to take hold.

"We shall." We made our way up to St James's Park, the buildings around us blackened by the dark smog as if the city was paying tribute to its old days – the days it had been called the Big Smoke.

We slowed in pace, approaching a corner of St James's Park off Birdcage Walk. The park was lined with trees, but the greenery had been taken from their branches, as had the grass from St James's Park's soil. I had a feeling London was no longer the greenest major city in Europe, as once told to me by Dale. Both Precious and I walked into the colourless park, taking to its path, hand in hand. We looked around at the leafless trees and the dark dirt patches, which stretched on and on like a wasteland. A parcel of soiled land, split by crossing gravel paths, lined by burned, black, wooden trunks with branches twisting towards the empty sky. Our shock factor was no more. We walked in silence. No words needed to be spoken.

Precious let go of my hand and started to walk off the path onto the soil. She took off her shoes, walking barefoot, and held them in her left hand while she held her dress up with the other.

"What are you doing, Precious?" I asked, as she sat down on the patch of dirt and placed the shoes by her side. "Your feet are going to freeze." Precious looked up at me and gestured for me to join her.

"Come. Sit with me." I walked over and sat beside her. She clawed her fingers into the dirt beneath us and breathed deeply. She looked at me, reaching over with her now dirt covered hands, grabbing either side of my face. "When we met, you saved me with a certain gift of nature. I've got one too." I sat curiously, awaiting further explanation.

Precious explained that when she was a little girl, living in a small house in Ascot, she used to play in the garden, picking flowers for her Ma. She further explained how her Pa used to take long business trips and that by picking flowers she thought she'd cheer up Ma, brighten her days while Pa was away. She'd place them in a vase on the centre of the table for Ma to see. But Ma never made a comment. Took no notice. Too occupied by her special friend that seemed to cheer her up while Pa was away. A man that only ever came around when Pa was gone. He used to scruff Precious' hair when he said hi. She hated it. She hated *him*. But Ma seemed to like him a lot. Now as a young adult, Precious thought back and knew what was going on. But as a young girl, all she knew was that this man took all Ma's attention while Pa was away, and when Pa was home, he and Ma spent so much time arguing that they had no attention to spare. Caught up in fury.

Although picking the flowers was for Ma, the garden was her happy place, where she could prance and dance with the garden spiders and bumble bees. Away from the arguments, and when Pa was gone, away from the man that scruffed up her hair. Her Ma may not have taken notice of the flowers in the vase, but Precious admired them each morning, until they would start to wilt. When they did, she would often replace them. Then one day, as Precious got a little older and learned that plants were living things, rather than throw the wilted flowers away, she thought she would take them back out to the spiders and bees, to bury them in the soil, by their family.

It was the moment Precious held the wilted flowers in one hand, while she dug a small hole in the soil with the other, that she discovered her gift of nature. It was at that moment she noticed the wilted flowers return to their flourished form.

"Like Aine," I whispered.

"Sorry?"

"The ability to nurture nature. I knew a girl. There was this group I went to. She could do the same," I explained.

"There are more people like me? Well Christ, I thought I was Mary frickin' Mother Nature!" Precious laughed.

"If you're right, I think you're enabled. That's what we call it. When you have an ability. What the Collective called it. And to nurture nature or move things with your mind. We're all connected. We're all one, Precious. We're like each other, you and I. Why didn't you say?" I asked. Precious shrugged.

"I'd just been saved from Mister super-strength and you were explaining how you did what you did. Then your life. Then Jade. It got deep quickly, Michael!"

"Fair point," I said, with a little chuckle to myself.

"Okay. Shall I try it? Shall I see if I can do it?"

"Go for it! No time like the present!" I shouted.

Precious dug her fingers back into the dirt beneath us. She closed her eyes, sat up straight and began to breathe heavily. I looked at her hands. She squeezed the soil between her fingers as I saw sprouts of grass starting to grow around them. The growth began to widen, from around her fingers, to around where she sat. I stood up quickly and walked back, witnessing a circle of grass grow fast around her. Her breaths deepened. She seemed as though she was putting all the energy she could into it.

"You're doing it!"

Sprouts of grass began to sprout up between the already growing sprouts, thickening the patch around her. But it seemed she had reached her extent. She opened her eyes and looked around her. Then around at St James's Park. She looked disappointed. She must have wanted to grow more. She squeezed her eyes shut and pushed her hands harder into the dirt. A thick vein formed up her neck and onto her forehead.

"I've got to reach the trees! I've just got to!"

"Precious, stop. You're going to hurt yourself." She didn't listen. She was determined to bring the park back to life.

"I've got to bring them back!"

As she screamed those words, her sentiment rang within me. She wanted to bring back what she felt she had the power to. Her own grown family, which had vanished from Leicester Square. I felt for her. I felt the desperation pour out from her. I quickly ran and sat in the patch of fresh green grown grass in front of her, crossing my legs and grabbing hold of her hands. The hands that had held mine and squeezed them. It was my turn to squeeze back. Precious opened her eyes, confused, and went to pull away. I held on tight and didn't let go. "What are you doing?!"

"Focus! Keep going! Don't stop!"

Precious closed her eyes as I forced our hands back onto the dirt together. I slid my fingers between hers, feeling the energy I'd felt between us before, but at full force. Multiplied. We both clenched the ground below us. I squeezed my eyes shut tight, channelling all the strength I could muster, wanting to pull out the sprouts from below us, out and up to the branches of the trees above us. "Open your eyes! Look at me!"

Precious and I opened our eyes and felt a connection surge through us simultaneously. In the background, I saw an explosion of greenery in the park. I pushed my fingers into hers and raised our hands pressed up against each other. A force pushed us apart. The pair of us were thrown either way about six or so feet. As I landed on my back, I saw green leaves appear on the branches above, reaching up to the dark emptied sky, adding colour to the saturated dark smog around us, accompanying Precious' vibrant red hair. The adrenaline rush I felt run through me was strong, and I felt Precious had felt it too.

I sat up and looked ahead at Precious. She was laid out on the ground. I panicked. I wondered if the connection had been too much for her. I gathered what little strength I hadn't expelled, pushing myself off the now grassy ground as I ran to her side. I stood, breathless, but relieved. Precious lay with a big grin on her face, tears of what looked like joy streaming down her face as she looked around at the trees, now with full, leafy branches.

"We did it. We actually did it. That was *us*. I could feel your energy inside of me, Michael." Precious stroked the grass beside her and asked me to join her. She was making a habit of that. It was a habit I was rather taking a liking to.

I rolled my back down onto the green grass beside Precious. She grabbed my hand and turned her head to face me. I turned mine to face her. She leaned forward and kissed me. It took me by surprise. But I leaned in and kissed her back. The two of us lay on the grass we'd grown together, and turned our eyes back up to the trees around us, both with a smile on our face. We spoke about the connecting energy that we each felt. The energy which joined us. Came from us. Into the park around us. We talked about what else might be possible. What else we could do. For what we had just done was achieved in a state of panic on my half, jumping in to form a spontaneous natural connection in my desire to help her. I hadn't even known it was possible. And for a few minutes, we forgot about the dark world around us, leaving the blackened and defeated buildings, emptied streets and creatures of the underworld behind us.

"So, if you don't mind my asking, what *were* you doing, before you were chased by a man in a black cloak with super strength? How long was he after you?"

The pair of us lay out on the grass we'd grown, rolled onto our stomachs, laughed, cried and flapped our feet about. We spoke a little more about our experiences leading up to those colours in the sky. We got to know a little more about each other, too. I felt this was the time to tell all. No vague details. Precious had chosen to take this journey with me. I owed it to her. To divulge who I was and what I had done. Let her decide, for herself, if it was a journey she wanted to continue. Although, first, I listened to *her* story.

It sounded as though only one day had passed since I fell into the bloody River Thames. It was an awfully short time for Lenroc's Dark Enabled army and creatures of the underworld to have brought London to the ground. But they had certainly managed. Precious began to explain that she and her friends had been walking along Leicester Square mid-morning. They'd stumbled out of the club at six o'clock, and found a cheap kebab shop, where they got food and shakes. She remembered thinking how odd it was, that no sooner had the sun began to rise, it seemed like it had set. The sky darkened around the city. My mind flashed back to when I'd completely lost myself at the fountain of Buckingham Palace, my carnage taking to the Mall, as I blew the emergency services and royal soldiers off their feet. Walking the Mall, leaving a trail of dark, gloomy sky behind me, which quickly saturated the heavens. For the moment, I kept the information to myself. But I knew it was in that moment, when Precious and her friends ate kebabs and drank shakes, that my wrath had begun.

She further told how they had had such a good night that they weren't ready to part ways. Once they'd got their food and shakes, they'd laid over each other, on and around a bench. The one to the side of the Charlie Chaplin statue in the centre of Leicester Square. Cackling about stupid moments they'd had on the dancefloor. Moments later they were mesmerised by the changing fluorescent colours of the sky. The sky soon after had emptied of everything and anything – alongside the zapping of life around her in Leicester Square. Precious spoke of how she'd stood and looked around for what must have been fifteen minutes. She was in disbelief. Waiting to wake up. But as the lifeless surroundings settled in, she snapped out of her self-induced state, as she hoped to wake up. She'd patted down her jacket and thighs in search of her phone. She felt it on her right hand thigh and pulled it from her pocket.

In taking out her phone, Precious hoped to find news coverage, footage or stories on social media, about what had just gone down. Although Precious herself had wanted to take in the bright colours that formed in the sky with her own eyes, a couple of her friends at the time pulled out their phones to capture it. She wondered if there were others out there, like her, that had still remained. However, as she pulled her phone out, the screen was plain black and she'd felt a pulse of electricity run through it, into her hands. *Saw* it, even, claiming it was a purple surge. She'd dropped it and stretched out her fingers, with a spark of slight pain, kicking the phone softly with the side of her foot to ensure it was just a surge. She said when she picked it back up it was completely dead. She recalled looking at her phone just before they'd gotten their food, and she'd still had half a battery. She felt sure the battery wouldn't have died at that time. Whatever zapped everything from the sky, and the people around her, must have also zapped the life from her phone. She was completely on her own.

Precious said she'd put her phone back in her pocket for safe keeping. She'd started to stroll the empty streets. With no sign of other life at ground level, she'd decided to head down into the underground – but not a single person was in sight. Not a tube ran. Not a sound or footstep was to be heard. Just the wind whistling through the underground tunnels, taunting its emptiness. As Precious had made her way back up to London's city level, she'd started heading towards Stratford. She said this was where her flat was. She couldn't think of what else to do or where else to go, thinking that maybe if she went home to bed she would wake up and it would all be over.

Passing through Covent Garden, she saw her first sign of other life, as an old eratic woman in scruffy clothing and tattered hair ran mindlessly – spotting Precious ahead. *Child! It's the end of days! The river's run red! A dragon has taken to the city! Get out while you can! Be gone child, be gone!* Her first sign of life spoke gibberish, and as quickly as she'd appeared, she'd vanished before Precious' eyes, as the eratic woman ran off down a side street which, in its emptiness, echoed her mad laugh. Within seconds of the encounter with the woman, Precious said she stood further shocked, looking up above her as the winged creature flew across the sky, staring in further disbelief.

Seeing the winged creature, Precious had to sit down for a few minutes. She'd taken a seat on the pavement, describing staring at the cracks in the black tar in the road beside her. She remembered thinking to herself, *what cracks in the world had let such a creature leak into it? What cracks in the world had sucked the majority of humanity into it, and why on earth had the cracks in the world spared her?* Her thoughts had been broken by the sound of a young girl crying. *More life*, she'd thought. She'd made her way around the corner of the block towards the sound of the girl and saw her sitting against a red post-box. The girl was hugging her legs up to her chest and crying into her knees. She'd walked up to the girl and crouched beside her.

Precious recollected the conversation she had with the girl as best she could.

"Hi, sweetie." The girl had stayed huddled into her knees.

"Go away! You're not real! You're! Not! Real!"

"Sweetheart, I *am* real. I won't hurt you, it's okay," said Precious, as she placed her hand gently on the girl's back. The girl uncoiled, pouncing back towards the post-box, glaring at Precious with mistrust.

"You can touch me?" Precious laughed.

"Of course I can touch you. Sweetie, do you know what happened here? What did you see?"

"I was with my big brother, Tony. I was holding his hand. He was mailing a postcard home to our parents. He wanted to get it done first thing in the morning. And quickly, because he thought a storm might be coming. Then he told me to look up at the sky. There were pretty colours in it. Then I dropped my dolly. Jasmine. Then when I looked up a big flash of purple made everybody disappear. I went to grab hold of my brother's hand again but he was gone too," said the girl.

Precious said how the girl thought she had gone to hell. Maybe because of the time she took her friend's bracelet that she really liked after a sleepover. That her brother had probably gone to heaven because he was a good big brother. Then Precious described the most absurd thing. She said the girl's eyes widened as if something was heading straight for her. She squeezed her eyes shut and disappeared.

"Wait," I said. "Hold up. The girl disappeared? Like the rest of the people?"

"No, I don't think it was the same. It was like she *wanted* to disappear."

"Do you think she was.."

"Yeah. I think she was.."

"Enabled. Do you think...?" I paused in thought for a second.

"What? Do I think what?"

"Do you think that..." I paused again, thinking through what I was about to say. Really thinking it through.

"What, Michael? What else do you think?"

"Well, that the only people left in London could be enabled," I suggested. Precious looked at me as if a lightbulb had just been turned on inside her head. Her jaw dropped.

"Jesus. Do you think?"

"It's possible, isn't it? What's the chances that I run into you, someone with the ability to nurture nature, of all people left in London? And you, me." As I spoke, Precious nodded in absolute agreement. "That crazy lady, god, who knows what she could do, but I'm sure it was something incredible. The girl, whether she knew it or not, made herself disappear. Invisibility, or teleportation maybe, I don't know. Wait, wait, wait, you said she looked as though something was coming towards her. What did she see?"

"Mister super-strength. That was when I encountered him. I don't know what he was doing behind my back to scare her like that. But the moment she disappeared, I felt his hands around my neck, pressing a knife up against my throat."

"Fuck."

"Yeah. He told me not to move. Asked me where the little super-freak had gone. Asked me what I could do. I just fell onto my knees and said I didn't know anything."

As Precious spoke about the cloaked man with super strength, she began to tear up again, so I held her. She said that he told her it was just him and her now. That there was nobody around for her to scream out for help. No police about to interfere or get in his way. Just two mammals, on God's green earth, back to the primal days. The chosen ones left to re-populate and do things right this time. "He let go of his grip on me and scraped his knife down my back. He asked me to bend over and show him my junk. I quickly made a run for it and turned back to see this old, frail man. It gave me confidence that I'd get away. But I couldn't expect what happened next. As I kept running I heard him shout *fucking bitch*, then the loudest ring entered my ears. I kid you not, the fucking post-box had hit the building beside me, and clanged like an iron bell down onto the street."

It was a pretty unbelievable thing to hear – had one not experienced everything that I had – but all things considered, I believed it. "Yep. He'd thrown a fucking post-box at me because I wouldn't show him my junk. And he thought he was one of God's chosen ones. Yeah right son. Fuck, did I run."

"Hang on. So, this happened only a few hours after you left the club? At six in the morning? So, you were running from this guy until I ran into you?"

"The whole day, Michael. The whole damn day. I found spots to hide. But the guy just kept finding me. It's kind of hard to hide when someone is bashing walls of buildings down around you. Not knowing if you're standing under the eve of a building he's just hit with his fist. This guy had some serious undealt with anger management issues. He couldn't just let me be."

Precious finished by saying there was one guy she ran into on the street. He was sitting on the curb down near Blackfriars Bridge. Seemed he had given up hope on the return of any other human life, as he sat, playing with a deck of cards. Precious described running towards him as he caught her eye with returned hope. But she quickly stopped, as the old cloaked man with the knife walked with a quick pace towards the new found guy playing cards. Precious started to back away, as mister super-strength took to the guy's neck with his knife, slicing the life from him, then grabbing him by his shirt to throw him onto Blackfriars Bridge.

Precious' story continued to hold tales of shock and horror, as she ran through the city of emptied streets, with the old cloaked man tracking her down. The only bodies she'd come across, between the guy at Blackfriars Bridge and I, were dead ones. "So, Michael. By the time you appeared and tore that man in half, I was rather grateful. A little nutty, as I'm sure you picked up on, but grateful."

14 MEETING MELISSA

Dale told Dan she wanted to meet Melissa. She asked Dan for her phone number and began calling her for little chats. Initially it was a call to just say *hi, I'm Dale. I've heard lots about you. Thought it might be nice for us girls to meet.* Melissa asked Dan if it was okay with him. He said he thought it would be good for Dale. Selfishly, he hoped like hell they would hit it off right away. Maybe then, he could start to live the open and honest life he once prided himself on again - without feeling his head might be bitten off for it.

Dan originally met Melissa when she'd had a summer day trip to Brighton with her girlfriends. They met at the BMB. Dan opened up about his life, as Tracey was with him at the time, and as Melissa was intrigued, they exchanged numbers. Melissa thought it sounded like an exciting life and took to it rather quickly. She kind of loved the novelty of having a long-distant, polyamorous-relationship with a musician in Brighton.

The nights Dale spent on her bed riddled with anxiety, wondering if Dan had taken Melissa home, you can bet that was the case. The images she'd seen of them rolling around in bed, clawing at each other's skin, were indeed actuality. Starved of each other. The time the two spent together was precious. Because it was so scarce. Which is why it had been so easy for Dan to let Dale become more central in his life – because she was right there with him. But on reflection, Dan had made it paramount that he put the extra effort in with Melissa. In response, Dale felt it was only fair that she did too. So, she wanted to travel to Cardiff to meet Melissa, in her very own territory.

Dale sat on her shift as maître'd, feeling confident about organising her meeting with Melissa. Then, the desk phone rang. She answered it. It was a voice she hadn't heard in a long time. A voice she'd rarely heard back when she was around it. It was Henry. Her father.

"Dale? Dale, it's me." Dale sat silently. Goosebumps took to her body. "I know I'm probably the last person you want to hear from. But I thought I should call. Mrs. Douglas' daughter thought she saw you, zipping out of a hostel in Brighton last Summer, and so I've been just about ringing all of them."

He laughed hesitantly, quickly stopping himself, knowing it wasn't appropriate. Dale didn't find anything funny about it. "I'll just cut straight to the chase then. Your mother's dead, Dale." The truth was, he was exactly the person Dale wanted to hear from. But he was nineteen years too late.

"Don't ever call me again," said Dale, and then hung up the phone. A range of all new emotions flocked her body. She felt physically sick. Sick that it took him so long to get in touch. Sick that it took Melody dying for him to have done so.

Dale sat for a few moments as a tear dropped from her eye. Just the one. She picked up the phone and called the operator to ask to be connected to the local cemetery back home. She asked after the date and time for Melody's funeral. It was in one week. She wrote the date and time down on a piece of paper, tore it from her notepad and folded it, and then put it into her jacket pocket. She picked her phone back up and called Melissa. "How's this weekend?"

Dale had two occasions ahead of her. The first being a meeting with Melissa. The second being a trip back home. Not to see her father. Not to see off her mother. But to say goodbye to a part of her life which she'd never had the opportunity to confront. To make her peace, and then leave. Storming up to her father had never been part of the plan. It was just something that felt right at the time. It was something that her weekend meeting with Melissa had fuelled her to do. Her way of release. The meeting with Melissa had gone alright, initially. Dale sat on the coach and looked out the window as the British scenery changed from Brighton's seaside to Cardiff's docks. She listened to a message on her phone from Dan, which said *hey babe, really hope you have a nice day with Melissa. You'll adore her. Love you.*

Dale waited on the coach while all the others disembarked. Her nerves were racing. The line of passengers piled off. The coach driver walked back in, after helping passengers with their luggage, and asked if Dale was getting off.

"Yeah, give me a minute." She took a deep breath, unbuckled her seatbelt and made her way off. As she walked out from the coach she looked straight ahead, to where a female was standing. She was in a dark top and short skirt, with long, bleached blonde hair blowing in the wind. Dale knew it was her. The comparison between the two of them was too unsettling. Dan clearly fancied a certain type. *A collection of blonde girls in his harem,* she thought. A shudder ran down Dale's spine while the female who was most definitely Melissa approached her.

Dale plastered the biggest-come-fakest smile on her face. Melissa reached out with her arms.

"Dale?" Melissa questioned, to make sure as she approached her.

"That's me!" Dale shouted, with fake enthusiasm, to accompany her fake plastered smile. This moment was a real swallow of pride for her, that was for sure, but she was in the deep water now. Melissa joked about how they could be twins. Dale laughed reluctantly – but believably as she agreed.

"Typical Dan!" Melissa exclaimed. "Aw Dale, it's so nice to finally meet you. It's nice to put a face to the name after chatting on the phone."

"Yeah," agreed Dale, slowly settling into Melissa's warm vibes.

Melissa linked arms with Dale forcefully and began to walk her out from the coach station. She told Dale they were going to take a stroll around the city block, and finish back up at Cardiff Castle, as it was right near the coach station. There was a nice area within the castle's grounds which was open to the public. It was a large grassed area. They could finish their day sprawled out on the grass, with a few tinnies in the afternoon. It sounded like a well thought out plan. A little walking to get rid of the nervous energy. A little chatter while circling the city. Then relaxing into the afternoon, sinking into a patch of grass with a drink in hand.

The day hadn't started too badly. In fact, apart from Melissa's initial greeting, Dan's name hadn't even been mentioned once. The two girls strolled the streets of Cardiff getting to know each other. They spoke of silly things. General things. Things of passion. Their favourite television shows. Their love of music. Their opinions on British politics and unbelievable hate for the Tories. The two girls actually got on effortlessly. It would have been pleasing for Dan to have seen. As the day came to an end the girls bought their tinnies and made their way over to the open grass within the walls of Cardiff Castle. Sinking into the grass they cracked open their drinks, while Dale awaited the arrival of her coach back to Brighton.

Dale looked around at the large medieval castle walls. Then onto the small castle which sat inside with them. It was a tiny thing. Just one small build on top of a tiny mound. Melissa told Dale it was a Victorian Gothic revival, smack bang in the middle of the city, built in the late eleventh century on top of a third-century Roman fort. Dale said she thought that it was neat. But having taken a seat and no longer in the pace of stride, Dale's mind started to wonder. She looked at Melissa as a flash of her bare open breasts bounced above straddled Dan. Dale squeezed her eyes shut and winced away from Melissa.

"You okay?"

It was a funny thing, being occupied with a rhythm that let Dale immerse herself into the day. Whether it was the desire to have made an effort, or the genuine great day that she had with Melissa, her ability of sight had been blocked up until this point. Sinking into the grass provided a moment's thoughts. Thoughts on the girl who she'd just spent the day with. The girl, being Dan's girlfriend. The girl, being what had made the last few months of Dale's life, at times, unbearable. Dale's mind let go of her good intentions as the jealousy, anxiety and insecurities set back in.

Dale looked up at Melissa without answering her question, and instead blurted out her own.

"Do you love Dan?"

"Well, that was out of nowhere!" Melissa laughed. She paused for a moment as she was aware of the trouble that Dale had settling into this new dynamic with Dan. When Dan and Melissa spent their precious time together, their meetings almost acted as a platform for Dan to vent and confide in Melissa. But Melissa didn't want to subject herself to the tiptoeing that Dan had. She thought it was important that this day only held truths, to be able to move forward. "Yes, I love Dan."

A shot of anxiety ran through Dale's body as shudders and shivers took over it. Dan's lips pressed up against Melissa's lips flashed into Dale's mind, as he whispered the words, *I love you.*

"Has he said he loves you?" She hardly wanted to know. Funny thing was she did already know. She'd just seen it. She felt in her gut these were visions, as opposed to imaginary concoctions.

"Yes Dale, Dan has said he loves me. We've shared those words for a while now." Dale's stomach turned. It felt like it flipped right over like a pancake. She couldn't handle the thought of it.

"He should have told me that. Dan had no right to not tell me that!" Dale shouted, as her anxious energy got the better of her. "I don't think the guy is polyamorous at heart. I think he's battling with himself internally," said Dale, trying to justify why Dan might have kept such words from her. Melissa sat awkwardly for a few seconds. She'd wanted the day to be about truths, yes, but she saw a girl in front of her who looked as though she was about to pass out in clear need of comfort. So, although she felt it was stupid to do so, she just agreed in that moment.

"Yeah, I don't know that he is polyamorous." In hindsight, as someone who had taken to Dan's lifestyle with ease, Melissa internally thought *no girl, he just can't be polyamorous with you.*

Dale couldn't take it any longer. The anxiety that had set in was too much. The anxiety sat on top of the nerves that subconsciously crept in with the funeral of Melody approaching. It festered its own anxieties, with the thoughts of seeing her father again, the man that never came after her. A father that needed the death of his wife to have the courage to call his own daughter. Images of her father's face, Melody's abusive hand, her disgusting foster dads and Dan's lips up against Melissa's lips flashed through her mind. Melissa went to reach out to place her hand on Dale's knee, for comfort, as she looked on at the distressed girl in front of her. But Dale clocked her hand approaching and took control of Melissa's mind in an instant. She didn't want to be touched by the bitch. She had Melissa hold her hand in mid-air between them.

Dale looked around at the other people sitting within the castle walls. The two girls had pretty well nestled themselves into a secluded spot. Families and couples were caught up in their own company, in the far distance. Dale swung her face back to Melissa with her hand frozen in place. Dale looked into Melissa's eyes of confusion. Melissa went to speak, to ask Dale what was going on, but Dale stared Melissa down and clenched her fist as she made Melissa mute.

"You, Melissa. You don't get to speak anymore. You little slut."

As Dale looked into Melissa's eyes, she noticed they had started to tear, with Melissa realising her hand and lips were held at Dale's control. Dale smirked. It wasn't like the instinctive takeover she experienced with her foster dad. It wasn't another spontaneous dancefloor moment, keeping Derek from leaving her. It was forced and purposeful control – and she got off on it. She didn't *want* Melissa to touch her with her dirty slut hands. She didn't *want* Melissa to speak with the tongue that had slid over Dan's cock. She wanted the bitch to die.

Dale continued to stare Melissa down. She looked at her hand mid-air and then to her folded legs. She saw Melissa's exposed knickers with her skirt hitched a little too far. *You probably fucking love it like that.* Dale looked back up at Melissa's face and squinted her eyes as she tilted her head. She took complete control of Melissa's will, tapping further into her ability to control Melissa's mind.

"You *are* a little slut, aren't you, Melissa?" She sought no reply. Dale watched as she had Melissa take her hand and move it towards her exposed knickers. She watched as Melissa's fingers slid behind them and started to jam their way inside her. Dale looked back up at her face while her body jolted, to her dry fingers forcing their way into her pussy. Her eyes welled with tears with a face full of obvious pain.

Dale cracked another smirk as she watched Melissa finger herself. *You fucking love that too, don't you?*

"What do you and Dan do when you're in bed together? I've seen you clawing at his skin, you know. In my head." Dale laughed as Melissa's face filling with dread. "Have you ever tried asphyxiation? I'm sure you just love a big boy with his big firm hands gripped around your neck, don't you, Melissa? Yeah, you fucking love it." Dale watched as Melissa raised her hand and now bloody fingers to her throat. "Lay down, Melissa. I want you to enjoy every second of this." Melissa laid down on the grass, sinking further into it as she took both hands to her throat, strangling herself on the grass beside Cardiff Castle.

"I do have a coach to catch. But it's been a time!" Dale stood from her place as she watched Melissa drain the life from her own eyes at Dale's control.

"Help! Help! Someone help!" Dale cried. A few people enjoying their day with family and friends ran over. "She's strangling herself! She won't stop! I don't know what to do!"

Dale cried out, while holding her smirk inside her mind. A dad who had been playing ball with his two sons tried his strength at pulling Melissa's hands and bloody fingers from her throat. But it was no use. As Melissa took her final suffocating breath, Dale watched as her body became lifeless, and the man let go of her hands which dropped from her throat and fell beside her, her knickers red from blood. Dale walked up to Melissa's dead body beside the man that had tried to save her life. She crouched down and pulled Melissa's skirt down so her blood infested knickers were no longer exposed.

"Let's keep some dignity, shall we?" Dale asked the man. He looked at her sympathetically.

"Yes. I'm sorry about your friend."

"Can you please call this in? I've got to go and break the news to her mother. She'll be devastated. I want someone who knows her to be with her when she finds out."

"Yes, yes of course. You go. I'll look after this."

The man called out to his onlooking sons, telling them to go sit with their mother, as he pulled out his phone. Dale craftily made her escape, leaving behind Melissa's corpse as the smirk inside her mind emerged on her face. As she walked back to the coach station she pulled out her phone. There was a voicemail from Dan again. *Hey Dale, I hope you've had a wonderful day and I'm looking forward to hearing all about it. Give me a call when you get a chance.*

Dale dialled Dan's number. She put the phone to her ear as it rang. Dan answered.

"Dale! How are you? Had a nice day?"

"Not really; it was suffocating. On my way to the coach station now."

"Oh. I'm sorry to hear that."

"I want you to do something for me, Dan. I want you to pull out your dick, and wank yourself the last load you're ever going to get, knowing that you're about to die. I hope it feels miserable. Then, I want you to make your way to the kitchen and grab a knife. Stick it in your heart and twist it for me. Like you've been doing to mine all this time."

Dan did as he was commanded under Dale's control. Her ability had reached an infinite new level. She was able to control the waves through the phone signal, to control Dan's mind, without the need to be with him. Her anxieties and nervous energy had been channelling her ability her whole life. Ultimately, every new anxious experience unlocked Dale to a new extent. Although, at nineteen years old, this was only the beginning. For she had now tasted blood. Yes, she tasted it the day she'd turned sixteen, but the blood she tasted on this day was a new kind. At sixteen she spilled blood out of instinctive defence. At nineteen, she spilled it out of jealousy and hatred. A hatred that trickled in like a virus. A hatred for the world, and everyone in it.

15 COVERAGE

Precious and I sat up from where we had been laying, on the freshly grown grass of St James's Park, thanks to our combined abilities.

"Well, that's my story. In a nutshell. I'm glad you found me." Reflecting on what she had been through, it was intense. The cloaked man that had tracked her through the city hoping to do god knows what with her. Killing anyone that got in his way as he bashed down walls with his fists. The disappearing child by the post-box. The very possibility that the only remaining people in London – maybe the world – were enabled.

It made sense. The two of us, finding each other, what were the chances that we would both have been enabled? What were the chances the only other people Precious had run into before me were enabled too? The cloaked man and his super-strength and the post-box girl's invisibility. The tatty old crazed woman that screamed the river had run red, and the boy that Precious saw playing cards by Blackfriars Bridge, they had to have been enabled too.

"I'm glad I found you too," I said, as an unsettling feeling started to sink into me.

The very people I had brought Precious on this journey with me to find, Pree Possessing and Rubis Rouge, were not the enabled kind. Not that *I* knew of. As I realised this, I hoped to god that the tatty crazed woman running a riot in the streets of London, and the boy by Blackfriars Bridge, were of the regular kind. If so, then just maybe Pree and Rubis were still out there too.

"Are you okay?"

"Oh, I'm alright. It's just a lot, all this, you know?"

"Yeah. It is. At least we have each other now though, right? To get through it." Not knowing the thoughts that had just run through my mind, I smiled at her.

"That we do."

"Should we take a lap around the park? Take a look at how far we reached?"

"Yes! I think that sounds like a great idea!"

"So then. It's your turn. What brought you up to the point you found *me*?" We got up from the spot we had joined hands, to grow the roots of the grass on which we were now standing. We brushed off our jackets, which kept clean the garments we had chosen for each other, for our trip to Café De Paris.

When asked by Precious to share my story, I didn't quite know where to start. I wanted to speak only truths. I wanted full transparency. I owed it to her, and I owed it to myself. But where to start – my story didn't begin the morning the fluorescent colours took to the sky. My story started much earlier. Years earlier.

"I'm going to take you back. There have been a few details I've been skimping on with you. I'm going to take you right back to a time that I believe led to this moment. If you're happy to listen, I think it needs to be told. What you choose to do after I tell my story is up to you. But I hope you'll stay. I hope you'll see that I've awoken with a new spirit. That all I want now is good. All I want now is to make things right."

"I'm all ears, Michael."

As Precious and I started to make our way around St James's Park, we both looked around at the fresh green grass and trees with bright green leaves. We walked. I talked. I started my story with how close I'd been to my mother as a young boy. How as the eldest child I looked after my younger brother and tried as best I could to play man of the house while Dad was away. I strived to keep a balance in the house while Mum struggled on her own. I spoke of how I experienced bullying in primary school. How I kept a knife in the back of the bathroom cupboards, ready for the day it just all became too much.

I told Precious how I was all too happy to have finished my primary years as I said goodbye to the smart arse who always cracked jokes at my expense. Humiliated me as he had my peers chant *ranga ranga ranga* as I turned up to my school dance. I started to speak of more fond memories as I told Precious how I was accepted into Lumiere, College of the Arts. That I finally found my people. That I'd made best friends with a brilliant guy named Andrew, who I missed dearly. Who really, I should have tried to get in touch with a long time ago.

I also spoke of the not so fond memories. The memories of Gus and Tom. The boys who taunted me. The boys who suffocated me with dirt behind the school bush as Gus slapped his dick on my face. Speaking of the moment, that I hadn't realised at the time, when I'd first tapped into my ability. The night I watched my boyfriend Victor fucking Tom in a toilet cubicle. The night I watched Gus smoothed out clean on the road.

"I made it happen. I made that car hit Gus," I said, as I started to cry and breathed in deeply, trying to clear my tears. Knowing that was the start of it all. The start of so much more. Precious grabbed hold of my hand and stopped me from walking to turn to face her.

"It's okay. He was a dick. He had it coming. It sounds as though the guy was drunk as a skunk that night anyway. Reckless. He probably wasn't a very happy guy. He probably wasn't very happy with himself. He knew he wasn't a good guy. You probably just, I don't know, nudged along the inevitable."

"Thank you. But I did so much worse."

"Hey, none of that." Precious pulled me into her and held me. Then leant back and lifted my caved head by my chin to kiss me. "Michael. It's all behind you. As you say. You want to put things right now. That's all that matters.

As I said when I met you, we all have a history. Let's make sure you don't repeat it."

Precious' words were full of warmth and comfort. I squeezed the last of the tears from my eyes as I looked up at the green leaves on the tall twisting branches into the darkened smog sky. I felt at ease to carry on. Precious ensured I felt at ease to carry on. We continued to walk surrounded by the green grass of St James's Park and the dark smog of the city. I picked up my story, reiterating to Precious that I didn't know I had tapped into something called an ability at the time, and that it wasn't until much later that I found out I was what was known as enabled. But something I did discover about myself, while my parents sat by my side with a brain scan sat up on a lightbox, was my plague of the brain. A build-up in clusters of protein fragments. I'd been told to contain it, if I hoped to put off my dizzy spells, blackouts and possible early onset symptoms of Alzheimer's, and that I needed to reduce any stress in my life. Precious stroked my arm and went to sympathise, but I told her I was okay, there was so much more to tell.

I continued with speaking of my integration into the scene. Finding a place I thought, at the time, I belonged. A place that held every colour of the rainbow - and then some! *Para-dice'etc.* That my career as a drag queen had taken off quickly. But that it was cut short as I became consumed with anger, witnessing mother superior Miss Angelica Absolute and her gaggle of queens fuck a drugged-up twink. I described to Precious how I sat in my car distraught. That after all the torment I'd received, and the things I had come to know, I wanted the lot of them to suffer at my hand. And, that they did.

I revisited the hardest moment of my life. That moment when the police came to my door. My family were zapped from my life, and so I explained how I could relate to how she'd felt, when hers had been zapped from Leicester Square. The tears in my eyes started to build again. Precious offered to take a break. But I insisted I just wanted to get it all out. I explained how when I closed the door on police, I lifelessly walked to the bathroom, bumping into walls and walking into the doorframe. That I screamed into the bathroom sink – pulling chunks of my hair out as I did. That I looked up in the mirror covered in glitter, blood and tears. That I'd lost an entire day curled up on the floor, waking to a phone call from Absolute the next night, screaming down the phone at me, that I was supposed to have been at the club and had a show.

I explained how in my rage, and disregard for everything, my love of anything lost within the emotions of losing my family, that I'd hung up the phone and sat at my dresser. Readied myself to indeed head in for my show at the club. While forming the conceptualisation of the massacre that I ended up seeing out.

"I know, Precious. I know, it's sick."

"No. It's fitting." She squeezed my hand. She was still with me. We continued to walk. I explained how I still had no knowledge of my ability. Had I known I held the ability to move things with my mind maybe I would have glided in with the trail of my dress behind me and crunched their throats with the clench of my fists.

I ploughed on, sparing her the gritty details, then told of the moment in the dresser, looking in the mirror soaked with the blood of the drag queens, ready to end my own life. Feeling like the boy that kept the knife at the back of the bathroom cupboards. Everything having become too much. But I stopped myself, as the knock sounded at the door. Ric. Absolute's fiancé. The ignorant jerk living his life with the HIV virus and knowingly transmitting it to others.

I explained how what happened next, at the time, felt like it was my subconscious memory with a hallucination, jerking me to carry through with just one more act of justice. Justifying that it would be putting things right. As I envisioned my teacher Mrs Cornel popping up beside me, placing her hand on my shoulder, reciting something that re-fuelled me.

"Throughout history, it has been the inaction of those who could have acted that has made it possible for evil to triumph."

I explained how I slipped the knife into Ric's throat, as I opened the dressing room door, and walked out in my blood drenched dress, my body in agony. Tripping on my dress. My fall. Taking my final bow on stage as my alter ego, Sacrifice. I further explained how Mrs Cornel had *not* been a hallucination. How I had received a visit from someone who I later learned was known by the name Lenroc. Someone who had harnessed their ability of sight, to not only see what was in one's mind, but clearly force their way into it. I told Precious that it was all part of Lenroc's greater plan to see a prophecy come to light. The prophecy that *the dark enabled will break the boundaries of earth and the underworld by spilled blood of a torn lover.*

There was a sure change in the air as I told this to Precious. She broke my story for a moment.

"This is what this all is, isn't it? We're living in a prophecy right now, aren't we? It happened? The dragon... The boundaries of earth and the underworld have been broken. That means..."

"Yeah. Blood was spilled. There was a torn lover."

"It was you. Pree, Rubis and Jade. The one that tore you away from them. Fucking hell mate. You're the torn lover!" Precious had put two and two together. When I'd opened up to her as we first started this journey together, when I'd spoken of Pree, Rubis and Jade, she clicked. I thought back on the words of the prophecy, particularly on the words *the boundaries of earth*, and I was certain that the dark smog we stood in wasn't just London: its coverage was the world.

Precious pressed me for answers on *who* Lenroc was. *Why* was it their plan to see the prophecy come to light? *What* were the Dark Enabled? It was almost like she'd forgotten I just told her about the drag queen massacre. That, or she really did think it was fitting. I still believed she was Miss Independent. That she'd suffered her own trials and tribulations. I still didn't know what led to her cutting away her family and running to London to form her own. To be honest, I didn't know *her* story. I only knew how she'd come to realise her ability, picking flowers for her neglectful mother, and of course, the story that led her to me.

16 BOXED-IN

After leaving behind Melissa's dead body within the walls of Cardiff Castle, commanding Dan to his death, and confronting her father at Melody's funeral, where she let out every emotion she had left, leaving him to suffer in his own pathetic self-induced misery, as opposed to ending his life, Dale carried on. The innocent girl that had once laid under the bed covers in foster homes, that had cried on the curb of her childhood home when Mrs. Douglas jogged towards her, and that had kept quiet at the dinner table, was no more.

A force had entered Dale's veins. A power which had overcome her. Overcome with darkness. A darkness she once entered as she escaped the touch of her foster dads, as she escaped the household of her mother, using music to lift her away. Music, however, could not lift Dale from this new darkness. The darkness, from which Dale had once fallen in and out, was now here to stay. It clouded her head and consumed the cells in her body. This darkness became Dale. This darkness would see nineteen year old Dale Cornel become Lenroc. The Lenroc who flew above Tower Bridge and sliced into the wrists of a torn lover, to ensure the prophecy of the boundaries of earth and the underworld came to be.

Dale left her life in Brighton behind. There was nothing left for her there. She'd gone back after Melody's funeral to collect a few of her personal belongings. But she packed light with a small shoulder bag of clothing and bits on her back. She cackled to herself as she read the newspaper headlines on the train out. *Polyamorous Suicide Pact as Three End Their Own Lives.* Dale was impressed with herself; she hadn't been the culprit of Tracey, but she was surely the reasoning for it.

"Poor Trace couldn't live without her Danny," Dale murmured to herself. Dale threw the paper to the other side of the carriage and laughed.

"You can't make this shit up!"

Dale sat on the train, fleeing, as she once did as a young sixteen-year-old girl. Although when she'd come to Brighton, she'd travelled without feeling, without anything but the clothes on her back, arriving not knowing where she would end up. Three years on, she looked out of the window as she left Brighton behind her, feeling so many things, with her bag of bits on her back, knowing exactly where she was going and what she planned to do when she got there. Her destination was Victoria Station, London. Thankfully, as the hardworking young woman that Dale had grown to become, she had saved up a healthy bank account to see her through the coming months. She'd made a call to an ad in the paper for a flat-share she saw in an area called Cricklewood. Once she reached Victoria Station, she was headed straight to it.

When Dale reached Victoria Station, she stepped off from the train, looking around at the large grandeur of its overarching structure. People piled off around her with places to be, walking full steam ahead. She walked at a slower pace, thinking to herself *London: my new home, baby.* This was where the people were at. This was the city outsiders ran to. This was the city where misfits fit. The city where they found each other. The city where they found a sense of place in the world. Ah yes, the people of Brighton had spoken all lovely words about Londoners to Dale.

In London, Dale planned to find others like her; she was sure there had to be more. More people who could see things. People who could read minds. Control minds. Dale was going to find them, assess them, then seek out the vulnerable and pray on the weak. Battered and bruised chorus members seeking validation and approval through the audience's applause on the West End. Underground cabaret artists living their Liza Minnelli fantasy in a badly wired flickering spotlight with a half-empty room of ticket holders. Hollywood wannabes being treated like cattle on early morning getups just scraping by with extras work. Make them realise they're working towards nothing and offer them something more. Offer them a chance to kick the dirt back in people's faces that kicked it in theirs. With their powers as one, the damage that Dale felt she could do to the world would be unstoppable, and the idea of that almost brought a little joy back into her clouded head of darkness.

But before Dale could make a start of any of this, she had to set herself up. Get a haircut and a real job, as Melody used to say to Dale's father. As she walked out from the main thoroughfare of Victoria Coach Station, she looked up at the large clock suspended in the middle of the entrance, noticing she had some time to spare. Dale had done her research, and Victoria Station just happened to sit below Belgravia, a ritzy area of London nestled neatly beside Buckingham Palace and Park Lane's Mayfair. Here, she wanted to nip into a boutique salon and create her new identity.

Dale needed her nails filed, shaped and polished to perfection. *A French tip*, she thought. Her hair needed a do over too. But not just a trim. She wasn't going to be Dan's long blonde-haired bimbo anymore. Equally, she needed a cut and style that the people she'd come to gather would take to. That they would warm to. It had to be the perfect fix of appealing and stylish yet neat and petite. To Dale, the answer was a bob. Very nineteen-twenties to capture the attention of the artists in town. But it had to stay blonde. To go any darker would be too much of a statement. She wanted to be intriguing. But not too intriguing she might seem to have a darker side. Dale wanted to stay warm and approachable. Blonde was as warm as it got, in her mind.

A blonde bob it was. Nails were done, hair was set and a few subtle touches of makeup were placed - to add to her warm and approachable new look.

Eye lashes were definitely a no go when the beautician suggested it - too striking. But she accepted some light mascara that allowed her eyes to pop. Dale spun her chair around and asked if there were any jobs going. As luck would have it, they were looking for a hair-washer for peak periods and someone to assist with the sweep-up and clean-up of work stations. Dale thought it was as fine a job as any, accepting a trial shift offered to her for the very next day.

Next, it was on to Cricklewood. An area with no such luck of being as charming and picturesque as the likes of Belgravia. But unlike Belgravia, it was affordable. You would have had to be a Chief Exec of a company to even afford a *flat-share* there. If the area of Belgravia even had any flat-shares. The people of Brighton had referred to Cricklewood as a lively area – if you lived on the street with the corner pub! A place predominantly made up of Irish workers. Dale had a soft spot for the Irish. There was an Irish band with a resident night at the BMB Dale just loved. They talked, they joked and they knew how to drink. But god forbid the barman poured their Guinness wrong – it had to be slowly done with care and it had to have time to settle before it was finished.

After having made her way squished on the tube and squeezing her way onto a bus, Dale got off a few steps early and walked the rest of the way, glad to be free from the scent of body odour. When Dale arrived at the address she looked up at the large three-storey house. A big gate was built in front of it. Unlike the many doors in Belgravia, which had but one doorbell, this gate had many. Dale pressed doorbell number nine. A large lad with a scruffy beard, thick specs and a green plaid patterned robe walked out from the house. He stood by the front door while the gate began to electronically slide open.

Dale walked into what was a small car park kind of area. It looked fit to hold six cars but only held two. The large lad in the robe called out as Dale walked towards him slowly.

"You coming in or what, love?"

"Yes, yes. I'm coming." When Dale reached the door, at a quick glance the lad looked her up and down, which sent a quiver of repulsion down her spine.

"Agent says you're here to see the vacant room."

"That's correct." But what she really wanted to say was *that's correct, you simple minded wandering eyed pig — do you state the obvious to every person you meet?*

The robed lad walked Dale through a small foyer area, which held two doors ahead, but otherwise it was just a room with a line of shoes either side.

"You can take your shoes off here if you want but not everybody does."

"I can see that. I think I'll keep mine on." They continued on through the door without a key lock of the two, a door which opened to a tight, closed-in staircase, with aged carpeting covering it. The stairs creaked as they walked up them. A slight musty stench lingered in the space. On the first landing of the staircase there were four key-locked doors. Dale followed the lad, passing the doors as he ran his hand along a rickety wooden bannister, continuing up another set of stairs. Dale imagined how the house might once have looked. Before the additional walls which closed in around the staircase and key-locked doors were put in place. She pictured its once open plan - now a boxed in house of rooms to fill the landlord's pocket.

As the two of them reached the second landing, it also held four doors. The lad led them to the last one at the other end of where they'd popped up from the staircase.

"My door's the one at the bottom in the foyer. This one's yours. If you decide to take it." It clicked to Dale that he was the landlord. Probably living his ground level life with a garden and living space while he locked everyone in their rooms upstairs.

"I thought this was a flat-share?" Dale asked.

"It is," said the lad, as he opened the door. "Knock, knock, we're coming in!"

Dale followed behind the large lad as he walked them down a small, closed corridor with a line of four other doors. One was open with a girl standing under its frame. She looked at Dale with a smile and nod. She had long black hair, a large shirt which was much too big for her and came down to her thighs, with metal framed glasses on the edge of her nose. The lad introduced Dale to her as Katrina. The door opposite he said was the bathroom, and the two doors at the end were bedrooms. "It can be yours as of today."

It wasn't brain science that rooms in London got snatched up quickly – even in this box-like setting.

"I'll take the keys please," said Dale, literally throwing her bag into *her* new room. It held a bed, a wardrobe and a small desk with a chair. Dale could see the landlord's eyes light up – *money in the bank*. He explained a few bits and bobs about when rent was due and a required safety deposit, to put against potential damage or financial loss from unpaid rent, then left her to it. Katrina loitered in the corridor, moving from her own door frame to Dale's one.

"Just like that, hey?"

Dale sat on her bed while she engaged with Katrina. It was time to start making the pleasantries. To get people on side. Start a network that would lead on to potentials. A guy walked past Katrina, then took a few steps back, to peek into Dale's room. He wore dark skinny leg jeans and a black turtleneck with slicked back mousey blonde hair.

"Hey, new roomie?"

"Dale! Pleasure."

"I'm Kent."

"Ha! Katrina and Kent! Love it!" Dale joked, their names both starting with *K*.

"Well, see you around, Dale!" Katrina and Dale kept chatting while Kent took off. It so happened that Katrina was also a music buff. She was in London studying it. Composing was her forte. She and Dale clicked instantly. Katrina spoke a little gossip on behalf of Kent – telling Dale that he had a boyfriend who popped in on and off, but that they were in an open relationship, so it wasn't uncommon to see a strange man in the flat. Katrina had once opened the bathroom door to a random naked man, with a dick the size of the Great Wall of China as she put it, and took to a fit of laughter.

Dale sat a moment while laughing with Katrina as a subconscious grief began to rise to her surface. Not that she had been in an open relationship - Dan's circle was tight. But she knew the question was coming.

"Are you seeing anyone, Dale? Any late night booty calls from a certain someone to be expected?"

"I was. That's done now," replied Dale, trying to keep the details minimal.

"Oh, I'm sorry. Well, you're now in the house of KDK!" Katrina joked, wedging Dale's initial in-between.

"Say, you wouldn't be interested in being on a board, would you?" Dale asked. It was an interesting moment of choice to do so, but the girls had gelled so well, alongside Katrina's music interest, that Dale thought it was the perfect starting point.

Dale's plan was to form a registered charity. A charity with a mission statement *to nurture and support emerging artists and talent.* A charity that would see Dale reach the most weak and vulnerable of the arts sector. A charity that would see Dale become quickly connected in London. The UK too. She hoped to get this charity to the point where they could grow the project to regional cities and secluded parts of the country. Certainly, London was where the people were at. But small towns and districts held the suppressed and aspiring. If Dale hoped to see the world burn, she would need to build it to a national profile, and to do that she would need a board of appointed trustees that she felt she could hold under her subtle direction.

"Yeah sure, can't hurt the CV. Why the hell not!" Katrina replied, and with that, the motions of Dale's plans had begun.

17 THE MALL

Precious and I continued our walk around St James's Park, taking in the vibrant greenery that we'd drawn up from the dirt below our feet, among the dark smog. Although I didn't know Precious' full story, with her having shared her story which led her to me, it was only fair that I finished mine. Even though it was much longer. Even though it monopolised my life's story. I was sure, in time, I'd come to know what monopolised hers. Having told her up until when I was visited in the mirror by Mrs Cornel, with Precious not batting an eyelid at the gruesome details, it was time to delve into the details from when I'd awoken in Brixton Prison, answering the questions for which Precious had started to press me. About the Dark Enabled, and, just who Mrs Cornel – Lenroc - was in this story. Who *I* was in this story. How the prophecy came to be, and how it had been the spilling of *my* blood above Tower Bridge that saw the boundaries of earth and the underworld break. How I hadn't the faintest idea how to stop it. The people that just may have, being the Collective, were now dead. Yet alone, the stories the Collective had shared with, of the Dark Enabled times.

I spoke of how I'd woken in a ward at Brixton Prison, although I hadn't of course known that at the time, tormented by the morbid memories of the murders I committed. How my mind went spinning as I was wheeled into the Warden's Office to find Mrs Cornel sat behind the desk. I spoke of how I was thankful to have seen her at the time, spun mind or otherwise, because I'd soon started to break down with my acts of violence weighing down on me. Dale had really stuck her neck out for me at Lumiere, no matter what the reasoning I later came to learn, so I held great comfort in her presence.

I told Precious how Dale took that moment to have me reflect. To realise that it was my will for the car to hit Gus that had made it so. That it was not my physical strength that had seen me drive a knife into the drag queens of my past. It had been paired with – or more so, powered by – my ability. Enabled, to move things with my mind, as I'd enlightened her a little when we met. Now, I further elaborated. Continuing to tell my tale, I explained how Dale had performed something called *the clearing*, allowing me to move forward with a clean slate. The clearing, not erasing what I did, but erasing me from the minds of those I'd had contact with in my life, allowing me to walk on from Brixton Prison a free man. Mrs Cornel had taken care of logistics and practicalities.

I let Precious know that the stories Mrs Cornel went on to tell were a bit hit and miss. Fabricated truths, not known to me at the time, concocted to cover her own dark past. But what was clear was that the *enabled* were those with abilities, that I was enabled, and that there were also *dark enabled*. The dark enabled being people with abilities that had lost their path. My massacre had seen me on the verge of this. But I was later to find out that Mrs Cornel needed to guide me back into the light, as part of her inevitable plan to fulfil the prophecy.

At the time, she had also told me that when I tapped into darkness through my abilities, I'd caused a shift in motion to the universe, and raised concern with the Collective. Although I now knew it wasn't the case, as I was sure the Collective would have reached out to me, rather than me to them. It seemed I'd been cloaked from them, as they'd later come to foretell my meeting with them. What I did take as truth on meeting them was the explanation *of* the Collective, being an appointed group of people with abilities, who had proved their loyalties in miraculous ways, to enable light in other enabled. The Collective kept the enabled in line and within boundaries set out to not disrupt the order of all worldly things - mother nature and society as it had been created. Everything that had now been destroyed.

"You keeping up?" Precious blinked her eyes widely.

"Just about. I'm sure I'll catch up. Please, carry on."

I did, speaking of how Dale wheeled me out right past the prison guards. On to the discovery of the glorious city that was London, my eyes widening at the sight of red double deckers and the – unshattered - Shard in the distance, then on to Primrose Hill. The place of healing. Oh, how I recalled the beauty as dusk set in around us, wheeled up the hill among the soft warm haze of lamp lights. The gasp I took as I turned in my chair to face the city skyline.

"I hadn't seen anything like it."

"So, what made Primrose Hill a place of healing?"

I told Precious, as it was told to me. I explained that there was a time when the dark enabled rose to power. The timeline hadn't been clear, but it'd spawned from a time when one particular individual had gravitated into darkness, so bitter and sour with the world, that they had collected a following of people with abilities that lost their ways, to enslave humanity. This individual preyed on people with abilities' loneliness and hatred of their lives, feeding them with promises of a brand new world, which would rise from the ashes they would create. Together, the dark enabled wanted nothing more than to see the world burn, and an army of dark enabled was needed to see that day come. That individual, as later explained to me by the Collective, was Mrs Dale Cornel, who led the dark enabled by the name of Lenroc.

I explained how there were many casualties in the days of the dark enabled, both enabled and non-enabled. The world had come to its darkest point. Greater than any world war or pandemic. Bodies had been left for dead on the streets all over the world. The Collective defeated and banished the dark enabled, to a realm created by themselves, to be sealed off from all things. When light was restored the world remained in balance ever since – until now. I told how, once the Collective had banished the dark enabled, there had been a worldwide stage of grief, followed by a worldwide clearing. As Lenroc had cleared my existence, from the minds of those I encountered, the Collective had collectively cleared the minds of the world, clearing the events of the Dark Enabled times.

The Collective allowed people the time to deal with the grief of their lost ones, and the shock of being witness to some of the unexplainable and horrific events that they did. But it was important that society, both enabled and non-enabled, worked as one to restore the world to some form of normality. I described how it had apparently been a beautiful moment, to see every day non-enabled people working together with the enabled. Restoring damaged sites. Elevating fallen down walls back to position. Clearing rubble and debris into the air and into skip bins. Much like the plague, but on a worldwide scale, pits were set up to use as burial grounds for bodies, Primrose Hill being one of them.

I told Precious how Primrose Hill, like many other of the pits created, were now places of healing for us enabled. Drawing from the earth and the universe's force, by drawing the remaining energy and life forces left in the dead that lay there. Their will to have lived. Their spirit to have fought. Their abilities as enablers and, likewise, the remaining energy of the non-enabled. I also told Precious, however, that it could only heal inflicted matter, that sadly as a natural progression, the clusters on my brain were not part of the deal. Precious tightened her grip around my hand. *It's okay, I'm here.*

I carried on to deflect, telling how before the worldwide clearing when the enabled and non-enabled began working together, it had been part of a campaign. Civil unrest had spread, directed towards the enabled, deemed evil and inhumane, those that were not yet discovered keeping their abilities hidden. But the ENABLE THE ENABLED campaign saw society come together as one – in time. Then, just as society had rebuilt itself, and the grieving had neared an end, the Collective performed its worldwide clearing, restoring the world, satisfied that it had dealt with its grief.

"Life carried on. As for me, Primrose Hill saw me stand, and on I ventured for my first visit at Café De Paris."

As I told Precious, when I'd first walked down into the glimmering golden entrance with deep blue crushed velvet walls, I felt myself reliving the experience. The most compelling human I ever did see. Radiating positively undivided femininity. Their bubble-gum pink holographic shoes. Royal purple trousers twinned with a button up vest and open but again, oh so well fitted, matching blazer. The buttons on the vest sparkling their deep pink, trailing up their chest to an embellished and ornamental neck piece that sparkled like diamonds. Their puff of baby pink candy floss hair and contoured face with black lashes and pink glittery lips. Rubbing together their hands full of pink and purple jewelled rings. Making an exception to personally take Dale and I to our table. Charging pompously in front of us. Remembering the parched sensation they had on me. Pree. Pree Possessing.

I relived the sparkle in my eyes as I looked around at the splendour of Café De Paris and knew it was a world I wanted to be part of. How the Café Girls and Miss Rubis Rouge saw my brain ignite. Oh, how Miss Rubis Rouge saw the ignition hold a lasting effect. How my mind had first opened up to the idea of polyamory over a late-night bite with the cabaret folk. How I formed an interest in two new beautiful people. How, that night, I ended up back at Pree's place. How the next morning, Pree had angered me on a purposeful endeavour to see my ability come to be after opening up about it. How I quickly held absolute trust and faith in Pree as they accepted me into their life.

I relived and told Precious how Pree took me to meet with Dale at Trafalgar Square. How I spoke of polyamory when I saw the three linked sex-symbols on the traffic lights. How Dale opened up to me about her own experience with polyamory, before taking me onwards, as we walked underneath the monstrous and gigantic Admiralty Arch leading on to the Mall.

I stopped for a moment in my re-lived experience, jarred by memories I wasn't so keen on reliving. The flash of the golden shining centre to the Queen Victoria Monument. The Golden Winged Victory. The personifications: Constancy, holding a compass with its needle pointing true north; Courage, holding a club; Empire, the two eagles with wings spread out wide. Queen Victoria facing the Mall. The pools of sparkling crystal water either side.

Precious and I had walked St James's Park and now we'd reached the other side, and standing before us were large black and golden tipped gates. They opened on to the Mall. I let go of Precious' hand and fell to the floor as a flood of images came rushing back to me. Falling into the water as I'd stood above it with Pree – with Victor on my mind. The explosion of blood and guts that followed as I ended both his and Buttocks Boy's lives. Jumping into the water - with the Collective on my mind. The white nothingness. The first moment I laid eyes on them. Then, the last moments I'd seen each of them. The moment the sparkling crystal water of the fountain turned to overflowing, boiling blood. My lips, speaking the word *boo*, as every officer, soldier, medic, bystander and vehicle blew down the Mall. The air filling with smoke and fire. The bold pumping blue veins under my skin. Queen Victoria's Monument cracking and crumbling at the wave of my hand. My reflection in the burning police vehicle's window - splattered blood with white rimmed eyes.

Precious ran to my side and held me, jolting me out of my flashbacks. I looked up at her with tears in my eyes.

"Oh, Michael. Michael, Michael, Michael," said Precious, as she held my head to her chest and rocked me.

"I haven't even told you the worst of it. I shouldn't be here. I don't deserve to be here." Precious grabbed either side of my face and turned me to her.

"That's just silly talk. Of course you deserve to be here. What happened to what you are doing *now* that matters, hey?"

"I know. I just.."

"No. That's it. I get that you've done some messed up shit. I get it. But what are you doing right now? You're on your way to find two people you love. You rescued me from a super strength maniac. You're speaking your truth with me. Michael, you're back on the right path. You're with me." I looked at Precious and forced a smile as I squeezed the tears out of my eyes. I held her hands and squeezed them with mine, then looked over at the Mall ahead. I inhaled deeply and exhaled in one big breath.

"That road. That damned road. It led to all this. That road was literally the path that paved the way to the world's destruction."

"Well. How about you stop being mister dramatic and finish your story about where you went next with Dale, why don't you?"

I took another breath and started to exhale slowly.

"How about I take you there?" I suggested. Precious was silent. I stood back up on my two feet, offering her my hand. She took it.

18 THE CHARITY

Katrina and Kent had adopted Dale into their household with an openness which made Dale sick. They were the kind of people that hadn't faced a rough day in their lives. They hadn't hardened yet. Their spirits remained bubbly and uplifted. They invited Dale to tag along to drinks and nights out on the town. Dale latched on to each event as an opportunist, taking advantage of mixing and meeting with the people of London: composers and musos through Katrina, and the queer community through Kent, opening Dale to the battered and bruised folk of West End, the Liza Minnellis of the city and the Hollywood wannabes.

Dale took to the bright party lights of London with pleasure, mixing with emerging creatives and the up and coming of its arts sector. For a time, she spent her days laying in after a hard night out, popping down to Belgravia to assist with the lunch hour rush, and hitting meetings in the afternoon while she set up the charity to be known as *The Uprising Arts Society*. The more networking Dale took to, the further support and justification she received for the charity.

Dale listened to the wants and needs of the sector through the eyes and voices of the emerging. There was demand for more affordable performance spaces, the need for more funding pools to get work off the ground, a desire for wider subsidised arts training programmes, and even assistance purely to help artists living in London do just that – be able to live in London. Dale took her time to make her connections, getting hold of supporting documentation from them, and created her case.

Just over one year on and young Miss Dale Cornel, at just twenty years old, was CEO of UAS – the Uprising Arts Society. Her board of trustees was formed, with her flatmates Katrina as Chair, and Kent jumping into the seat of Vice-Chair. While Katrina represented the music industry, Kent represented the theatrically inclined and independent performance artists. Also elected on the board were members with the likes of financial and fundraising expertise, operations, and health and safety, recruited and appointed through mutual networks of the web that Dale had curated.

Health and safety was paramount for representation on the board, as Dale had worked a social housing partnership with the City of London, for the occupation of a large abandoned mansion in Marylebone. The mansion had seen several years of illegal squatting, as a lost and forgotten boarded up building that gathered cobwebs on its dulled crystal chandelier above the grand entrance staircase. It was worked into the agreement that the squatters could remain as residents – providing they contributed as paid workers to the restoration of the property. With a mix of government and privately obtained funding, the old mansion was to be converted into accommodation for performing artists and act as UAS Headquarters. The headquarters included an office, meeting room and function room to act as a hireable space, allowing the charity to have an independent income revenue stream.

Another year passed by, and at twenty-one years old Dale had put her darkened heart and soulless energy into the grand opening of the Uprising Arts Society HQ, doubling as her twenty-first birthday celebration. The journalists of London and newspaper headlines took to it as if it were the event of the year. *Twenty-one Year Old Founder and CEO Unlocks Her Adulthood by Cutting Ribbon for Emerging Creatives of London!* As Dale stood on the steps of freshly polished marble under the sparkling restored chandelier, she raised her glass for a toast.

The gleaming grand entrance of UAS-HQ was filled with VIPs and patrons of London's arts industries, journalists and reporters of both the city's most well-respected papers and not-so-respected magazines with gossip columns, mixing alongside the appointed board – Katrina and Kent on the steps by Dale's side. The room of people turned to Dale as she began to speak.

"I want to start by saying, thank you. Thanks to each and every one of you. For your support in helping UAS get here; to this day. For raising awareness of an incredibly needed resource in the arts sector. In turn, for helping and taking part in assisting and nurturing artists being able to do what they were born to do. To be able to feed their souls with *life* through their talents – and feed all of ours. Whether people work in accounting, sales, customer services, manufacturing, security or the emergency services. People turn to the arts for escapism. Whether they clock off at six and head home to watch their favourite drama; whether they purchase tickets to a show on the West End for a gift to a loved one; or, whether they work until god knows what time of night and hit the town for a drink, coincidently catching a midnight burlesque act. The arts are everywhere. It's time we cherish that. It's time we support the artists of our future!" Dale raised her glass and the crowd followed with her.

Here, here! called voices from the crowd. Dale looked around the grand entrance of UAS-HQ at the people toasting her. The people lined against the banister of the staircase, the people above it looking over the railing, and the people below it looking up at her. She looked on at them in her warm, crafted appearance, with her blonde bob, in a gleaming rose-gold crystal coloured dress. As Dale Cornel, who had come to London to start the beginning of the end, looked on at the people knowing her plans to knock them all off their feet. A lot of them. Boasting patrons as eager for affection and attention as the chorus members on the West End. The journalists and gossip columnists who were just as likely to throw someone under the bus for a story as the Liza Minelli hopefuls would for their poorly wired spotlight. As she had walked the room towards the beginning of the night, shaking hands, she'd seen each of their dirty little secrets flashing into her mind. The cheating husbands. The cheating wives. The inside-traders. The drug dealers. The closeted folk, that had supressed their sexuality so much they bashed it out of their system onto another. The very foul personalities that created that suppression in others. Inside her mind, knowing what she had planned, she smirked with sinister intention. As an exterior front, standing tall on the grand staircase as someone of new hope, she smiled with positivity.

Dale looked on at the room of pathetic excuses for human life as they followed their toast to her with applause. She wanted to give them a reason to be drawn to her even more. A little touch of vulnerability. Something the papers could highlight. Something people could connect with her on a personal level. She started to speak once again.

"I chose to celebrate my birthday tonight with all of you because you've all shown this cause such genuine passion and love. But tonight's not about me. I want to dedicate this occasion to someone that was once very dear to me. To dedicate all the work that has been put into getting us here today. My reason for starting all this. As I stand here before you all, I dedicate this evening to a young man named Dan Segway. A former musician and lover of the arts. An ally of the queer community. My ex-lover and partner. Sadly, the support wasn't there for Dan. As a struggling musician he couldn't hack this world. Let's ensure we work towards making sure another artist doesn't feel like that again. To Dan!" Dale raised her glass once more, with forced gleaming tears in her eyes that matched the gleam of the warm, craftily picked dress that she wore.

The night rolled on and included pop-up performances by artists from joint partnerships set up by Dale. As the grand staircase saw movement to the rhythm of opera singers and circus acts it saw a slow filtering out of bodies. The night drew to a close as Dale, Katrina and Kent rejoined one another by the bottom of the stairs; both Katrina and Kent with a sense of fulfilment, after their night of praise and engaging in industry mingling; Dale, with a sense of much darker things to come. The legwork was done. Now the real plans were to come.

Dale continued to hold her smile of positivity and thanked Katrina and Kent for their hard work over the last two years.

"Honestly, I couldn't have done this without you both."

"Sure you could have. You entered this city with motivation and determination. If it wasn't us it would have been two other idiots," joked Katrina. Dale agreed silently to herself. She couldn't have put it better.

"So, thank you. Dale. Thank *you*, for bringing us on this journey with you. I mean look at this place. Can you believe it?" Kent asked, in full hearted spirit and admiration.

"Well now, let's agree it's been a team effort, shall we?" Dale suggested, in the attempt to continue her warm and selfless craftiness.

The days of Dale sweeping up a salon floor and shampooing people's hair were well over. As founder and Chief Executive Officer of the Uprising Arts Society, Dale had created her empire, and it was going to become a powerful one. With a representing board under her thumb, a full team of carefully employed staff and a now fully operational building, Dale had made the start of the end. The board of trustees had ensured Dale was very well compensated, with an extremely generous salary for her role as CEO, and of course her hard work in setting the charity up as founder. Naturally, Dale had ensured that the board were in agreement about that, with a little mind manipulation. Her office was as gleaming as the marble staircase she'd descended on opening night, but she'd gone about purchasing herself a modest apartment, wanting to keep finances for her personal objectives stashed aside.

Her apartment, although modest, held the scent of newly varnished wood flooring and freshly applied paint, as opposed to the musky carpeted flat she had shared with Katrina and Kent. It was on a quiet street. Dale kept the walls bare as decorating one's apartment was a small fish to fry – in comparison. The kitchen was grey and the hallway to the bathroom and bedrooms was lined with the newly varnished floorboards that filled the apartment with its scent.

The apartment held two bedrooms - one for her and one for guests. She felt it important to have a second space. One that she could invite vulnerable creatives to stay if needed, building closer relations to those she suspected might be like herself. She kept the furnishings simple and purchased a bed, bedside table, and set of drawers for it. She wasn't opposed to being a half-way house and thought the drawers would serve well. She kept everything white: the walls, the blinds, the furniture and linens. All except for one room – hers. In Dale's room, she painted the walls yellow.

Dale had been able to tap in at times to other people's futures with her gift of sight. But not her own. Yellow walls were the only things she ever knew were in her own future. A personal rebellion and stand up to her past. They had been the one thing in her life she was certain she would get, and no, there they were. The one bright thing in her life. At the base of her plain white bed and linen Dale had purchased a large trunk. A treasure chest of sorts. In it, she placed some of the bits and bobs she had taken from Brighton with her in the bag on her back as she fled to London.

In it, her shrivelled and dried-up lavender corsage, as a token which kept her envy fuelled with what she had wanted with Dan but never got. A chunk of glass from the thrown champagne flute kept from the night she first saw Derek with another woman in her mind, which kept fueling her distrust in creatures named humans. Her blood splattered headphones, which on walking into the waves of Brighton sea stopped working, but kept fuelled no longer needing to escape this world once she had rid it of the people that made that feeling so. They each sat in the corner of her newly acquired trunk, after having sat at the bottom of a shoulder bag for so long, ready to be joined by other tokens Dale just might have collected along the way. Serving as fuel. Fuelling her purpose. Reminding her why she wanted to rid herself of everything in the world.

The morning after the grand opening of UAS-HQ, Dale awoke within her white linens rather chuffed with herself at what she had accomplished thus far. She rolled out of bed, showered, set her blonde bob, applied a smidge of mascara and dressed herself ready for the day. It was back to HQ for the beginning of a new chapter as she felt ready to turn the page. She arrived back at the building at midday, greeting reception with a smile and many thanks for their help with the previous night's momentous occasion. It was important to her to keep acknowledgments positive. Keep people on side at whatever level. Although she broke her smile instantly as she left reception, entering the now emptied grand entrance, with her heels' echo bouncing from the marble steps as she walked up them towards her office.

Dale reached the top of the stairs to a rather unexpected greeting. She turned to face back down the staircase as she heard a young man's voice echo up from it.

"Dale Cornel?!"

"Yes, that's me. Who's asking?" Dale questioned the mysterious gent. He was dressed in a long black coat. It fell to the back of the heels of his shiny black pointed shoes. He also wore a brimmed hat, stylish pair of sunglasses, leather gloves and shirt and tie – all black.

"Let's just say, I'm an artist of a kind," said the gent. He started to walk up the staircase towards her as he took off his sunglasses, placing them in his coat, then took off his brimmed hat, holding it to his chest.

"If you're here to register for accommodation you'll need to leave your details with reception."

The gent stopped walking mid-way and held on to the bannister with his spare hand.

"Oh, I'm well accommodated, thank you. I'm here to see you, Mrs. Cornel. That is right, isn't it? The papers refer to you as Mrs, but I see no ring."

"Yes, well. It's more a self-possessive move on my behalf, thank you. Listen, I've got quite the day ahead of me with a new building to run. If you don't mind, can you arrange an appointment with reception? They've got my calendar. Good day." Dale began to walk off down a right hand corridor on the first landing of the staircase.

"Got quite the coverage at the moment haven't you, Dale?! Imagine what the papers would say if they knew you were enabled with the gift of sight!" The young man's words saw Dale stop in her tracks. She turned back and walked down the steps to meet him mid-way, as she responded to him in a cautious whisper.

"Now what are you doing coming in here shouting a bunch of nonsense like that?"

"It's okay, Dale. Nobody can hear us. I've taken the liberty of forming a bubble of energy around us. You can't see it, but I can assure you it's just us right now."

Dale looked around the two of them at the empty grand entrance and then back at him as she began to laugh.

"You're pulling my leg! Right? Who put you up to this? Was it Kent? It's always Kent."

"Dale, I assure you nobody has put me up to anything. Try and call out to reception," suggested the young man. Dale began to call out. No response. She stood and looked awkwardly at the gent in front of her. He was a young man, but a confident one.

"Okay. Just wait right there." Dale stormed down the stairs and poked her head around the corner at reception to address them, but they went about their work at the desk, oblivious to Dale's presence. "Come on, people. The joke's over, you can stop ignoring me now!" No response. "You're all fired!" Still no response. Dale laughed. Dale looked towards the entrance as her personal assistant walked inside. "Grace! Grace, hello!" Dale continued to try to get Grace's attention as she walked towards her.

Dale had started moving her arms frantically in front of Grace as she walked right towards her, and then completely through her, as if she were a ghost. Grace walked up the staircase and Dale stood frozen – although she had started to believe it. She turned to the young man on the staircase.

"Sorry about that. I probably should have said when we're in a bubble we're not technically on the same plain as the people around us. And yeah, that can happen."

"We're *what* now?" Dale took a few steps back and leaned against the wall to catch her off-guard breath.

"Shall we take this to your office?"

Dale had caught her breath just enough, and as the young man suggested, took him to her office. She closed the door behind them as he hung up his coat and hat on a stand beside Dale's desk. He then pulled up a chair placed in front of Dale's desk and sat down.

"Can I get you some water or something? I know *I'm* having one..."

"No, I'm quite alright, thanks." Dale walked to the sink beside her desk, sunk into a little kitchenette, and poured herself a large glass of water. She downed it as if it was a pint of lager and was being encouraged by a clan of lads, then sat behind her desk to face the mysterious young man.

"Right, so. What brings you here?" Dale asked.

"How about we start with, hi. I'm Shane," he said, as he reached out to shake Dale's hand across the desk.

"Hello Shane, it seems you know *my* name. How is that? And what the hell was that out there?"

Shane went about explaining to Dale that what she had just experienced was *his ability*, as an *enabled person*. Like she was *enabled*, with the *ability of sight*. Dale nodded her head along, taking in what he was saying.

"Got it. Enabled, someone with power. The ability, your power. My power, sight. Your power, making some kind of bubble that turns everyone in it into a ghost?" Dale said, trying to make sense of it all.

"You've got the basic gist of it all." Shane went on to explain that what his ability was, in actuality, a bubble of energy created from energy drawn from other realms, virtually bringing the people within the bubble into an interim temporary world.

Shane followed with addressing Dale's first question, before she had time to interject with more questions on the newly acquired knowledge of other realms, and went on to tell her that he'd felt her presence for some time now. The day that Dale's birth had sent a strong unsettling movement through the air. When the woman reading her book in a Manhattan coffee shop saw her pages burn and turn to black. When the man on his daily jog through Myslenice town square collapsed. When the mother enjoying a picnic looked over at her children playing in Greenwich Park as her vision blurred and her head felt faint. Shane had been on his morning commute on the London underground, squished in with other commuters as he held on to a metal bar in the middle of the carriage. He'd let go to grip his chest as he lost balance in the moving carriage, falling down to fellow Londoners' feet, as he felt all kinds of unbalanced energy shift and pulse through him.

Shane went on to explain that he felt her presence come into the world the day she was born. That her presence had lingered in his bubble of energy ever since. That the second he opened the paper and saw her photo, he knew it was her. He was drawn to her. Dale sat, a little confused, as the young man telling her he sensed her presence at birth didn't look much older than she was.

"Excuse me, but you remember feeling my presence as an infant?" Dale questioned.

"Ah, I'm a lot older than I look. One of the benefits of harnessing energy. When I form a bubble I don't age. I'm not *that* much older, but a bit." Dale didn't question his age. There were more urgent matters on the table to Dale, a priority to her mind: was he here to stop her from her sinister plans? That, and what exactly he *felt* about her?

19 ONCE GLISTENING

I held Precious' hand as we walked ahead through the black golden gates towards the Mall. The greenery we'd grown had stretched across to the trees on the other side of the road. The Mall was lined with vibrant green, unlike how I'd left it, as the images of the Mall lined with burning trees of fire came rushing back into my mind. I winced. Precious could sense my wish for disassociation with this road and my connection to it. She squeezed my hand tight as I pushed through the trauma and walked with her onto it.

As my foot hit the road I pushed my mind past the awful flood of memories that wanted to rush back in. I held deep breaths in my chest and turned us to face the path of destruction that I had paved. Police vehicles bent around tree trunks. Ambulances upside-down and squished into the very road on which we stood. But no bodies. The odd one, to be fair – police officers who no doubt hadn't realised they held an ability. But then maybe they did. Or just maybe there were still non-enabled people around after all – I sure hoped so in the mind of Pree and Rubis. But in comparison to the carnage I had left behind, almost nobody remained.

I walked past the crashed emergency vehicles, edging our way around them, and on to whatever laid ahead in the darkened smog of the Mall - now lined with greenery. As we reached the end of the Mall, the smog thinning in sight, I looked ahead to what seemed like nothing. It couldn't be. Our feet touched the first step which once led onto the now crumbled portal, which I had stared down into glistening water, careless for Buckingham Palace, although as I looked ahead to see what just might be no more, I never wanted to see Buckingham Palace more.

"Michael, isn't that where..."

"Where Buckingham Palace stood? Yeah, yeah it was."

Squeezing each other's hand, we walked around the crumbled monument. No more golden shining centre at the top of a central marble pylon. No more personifications. No more large lions with guardians or grand marble steps. Just a pile of rubble. Beyond it, just the same. A very clear attack had been put upon Buckingham Palace. What stood were little remains of what I imagined would have once been an elaborate interior staircase.

I stood remembering how the Collective had been slaughtered: Audrey's body thrown into the distance by Lenroc's illuminating hold; Demos and little Lee's bodies floating in the lit crystal water of the portal; Frank and Fiona sprawled across the golden spikes of the gates of Buckingham Palace; Margaret by my side, before being sliced up on the wings of the golden Winged Victory, falling in two. Unable to hop back to Trafalgar Square to help Gwen, who lay dying as blood trickled out from the back of her head. With the exception of Gwen and perhaps Audrey, they all laid among the rubble of Buckingham Palace somewhere. I let go of Precious' hand, falling to my knees as I held my head and let out a scream.

Precious rubbed my back and then held her hand in place. I stood back up and leaned into her. She wrapped her arms around me and started to rub my back again.

"What is this place to you, Michael? Share it with me. Let me help you carry it." I was honestly so goddamn thankful I'd found her. I didn't know if this was a journey I could have done on my own. I wouldn't have made it this far. I wouldn't have found the will or strength to carry on. I let go of Precious' hold and walked back towards the once decorative fountain which held a portal. I sat on a flat piece of broken marble and looked down to the now rubble-filled encasement, drained of its pristine water with the staining of boiled blood in its place.

Precious walked toward me. She took a seat on the ground beside me as she waited patiently for me to relive my pain. To share it – with her. Ready to carry it with me. I began to speak as I stared down at what was once glistening in a once glorious city. I told Precious how Dale had brought me here to start my first full-day in London.

"Sorry. Lenroc," I said, correcting myself. Looking around at the ruins of Buckingham Palace, feeling *Dale* was too humane a name for such darkness. Whilst I had seen parliament house crumble – Big Ben with it – and flew over the London Eye as I saw it dive deep below into the Thames, I also sat here remorseful. I could just sense Lenroc basking in their destruction. Who knew how much more they were going to do. What more was even left.

I told Precious how there was once glistening water where we sat as I closed my eyes and pictured it.

"I know, matey, I've been to Buckingham Palace," said Precious as she laughed. No doubt trying to lighten the mood.

"Yeah, but if you knew what that water could do... That glistening became hypnotic. Never-ending possibilities."

I went on to tell Precious how the Commonwealth, the British Monarch leading it, held ties with the Collective and the enabled. Lenroc had never gone into the full extent of the Queen's part in everything, but seeing Buckingham Palace destroyed, I could only imagine what significance the royal family indeed held. I explained how Victoria's Monument had been set up as a traveling portal for the Commonwealth. That there was a portal in each of its nations. That Lenroc had been using it to travel back and forth from Australia to keep their eye on me. Posing as a teacher who seemingly cared and only had my best interest at heart. Little did I know at the time that they were grooming me to see a prophecy come to be.

In retelling the story, I recalled how Lenroc had joked about the portals being handy when the apocalypse came to town. I wondered for a moment if perhaps it wasn't the water itself that was the portal. If perhaps, it was the isolated area in general that encased the water, the water just acting as a distraction or deterrent from people hopping in it. I stood up from the broken piece of marble I'd been sitting on. Precious stood quickly too in an instinctual reaction. I turned and stared towards the defeated monument, while remembering the stories I told Precious back in St James's Park, about the enabled restoring the broken cities of the dark enabled times. How they elevated loads of rubble and debris to move into skip bins.

"I don't know how strong I am right now. But I want to try something and I might need your help. For now, stand back."

Precious stepped back behind me as I closed my eyes and tried to re-engage my ability. My ability had usually come from places of spontaneous reaction. Even when I'd tried to help Greg, the other Aussie in the smog, I'd tapped into my reactive annoyance of his arrogant attitude. Darn right ready to have almost left him there when he'd opened his mouth. But right now, I had to focus. Lenroc had certainly helped me to channel my ability and use energy around me. But it had to be noted that any true moments of impact were always sourced from dark places. I held nothing but good intentions and supportive energy around me right now. I hadn't quite done this before. Who knew - maybe it would be stronger?

With my eyes closed, I tried to engage with the energy around me, to lift the broken pieces of Victoria's Monument from the ground. I squeezed my eyelids tight shut, tightening them still as I heard the beginnings of a rumbling. Paired with the rumbling, I felt the earth beneath my feet start to vibrate.

"Michael! You're doing it! You're doing it!" I felt my inner self connect with the energy around me. Connecting with the good intentions I held. It only empowered me more. My eyes sprung open as I engaged them with the rubble I sought to remove in clearing the portal. Slabs of marble and broken pieces of the monument's personifications floated in the air in front of me like eggs about to turn suspended in the water.

The slabs and broken pieces stayed floating in front of me. I held strength enough to suspend them above the ground. But to move them took strength I wasn't sure I had in me. I tried to further channel the energy I had engaged, trying to move what I'd suspended, even just a little to the side. I felt ripples of sweat forming on my forehead. I didn't know how much longer I could hold this.

"Precious, I need you!" I shouted. "Give me your hand!" I saw Precious approach me from my peripheral vision, as she grabbed hold of my hand, looking ahead at my doings. As our hands connected, I felt a surge enter my body, again, feeling sure she felt it too. All of a sudden rain started to pour above us, falling heavily. We soon became drenched. My clothes started to weigh down on my body, as did my ability as it became more and more engaged.

Both Precious and I watched as the suspended parts of Victoria's Monuments flew down towards the rest of the carnage of the Mall, leaving what remained of what encased the once glistening water, as the bucketing rain above us started to fill it. Precious and I disengaged, as a ruckus of slabs joined the crashed vehicles along the Mall. The rain continued to pour above us but its heaviness began to lighten. We both looked up into the sky while the rain started to clear the smog around us. I looked over at Precious while she smiled in her stare above. She'd poked out her tongue to taste the fresh water from the sky, water I felt sure the two of us had just produced. I pulled her in towards me and started to kiss her, feeling an all-empowering energy between the two of us.

I pulled my face back from our kiss, with my hands around her waist, as I thanked her.

"You need me, hey?" Precious joked. The rain continued to shower around us ever so lightly as we laughed. I turned to face the ruins of the monument. I let go of Precious as my eyes started to swell. There under the rubble, as I'd suspected, laid Demos and little Lee's bodies. I walked towards them and sat on the cracked ledging of the fountain. Precious followed and sat by my side.

"It wasn't supposed to be this way. Lenroc knew we were coming. How didn't he foresee that?" I questioned, knowing Demos had held the ability of sight. Naturally, Lenroc held the advantage, *unnaturally* harnessing more abilities than just one, Demos probably upholding the values the Collective had instilled into the enabled.

"Maybe he did. Maybe this *was* part of his plan? Maybe he saw things that are yet to come. Maybe there's light in this world yet."

"Maybe. But then, maybe sometimes evil wins."

"Maybe, shmaybe. Come what may. But I am sorry this had to happen." Precious stroked the side of my face. "So, how does this portal work?"

I looked down at the encasement which held Demos and little Lee's bodies. It had slowly refilled with water around them from the rain. I tried to think, but nothing came to my mind. All I could recall was the once glistening water. Its hypnotic effect on me. It was as if a blank spot sat in my memory.

"I - I don't know, Precious. I - I can't remember." I squeezed my eyes shut, pinching the top of my nose, trying to recall. I knew that I knew. But I just couldn't remember. Precious grabbed the side of my arm and rubbed it.

"It's okay. Take your time. You've shared a lot with me today; you must be tired."

"Yeah. I must be."

"Is it maybe something to do with *where* you're going? Or *who* you're intending to see? You say Lenroc used it to go to Australia to watch over you." As Precious spoke, I felt the blank spot refill.

"Yes. Yes, I remember now!" I recalled how I too once stood over the fountain asking how it worked. I told Precious as Lenroc's words came back into my mind. How you had to stand in thought of the person or place that you wanted to go. Hone in on it. Then, clearing your mind, completely focused on the person or place, you simply let yourself drop into the water, the portal leaving a rip in the space you entered on the other side. The rip staying open. To get back. You becoming the key to that doorway, closing behind you on your return.

"Michael! If it still works... Do you think, maybe, it might..." Precious stopped speaking. I was certain I knew what she was thinking. I was also certain I knew her hesitation to finish the sentence.

"It's okay. What were you going to say?"

"I just thought maybe it might take you to Pree and Rubis. Supposing they're not at Café De Paris."

Precious said exactly what I thought she was about to say. Sure, that she too had the thought they may no longer be with us – the enabled seemingly the only beings left on earth.

"We can only give it a go." I paused for a moment and looked up at her. "I'm not certain I can take you with me Precious..." Precious smiled kindly with understanding.

"It's okay. They're your loves. You deserve to reunite without me anyway. I'll wait. If anything happens, I can always hop in and think of my flat, right? Wake up in my bed when it's all over?" *Miss Independent.*

"I *will* come back for you. I think you're just wonderful. This isn't the end of our adventure. I really like having you around," I assured her. She smiled back at me kindly, again. I grabbed hold of her face and leaned in to kiss her once more. As our lips and tongues caressed, I felt the surge of power I'd felt when we connected hands a moment before, throwing the rubble from its place.

I held Precious' body in my embrace. I firmly slid my hands down her sides as we kissed, and gripped her tightly around her waist. I slid my hands back up her body, placing them on her face, then pulled away.

"You go get them. Bring these beautiful people back for me to meet. If *you* love them, they must be pretty magical people."

"I will," I said, smiling, hoping to God that I could. I got up from off the cracked ledge and stood facing the portal. I closed my eyes and pictured Pree. Their puff of candy floss hair and contoured face with pink glittery lips. I pictured Rubis and her plump red lips. Her neck and shoulders soft as silk. Her wave of bleached blonde hair lit by the spotlight. I looked at Precious one last time, as she sat on the ledge staring into the water. She looked up at me and forced a smile. I smiled back reassuringly. I turned back and closed my eyes with Pree Possessing and Miss Rubis Rouge on the mind. Then, I stepped into the water, beside the bodies of Demos and Little Lee.

20 COVER OF A MAGAZINE

Dale sat in her luxurious office behind her desk as the young man – who apparently was *not* so young – in his all-black suit looked on at her intriguingly. She felt a slight unease knowing that he'd sensed her. Not knowing exactly *what* he sensed. She tried to tune in to his thoughts or get a glimmer of sight. But she could not.

"Another rather fun side effect, with my little bubble of energy, is that I can block other enabled's abilities taking hold of me." Shane said this, too close for comfort in his coincidental timing to Dale's attempt. "And indeed, feel when someone is trying to do so." Dale froze. "It's okay, Dale. You'll be curious, I'm sure. I would be too, if a stranger walked into my workplace, knew who I was, and was telling me they were drawn to me."

"Yes. Well. Can't be too careful."

Shane went on to explain that there had been some other enabled in the world sensing what they started referring to as *disturbances* in the natural balance. That a few enabled around the world had been coming together to form a kind of council. To investigate these kinds of movements in the world's elements and keep a balance. Dale questioned what kind of a balance they were hoping to keep and what exactly these disturbances were.

"A balance of everything. Society. The world. The universe. These movements some of us have been picking up on. These disturbances. They've been felt in different ways by different enabled. Depending on their abilities, I suppose. But one thing I'm sure of Dale is that the majority of us know something dark lies ahead. Some force. Maybe, someone. We're going to need all the help we can get. I guess I'm here to ask you, Dale, can we count on you? Will you help us with your sight to seek out any darkness? Keep your eyes and ears to the ground? Call on me if you find it? I feel like you're a key part in all this. I just don't know how yet."

"Of course. And how would I call on you if I found any of this darkness?"

"You've been in my bubble now. I'm connected to your energy. I'll know if you need me. I'm a collector if you will. My bubble holds a lot of other people's energy. Think of me as the glue holding this movement together. The middle-man."

Dale felt further unease with supposedly now being part of his bubble. She was going to need to keep this one onside. Likewise, a man connected to other enabled, as he put it, could come in rather handy. Dale quizzed him on exactly what kind of energy this bubble of his held. He merely said that the world they lived in was not the only one. Other worlds and realms existed. There was an underworld, our world, and a few more adjacent. Dale's eyes widened with delight. *An underworld?* She thought, although she didn't want to seem keen and pry. Shane thanked Dale for her hospitality and wished her adieu as he put his coat and hat back on. As he reached the doorway to her office, he stood still for a moment and began to speak, although he didn't look back at her before he walked on.

"Be careful with that ability of yours. Many men have tried to develop them through greed and hunger for power and got lost along the way. Good day," he finished, just as *she* had tried to dismiss *him* back on the grand staircase.

Dale sat behind her desk rubbing her hands together as she pondered on the word, *underworld*. She stared ahead unfocused on any particular one thing, her focus trying to centre around what this underworld might be, what it held, and if she could tap into it to become stronger. Hell, if she could *break it* to spill out onto earth, not only enslaving humanity but destroying it. Her mind rattled. She would keep Shane on side, slowly assessing his energies and how she might take advantage of that. But she still needed to gather her followers. She still needed to create an army. She needed to lead her own movement just as Shane was doing... But for darker intentions. An army of *dark enabled*.

Dale paged her personal assistant who came rushing to Dale's office door.

"Morning love. Can you get me the applications of our unsuccessful applicants so far?"

"Absolutely. Which funding pot? Or was this for accommodation?"

"All of them. I want every application we've rejected for anything." Dale received a mountain of boxes with applicants that had been rejected for all kinds of reasons. From lack of demonstrable specifications that they were in fact an artist, to lack of proof of residential status. Dale sieved her way through them. She wanted to begin with the weakest of likely candidates. People who had just faced rejection – that the reflection was raw. Meet with them and see what made them tick. See if a tick resulted in other events.

Calls were made and meetings were held as Dale began to source out the enabled among the rejected applicants. Many were rejected. However, Dale didn't mind so much. She fed a little off leaving some false hope in the world along her path. She didn't feel meeting with non-enabled people was a waste of her time at all. It just threw the world more bitterness to work with. To help tear it down. Even so, Dale's first meeting with another enabled held a tick with an unimaginable knock-on effect, which saw dark burning flames of pure ill-intentioned desire take to Dale's eyes.

This particular meeting took place at a diner in Camden. When Dale spoke with hopeful rejected applicants on the phone, she always suggested they meet at a place of their liking, feeling that comfortable and familiar settings may take down the walls of any potential enabled, helping to set off their trigger. She'd met and held conversations with hopeful rejections in hostel common areas, hotel bars, corner pubs and even a library. Although in this particular diner, nestled into the happenings of Camden, Dale had a much different kind of conversation. One that she became rather fond of quickly.

Each meeting always started the same. Dale would thank the applicant for their time and coming to meet with her. She would extend her apologies on behalf of the board that their application hadn't been successful – for whatever reason. Then offering a chance to reapply, but in doing so, as CEO she wanted to understand what might have let their application go astray. She expressed the need to know more depth to their life. Moments which may have led to their lack of confidence or ability to strongly justify themselves. As to Dale, all an application was, was marketing. Being able to market yourself. The need to be confident in yourself.

Christopher Collins was this applicant's name. He had arrived extra early to make sure he wasn't late, sat on his own with a nervous shake to his leg whilst he waited for Dale. Sat across the table from her, even in his favourite diner, the young seventeen-year-old boy displayed anxious energy as he licked his lips and over-blinked his eyes. This meeting was imperative to him. His application had been rejected for accommodation at UAS-HQ because he'd lacked demonstrable proof of income and work as an artist, his art form being mime. His income being a hat on the pavement for pennies. In his last year of high school, he'd dabbled in mime after hours and on weekends. But it certainly didn't provide enough work to leave education for – like some fellow peers of his that had left for the likes of apprenticeships and such. There wasn't even really a form of formal higher education for his chosen artform. But Christopher's passion for the art was absolute, and he spent what spare time he had in-between schooling, study and busking, studying the origins and history of mime in public libraries.

His application for accommodation came about being kicked out of home for being gay. Christopher was homeless. He held pride in himself and hadn't come under the radar of child services. He utilised the school's showering facilities, kept a bag with a change of clothes, which also held his mime costume and makeup, and he managed a night or two on weekends at his best friend's house, although most nights, he managed to avoid the school janitors after busking, rugging himself up for the night at school.

Up until he became homeless, Christopher had lived a sheltered life. He was raised in a rather adequate home, with a father who worked in construction and a mother who worked in a sewing factory. Both parents were always home by six-o'clock and dinner was always on the table by seven-thirty. His mother came straight home from the factory, while his father always finished earlier, but made a pit-stop at the corner-pub. Such routine and regularity, with a few hours in the house to himself after school each day, allowed Christopher to prance about the house in heightened campness without hesitation – before his parents' keys slipped into the door. He was able to talk freely with his bestie – Miranda - and express himself with makeup and nail polish before taking it off promptly by six.

Before the day came when Christopher was told by his father that he was no son of his, Miranda was the only person in Christopher's life that knew he was gay. In fact, as a more masculine kind of a guy, it was often mistaken that Miranda and he were going steady. They walked around the school with linked arms most days, with their backpacks hanging off their opposite shoulders. Still, even as a masc guy, Christopher's peers managed to find reasons to tease him. *Charlie Chapskin* they'd call him. Highlighting his mime, next to his red and lumpy hormonal skin, as they taunted Miranda by his side, shouting that she'd catch something, as if his skin were a form of disease.

Christopher's skin weighed his confidence down, but when he took to the streets with that white paint pasted on his face, he filled with confidence at magnified heights. As Christopher, he was shy and hesitant to engage with a new face or make a friend. Young children stared and hid behind their parents in supermarkets, as if he were a monster, while he quickly tried to grab what he needed and walk away. But as a mime, he puffed out his chest and greeted the strangest of strangers, with a rose in his hand. Children applauded and raced to his side to tug on *his* trousers for more – filled with joy and laughter as they asked him to be their friend.

One day, after a morning of staring at his face in the mirror with disgust, something peculiar happened at school. He walked the school's main corridor as the head cheerleader Trixie gave him an unusual look up and down. Unusual, because usually she wouldn't have given him a second glance. Unusual, because this day it was as if she didn't know who he was. Unusual, because when she looked him up and down, it was as if she was checking him out. Seconds later, he walked up to Miranda to say hi and it took her a few seconds to click that it was Christopher.

"Chris, is that you?" Christopher laughed.

"What are you playing at? Girl, Trixie just totally checked me out. I'm not kidding!"

"I'm not surprised," said Miranda, as she looked him up and down herself. "You're looking good boy, what are you using on your skin?" Miranda squinted as she jutted her neck forward to look at his face more closely.

Christopher stood, confused. He'd been staring at his face with disgust just over an hour ago. He raised his right hand to his face and felt it. He could *feel* the bumps and blotches on his skin. He didn't know what Miranda was on about.

"Come on, Miranda. Stop kidding. This isn't the kindest of jokes," said Christopher, in disappointment as he dropped the hand from his face.

"Boy! I'm not kidding! You look fit as fuck right now!" Miranda scavenged through her bag and pulled out a mirror and handed it to him. Christopher put the mirror up to his eyeline and looked straight ahead. His skin looked clear. He looked into the mirror and felt something he thought he'd never feel in his life. He felt like a model. He even turned himself on a bit as he raised an eyebrow to himself. Unrecognisable, even to himself. But as he raised his hand to feel his skin, again he still felt the bumps and blotches. They just weren't visible. Feeling the bumps again, he handed the mirror back to Miranda in a startle.

"Thanks. Yeah. I don't know. A new skin product I'm trying out I guess," he said, unsure of what was going on himself.

Christopher spent the afternoon staring at himself back home in the mirror, this time with curiosity as opposed to disgust. He indulged in his looks, despite what he could still feel on his face. He pouted and posed like a model on the cover of a magazine. As he did, the tiles around him in the bathroom's reflection vanished as a white background with text popped up around his glowing face. Just like the cover of a magazine. Christopher jumped back and hit the tiles on the wall as the mirror flashed back to its normal reflection. His face returned to red and blotchy too.

When the mirror changed back Christopher just about cried. He couldn't stand the sight of himself. Not now. Not after a day of seeing himself with smooth glowing skin. He ran back to the mirror and gripped either side of the basin below it, squeezing it until his hands turned red. His tears dropped into the basin below him, each tear drop full with hope of seeing his face return to the smooth skin that it had appeared to be that day. As he looked into the mirror, the red blotches and bumps on his face slowly began to fade away until his face was again fit for the cover of a magazine. Christopher dried his tears and started to laugh.

He looked at the smooth skinned boy in the mirror. He stroked his face like one might do after a clean shave, though his fingers ran up and down the bumps under this illusion, rather than glide. He didn't care that he could feel them. He carelessly tossed his hand aside. All he cared about was that a new boy stood facing him in the mirror. A boy he thought was mighty attractive. A boy he could learn to love. Hell, that he already loved. A boy that could walk the streets proudly with his shoulders held back and chin up high – without a face of white paint.

Christopher looked ahead and stood a foot back as he imagined himself in stylish new clothes and accessories. A jock-like jacket and baseball cap. Seconds later, he was standing in them. Or at least, visually so. He blinked his eyes twice as a cap appeared on his head with sleeves of his new jock-like jacket rolled up his arms. The only thing was, as he felt the top of his head, and he couldn't feel the cap. His fingers ran through his scruffy hair. He really didn't know what on earth was going on. Then, he heard a loud knock on the door disrupting his curious state. His cap, jacket and smooth skin vanished.

"Christopher, I'm home! Did you manage to pick up the milk on your way home from school like I asked today?"

"Ah, sorry Ma! I forgot! I'll get straight to it!"

Christopher brushed past his mother running down the stairs and zipped out the front door. As he walked along the path, he looked around him for any onlookers. The coast seemed clear. He wanted to test just what the hell was going on. Test what he could do. As he walked, he looked down at his shoes, one stepping in front of the other. He wore old worn-out sneakers which had started to discolour around the edges. But not for long. As he walked, he thought up the most ridiculous shoes he could. Soon, he was walking in golden glitter sneakers. Then black leather boots. Then big ridiculous clown shoes. Then his trousers vanished completely as he pictured himself and appeared in leggings with high heels. Then, he bumped into an oncoming person that had just turned a corner onto the street. Christopher stumbled back and fell on his arse. The person looked down at Christopher with disapproval as his legs with leggings and heels on his feet were spread. He still didn't know what was going on. But he very much liked it.

The weeks that followed saw Christopher start to use his change of appearances more wisely. He tried to take control of it and started with smaller things like the colour of his shoe laces. Once he mastered keeping them the same colour for a day, he'd try for a week, and after a week, he'd move on to his socks. Then his shoes. Then his trousers. His shirt. His jacket. His backpack. He'd introduced the smooth skin back to his face slowly, putting the first time his skin miraculously cleared down to a really good reaction to a new scrub he was using. Not that many had noticed. If they did, most people hadn't realised it was him. Miranda, however, who absolutely did notice, held the pleasure of sleeping over one night when Christopher told her about it. He said as his best friend, he treasured her dearly and she could never know how much it had meant that she held his secret about his sexuality. He added that he had another secret to share.

The two of them sat on his bed in his room laughing, while Miranda joked that he was about to admit he'd lost his virginity.

"Let me guess! Let me guess! Was it... Mr. Cubin?!" Miranda teased. Mr. Cubin was a very old man that people joked looked like Santa Claus. Christopher laughed, not knowing how to approach it. *Out with it,* he thought.

"Miranda, I can change what I look like by thinking about it!"

"Ha, ha, ha! I bet you can. What did you look like for your night with Mr. Cubin?!"

"I'm not joking, Miranda. Watch this!" Christopher said, about to try the theory that seeing is believing. He waved his hands in front of his face and then pulled them away. Miranda looked at him in shock. His nose had doubled in size with a thick black moustache and thick framed glasses. Miranda started to laugh again.

"You are too much, Chris! What kind of prosthetic is this? Some kind of gimmick for your mime artistry?" Miranda asked as she went to tug on his nose. As she did, she let go of it quickly and flinched.

"You okay?"

"Yeah. It's just. The nose I just pinched isn't the one I'm looking at."

"I know. That's what I'm trying to tell you. It only looks different. Here, try brushing my moustache."

Miranda brushed her index finger across what looked like a thick black moustache. But, her finger just felt the bumpy adolescent skin above Christopher's upper lip. Now, with her attention, he asked her to suggest something. She tried to trip him, see through his trick by thinking up extreme gimmicks he couldn't have possibly been prepared for. But as he changed, sitting right in front of her, she began to rattle off anything that came to her mind as he made it so. A frail old woman that looked as though she was about to pass over. A tattooed man covered head to toe. A chimpanzee. A celebrity. Then, herself. She'd asked for him to turn himself into her. She looked ahead, seeing the unbelievable. But she believed it. Then she asked him to stop. She wanted Christopher back. Not the new fresh-faced Chris with confidence in his step that she'd come to know the last few weeks. But the Chris she knew well. He refused. The smooth faced boy she looked at was him now. At least, who he wanted to be.

As the days rolled on, Miranda took to Christopher's new chosen smooth complexion of an appearance. She also really made the most of having a best friend who could change how they looked. She laughed as Christopher took to the streets behind his hat of pennies now wowing both children and their parents alike with his new feats, as he hopped from one side in a can-can dress, to the other side in a rich man's suit with an unimpressed look on his face, then back into the can-can dress trying to out high-kick the other. The two of them came up with school pranks. Christopher made himself look like Trixie and broke up with her boyfriend, laughing as he overheard the couple having an argument about it later in the day. The boyfriend accused Trixie of playing with his head, while she argued it was the first time she had seen him that day.

After school, study dates became fun and daring, as Christopher made himself look older to buy alcohol for him and Miranda. Makeup and nail dates rolled on into late hours of the night, as Christopher tuned himself into reactively changing back to a makeupless-self, for when one of his parents knocked on the door. For a little moment in time, things for Christopher were certainly as colourful as the flag he identified with. But one night, they quickly turned to that red of the coloured blotches on his face. A little too much alcohol led to Christopher letting his guard down a bit too much. One evening, he and Miranda lay on his bed giggling with his nails painted bright red, with a covering of matching glitter. Miranda shaded and faded his eyes with a smoky black. Then, one missed knock as the pair of them giggled, and saw Christopher's father walk into the room.

Christopher sat up quickly in the bed. Miranda followed behind more slowly. Their giggling stopped. It was too late for a transformation. He had been spotted, and Christopher's father left the room. Miranda looked at him and he at her. They started to laugh as if it were a joke, but they quickly stopped as his father's voice – Daniel's voice - projected up the stairs. His voice was accompanied by something falling on the ground. Christopher thought it was possibly a chair. Possibly his mother's chair – Jane's chair - as she'd liked to do crosswords at the dinner table in the evenings. He was sure it had been as he heard his mother scream. Followed by stomping up the steps.

Daniel burst back into the room holding Jane by the back of the neck. He pushed her towards the bed. She fell onto it as Daniel stepped into the room and placed his hands on his hips. He started to point and shake his finger at Christopher.

"You see what you've done, Jane? You see what you've done? Kept him soft! Turned our boy into a little fucking Nancy!" Jane cried. The night heated as Daniel grabbed Jane by her hair and brought her face up to look at Christopher's face. "You fucking see what you've done?! Does that look like our boy to you?!" He threw Jane's head down onto the mattress and then grabbed

Christopher by the chin. Hard. "You like this?" Daniel asked, followed with a slap. "Yeah, you probably like being slapped like that too, don't you?" Christopher took it. Christopher always took it.

Miranda was howling with tears from fright, but pounced on Christopher and wrapped her arms around him.

"Leave him alone! He's done nothing wrong!" Miranda shouted.

"Ha! Being protected by another little girl! Can't fight like a man, can ya son?!" Jane got up from where she stood, reaching into the pair of them, pulling Miranda away while Daniel continued to slap at Christopher. Harder.

"Let me go!" Miranda shouted, as she kicked and squealed in Jane's grasp.

"He won't stop, Miranda. Not even with a woman in front of him, love," said Jane. As Miranda squirmed her way around in Jane's arms, tears streamed from her eyes as she saw Daniel take off his belt and begin to strike Christopher with it. She wondered how often this had happened before. Her impression was that it definitely had. The nights that followed saw Christopher crash at Miranda's place as the two of them made a run from the house. Daniel screamed at Miranda to run and get out, and when she did, he'd made a run for it shortly after her. The two of them cried, arm in arm, with bruises on their shoulders, as they made their way back to hers.

In Christopher's pride, he didn't overstay his welcome, although Miranda would have welcomed it. But Christopher assured Miranda that things with his folks would be fine. He secretly snuck back home, knowing his parents' routine, to grab some belongings that he needed, before starting his new homeless life on the streets. Following in his father's footsteps really, as Daniel had secretly snuck into another man's bed to get what *he* needed, before starting his new married life as husband to his wife. Drinking himself to numbness most nights after work at the corner-pub. Cracking the belt on his own back, before cracking it onto his own son. And as Dale sat across from Christopher, at a diner in Camden, while he shook his leg underneath the table, she saw a flickering of such events in her mind. Which was only the beginning of the dark burning flames in her eyes, for the images in her mind had been but a spark. What came soon after was the flame.

21 RED DIRT

I laid myself down into the shallow water that the remains of the destroyed fountain now held, produced from the rain which Precious and I had drawn from the sky, with Pree and Rubis in my mind. I closed my eyes. I could feel the light droplets of water still falling from the sky. The ripple effects it caused, rippling out to my cheeks. The droplets continued to fall from the sky onto the top of my face. I squeezed my eyes shut as I pictured Pree and Rubis, stronger still. I clenched my hands. But nothing happened. My body lay in the water as it rippled around me. I refused to open my eyes. I squeezed them shut even tighter, starting to bash my fists in the water as it splashed.

Tears pushed themselves out from my sealed tight lids. I let out a cry and bashed my fists down to the surface below me. I felt it crack beneath me and I felt the water begin to bubble. Then, two hands grabbed my shoulders and pulled me up.

"Michael, settle!" Precious yelled frantically, as she pulled me into her chest and held me tight. My head leant on her breasts. My tears began to stream. I crawled my fingers down Precious' back as I began to break down with the realisation that the sparkles of Pree and Rubis had been zapped from the world.

Precious rocked me in her hold. She started to hush me and kissed the crown of my head. I could feel her tightening her grip on me so I knew she was there. The tears I expelled fell, as the bubbling of the water around me settled back to its rippling, joining the droplets of rain.

"It cannot be. It cannot be. It. Can. Not. Be-e-e!"

"Hush, darling boy. Hush." Precious continued to rock me, trying to provide some comfort. I looked up at her, finally opening my eyes.

"They're gone, Precious. They're gone. Like every other non-enabled in the world-d-d," I cried. Precious stroked the back of my head.

"You don't know that, darling. We don't know that."

"I do. It would have taken me to them. The portal would have taken me straight there-re-re," I continued to cry. Precious didn't respond for some time. She carried on rocking me as I cried into her breasts. Then, Precious broke her silence.

"Michael. What if it's broken? What if the portal isn't working? What if, when the monument was destroyed, its traveling properties were too? Is there another you could seek?"

I thought about what Precious said for a moment. It was probably possible. It made some kind of logistical sense. I looked out across the dead bodies of Demos and little Lee beside us to the ruins of Buckingham Palace. Maybe it was worth seeking the Queen. If she hadn't been destroyed along with Buckingham Palace, that was. If she really was enabled, she was probably part of this fight. But a hesitant thought entered my mind, as I considered the possibility that the monarch could well be held captive by the Dark Enabled. By Lenroc. That wasn't such a wise move, if so. I took my time to think about it a little more. If Lenroc had no knowledge of my still being alive, I didn't want to lead myself straight back to her.

"I've got someone."

"Are you sure?"

"I'm sure. Okay, Precious. I'll come back for you." I laid my head back into the water and closed my eyes. It was a stretch. But it was all that I had left.

I thought back to hopping into Mum's car as *he* hopped into the back. I thought back to family dinners he joined. The bottle of vodka he snuck into my parents' house. The walk we took as I came out to him. The bonfire parties. The online chats. His disapproval of me meeting up with a stranger online. The way he looked out for me. The way he stuck up for me in the courtyard when Gus had a go at Victor and I. His presence in the hospital as I woke with the taste of dirt in my mouth. Stood together side by side in our suits ready for the school ball. His presence back in hospital as I was told I had a plague of the brain. The nights he joined me when I first started clubbing, as part of the scene. The scene that tore me away from him. My best buddy. *Andrew.*

My mind fuzzed. For the first time today, I felt a gust of air enter my chest as I opened my eyes in fits of coughs. It worked. The bloody bugger was enabled himself – providing it really was only enabled left on the planet. I found myself on an old tar road. I sat on a large crack lined through it, red dirt with dead dried shrubs and twigs either side of it. I looked up to find a rectangular white sign. Imprinted on it was a red circle and the black number eighty within it. A speed limit. Not like the cut out circular ones I was now accustomed to in London. I was back in Australia. Likely, had Andrew not moved states, in my hometown of Perth, Western Australia.

Although the dirt was red, the air held a dark smog. Looking around, I knew the dark enabled hadn't limited their destruction to the city of London. They had moved on, to defeat the world. But I was damned if I was about to let them conquer it. I had too soon given up on the world as I let Lenroc take the enchanted knife to my wrists. I had too soon given up on many things in my life. Pree and Rubis, who were now no more. Tears returned to my eyes as I thought of them. If I was going to ensure light was restored for anyone, it was in honour of them. I was ready to throw my life away after I'd found out my family had died in the accident. I needed to *live* for them too. I needed to restore light within myself. Not just the world. Hopefully, with my best buddy Andrew by my side. Again.

I stood myself up from the crack on the road as I looked out around me. The glimmer of speckled dust floated in a circular motion behind me. The doorway back. I looked on further. I certainly wasn't in the suburbs. Not a tiled pitched roof was in plain sight. The land of red stretched out for miles around me. I wondered where Andrew might be. I remembered how when I'd travelled to Victor I was spat out of his bedroom wardrobe – before he'd ventured in with Buttocks Boy. Perhaps Andrew was close by. Maybe taking a leak out in the bush. I didn't want to wander too far from the portal's gateway back. But I did start to walk down the empty road as I howled out to the open air.

Ahead, I saw skid marks on the road made from tyres. Ahead of those, a car which looked as though it had swerved off of the road and crashed into the shrubs. I started to run towards it. It was black. As if it had been on fire. The windows were blown in. *Please don't be Andrew. Please don't be Andrew.* I remembered the scarce few bodies I came across in London. In a city which held nearly nine million. How Precious and I had come to the conclusion that only enabled remained. I didn't come all this way to find another dead body of an enabled. I didn't come all this way to find that I'd left it too late to see my best buddy in this big wide world. I remembered how Lenroc had deterred me from returning back home as I looked down into the glistening water of the portal. How she'd said she knew what I was thinking, but there was nothing left for me. *Let bygones be bygones,* she'd said. I shouldn't have listened to her.

Once I reached the car I looked inside it. A black skeleton sat at the steering wheel. *Andrew?* I began to cry at the thought. It must have been. I thought of Andrew, and the portal brought me here. It had to be him. My tears streamed as I opened the door to sit in the passenger seat next to him. To tell him how sorry I was that I never said goodbye. That I was sorry I'd become so wrapped up in the scene and lost sight of him. That I'd become so wrapped up in my new life in London that I'd never come back for him. As I opened the door to the car it creaked. But I also heard something else take to the air.

I knew that sound anywhere. That was the sound of an old Aussie car zooming above the speed limit freely down a highway. *Andrew!* I thought. I ran from the charcoal car and back onto the road in front of the gateway. I saw two bright shining headlights ahead through the dark smog in the air. They were getting closer. I started to wave my arms in the air as if trying to get the attention of a plane in the sky from a deserted island. However the thought quickly came into my mind that the fast approaching car may not be Andrew at all. What if Andrew *was* the black skeleton in the car? What if I was waving down a creep like Mister Super Strength? But then I'd run into Precious too and look how that turned out. Andrew, creepster or Precious-like soul, I stepped back towards the gateway, ready to jump back into the waters of the portal should this go wrong.

As the headlights approached, the vehicle slowed down. It got closer. The headlights grew brighter. Then it stopped, the bright headlights beaming in my eyesight.

"Hello?!" I called out. No response. I heard the creak of a car door opening. Not quite as bad a sound as the charcoal door had just made, but somehow, more unsettling. The door slammed shut.

"What's your business?! You're not one of those purple glowing creatures, are ya?!"

"Not at all! I'm just looking for a friend!"

"And what's this shiny thing behind you?!"

"Oh, that? It's a portal! I travelled through it to find my friend!" I said, saying it how it was.

The voice stayed quiet for a moment. I could hear his steps getting closer from the heels of his shoes on the old tar road.

"Well, I've seen a lot crazier this last twenty-four hours. So, I'm inclined to believe it." He stepped in front of the bright headlights.

"Andrew!" I shouted at the top of my lungs. It was him. It was actually fucking Andrew. But he looked at me strangely. He looked at me as if he had no idea who I was. As if he'd never seen me before in his life.

"Well that's fucked up. But like I say, seen a lot the last twenty-four hours. How's it you know my name mate?"

"Andrew. It's me. Michael. Your best mate..."

"My best mate? I don't have a best mate, my friend. More of a solo rider." It was the strangest thing. He really didn't know who I was.

"You, me, Renae, Candice.. Heck, even back when it was you, me and Adam!"

"Okay I don't know who you are. But how the hell do you know my peers from school?"

"Andrew. I'm telling you. We are best mates. We were best mates. Before I popped up in London."

"London? Is this where you've come from?"

"Yeah. I was planning to take you back with me. I wanted my best buddy in the world by my side."

"Listen. I hope you find him, mate. But I'm telling you it's not me."

I stood in confusion. It crossed my mind for a moment that perhaps the clearing Lenroc performed on the people in my life included Andrew. But it didn't add up. Victor had known exactly who I was when I'd come back to him. Before his guts plastered the walls. Unless, of course, it was all in Lenroc's planning. I wouldn't have put it past her. With her gift of sight. Knowing Victor was a sore spot for me. Knowing the unfinished business I held with him. No matter. Andrew stood here clueless.

"Andrew. I'm going to need you to trust that I know you, okay?" He looked at me hesitantly. "You say you've seen a lot in the last twenty-four hours. Have you added to any of that? Have you seen yourself do anything strange or out of the ordinary? Have you been able to do anything strange or out of the ordinary at all? Ever?"

Andrew looked confused.

"Mate. I was in the city grabbing an ice-cream. Then all of a sudden everyone disappeared. The bright day turned to dark. Some freakish colour palette dispersed in the sky. This grey mist set in all around. I thought I was the only human left on earth. I wandered the streets for a while to see if anyone else was around. But nothing. No-one. I saw some medieval creature flying through the sky or some shit. That was a pretty epic moment. I kept my head low after that. I made my way up to Kings Park thinking I'd get a good view of any cars or people making tracks. Anyone left behind like me. Thought it was the best point of view to look down at the city. You can see it all up there. But what did I see? Some fucking big foot creature the size of Perth's tallest skyscraper bash it down like it was a cobweb in its way. I watched it navigate itself for some time. Not really believing what I was seeing to be honest. But it made its way North. So, I made my way South. Started to make my way down the freeway until traffic cleared up. Couldn't find a car I could actually drive off the road for miles that wasn't blocked in or crashed into something. Plus, I didn't know if that bigfoot thing might have doubled back and how far out it could see. Found this beauty behind me out around Baldivis. You, my friend, are the first person I've seen since yesterday. I don't know what you're getting at in asking me if I've contributed to anything. But I'll tell you one thing. I need the company. That, and I've never been to London! So, are we taking off or what?"

I looked into the eyes of my best bud while he spoke, not thinking twice about what he said. I'd seen my fair share, too. I was just so darn happy to see him. He filled my heart with warmth. I really couldn't help but think the guy felt some familiarity with me. He seemed to open up straight away, with no qualms about it. Whether he recalled me or not, at least there was that.

"You want to come back to London?" I asked.

"Mate. What am I gonna do here? Thinking of myself right now as Marty, and you're Doc, who's come to take me back with you. I meant, technically it *will* be traveling back in time, right? Ain't London like eight hours behind?" Andrew laughed. God it was so good to see him laugh.

"Would it be weird if I hugged you?" I asked. Andrew raised his eyebrow rather high and stretched his lower lip back exposing his teeth.

"Ah. Yeah. A bit. Sorry mate."

"Yeah, yeah. I suppose that's weird. If you don't remember me and all. Right, what next?"

"Are we going through there?" Andrew asked, pointing to the circular floating specks behind me. I looked back, then returned my gaze to Andrew.

"Yeah. I, ah... I've never brought anyone with me. I think we - I - I think we might need to be connected. Hold hands..."

"I see. Well, if it's for the cause!" Andrew agreed as he started to walk forward, his spirit still ever joking. Just how I remember him. He stood in front of me with his hand held out. I looked down at it, and then back up at him as I took it. We walked towards the gateway together then stood in front of it.

"So, shall we jump in on the count of three?"

"Sounds like a better plan than any!"

As we stood in front of the gateway, we counted one, two, three and then jumped in as we held each other's hand. I smiled a smile of comfort, knowing the adventures of Michael and Andrew weren't over. They were just beginning. My mind fuzzed. Blackness. Then, the shallow water.

22 THE EMPTY GLASS

Dale sat, looking across the table at Christopher while he spoke, with the spark of his experiences in her eyes. She'd started by asking him the standard questions about himself. Just as she asked anyone at these interviews. What experience he had working in the Arts. If he could describe his passion for performance and what made him unique as an artist. An explanation of why he needed accommodation over other applicants and how it would help improve his work. His answer to her question on what he would stand for as an advocate of the Uprising Arts Society was probably the best Dale had heard yet.

Christopher spoke of how he wanted to uphold and stand for truth. To ensure that nobody felt like they ever had to hide who they were again. That the night he'd made a run for it, before he fled his parents' house with Miranda, he stood under the frame of his door and looked back at his frightened mother and poor excuse for a father collapsed on the bed with his belt in his hand. Announcing that he was gay and that he was proud of it. That they should be ashamed they ever made him feel he had to hide it. It was at that moment his father chased him out of the house and yelled that he was no son of his. Christopher decided from that night forward he wasn't going to hide who he was, ever again. Not for anyone.

Dale looked at Christopher with a grin and the spark that had ignited in her eyes. Seeing his past's truth. The transformation he'd made on his skin. From the red, blotchy bumps to the smooth, fresh faced boy that sat in front of her.

"Now, now. No need to lie." Christopher looked at her defensively.

"I'm sorry, but I just shared a pretty vulnerable story with you…"

"Christopher, Christopher, Christopher. That you did. And how admirable your submission to UAS is. But it's not the whole truth now, is it? You wouldn't change, for anyone?"

"I'm not sure what you're getting at."

"How about, *everyone*? That's the truth isn't it? You change for everyone. Every day. So they can see you in a better light. So they'll like you. Respect you. Fuck you. So children won't whimper away at the sight of you. Am I ringing any bells?" Dale confronted him with the images that had flashed into her mind. He hadn't shared a word of his skin. Dale's knowledge made him feel uneasy - if he wasn't already jittery enough with his nervous leg shake.

Dale reached out across the table to grab Christopher's hands. He pulled away and backed up to the booth he was sitting in.

"What are you playing at, woman?"

"What am *I* playing at? Christopher. What are *you* playing at? You've got all these people fooled. Making out you're some stud when we both know what that face would feel like if I touched it."

"If you're referring to the skin condition I used to have, it's all cleared up, and I honestly don't know what you're on…"

"Chris. Cut the crap. I know. You haven't spoken it but I've seen your story. I'm just like you. But my power's up here," said Dale, tapping her head.

"You mean… You know what I can do?"

"I've *seen* what you can do. If you cut the shit and be frank with me, I think I can find a place for you at UAS-HQ. But you've got to level with me. Okay?"

"Okay," agreed Christopher, backing down and leaning back onto the surface of the table. Dale continued to speak.

"I believe you. I believe in what you stand for. You want people to live in a world where they can be themselves and not have to feel that way you've been made to feel. But right now, we're living in a world of people that aren't going to let that happen. We're living in a world where as soon as you take that coverage off yourself the next boy in line with a Hollywood smile at an audition is going to get the gig. I think you know that. I think that's why you keep yourself hidden. But you shouldn't have to hide, Chris. You should be able to practice what you preach. In full confidence. There's just one thing in the way. That's *people.*"

Christopher broke eye contact and looked away from Dale, turning his eyes down to the surface. He'd been justifying what he did to change his appearance by telling himself it was just like someone might apply makeup to their face in the morning. But deep down inside he did feel ashamed. Proud to be gay. But not proud in his own skin. He looked back up at Dale.

"What do you want, exactly?"

"To help you. Together, to make people realise their shitty views of the world. To give people like yourself a world they *can* be themselves. But first we're going to need to look at this power of yours. To guide you if I may. See what you can do. Push your boundaries. Find out what this ability of yours actually is. How does that sound?"

"Sounds fine, I guess," said Christopher, uncertainly.

"Oh come on. Let's hear some more spirit. We're gonna show these fuckers what shallow lives they've been living. How does that sound, Chris?"

"Sounds great."

"How great, Chris?"

"Fucking great!"

"That's the spirit! And do you want to make your dad pay for what he did to you?"

"More than anyth-" Christopher stopped speaking.

He looked back down at the surface of the table. Dale reached out and grabbed his hands. This time he didn't pull away.

"It's okay to *want* someone to pay for something. Just by saying so doesn't make you a bad guy."

"I mean... I feel like I want him to. But it doesn't feel right, does it?"

"Was striking you with that belt right?"

"You saw that?"

"I saw that. I told you to level with me here. We're talking about a man that has put you on the streets when he should have provided the one place you could return to every day to be embraced and encouraged to be yourself. I'll ask you again. Do you want him to pay?"

"Yeah, I kind of do."

"Frankness will get you a long way with me. Keep it up and I think you'll find your time at UAS-HQ a long standing one. A roof that you *can* come back to at the end of each day and be yourself. A place where I *will* embrace you."

Dale continued to speak with Christopher in her manipulative way, making his dark inner thoughts seem harmless as she provoked the worst from him. Provoked a hate that had been resting deep inside. She began to question him on his ability, asking what else he'd tried. Trying to see if perhaps he too might be pushed to harness a further developed ability in widening his channel of it. Just as she had developed herself from pure sight to mind control. She didn't know what else she might be able to get out of him. But she wanted to try. She asked him to describe what he felt when he changed. What ran through his mind. As he started to describe what he would go through in a moment of change, Dale began to see bright changing moving colours which morphed into prisms around him.

As Christopher finished speaking, Dale sat back on her side of the booth while the prisms around him vanished. She explained to him that she never quite knew what it was that she had but she knew there had to be others. That she'd encountered a visit recently from a man who explained those with abilities were enabled. That she was enabled with sight, the man was enabled with energy, and that she thought Christopher was enabled with light.

"Light? How can I be enabled with light? I thought of it like being a shapeshifter or transformer or something."

"No, No. To shapeshift or transform is to shapeshift into the shape you see or make a full transformation. With you, it's just what *we* see, isn't it? You're still *you* sitting there – it's just that I see what you want me to. What affects what we see? Light. I think you're enabled with light. I think there's a whole lot more you can do with that ability, Chris, and boy I'm looking forward to finding out."

Christopher took Dale's word for the thoughts she expressed. Dale wanted to test her theory. She asked Christopher to focus on something in the room. Something made from glass. Try to focus on the object and isolate his thoughts its way, as he had the first day he changed his appearance, thinking of nothing other than the desire for clear skin, repulsed by his own. But instead of changing the glass object, she suggested he manipulate the light in the room to melt it. Like a human magnifying-glass. Dale suggested a table that a family was sitting at in the corner of the diner. More specifically, the empty glass on the corner of it. She guided him with her words, reiterating to isolate his thoughts and focus on it. She even tried to tap into his mind herself. Boost his intention. Drive and control his thoughts.

"Sorry. I can't do it. Maybe you were wrong. Maybe this ability, as you call it, is just trickery. Illusion."

Dale refused to accept Christopher's counter suggestion. The prisms of colour and light she saw shine around him were too strong. She felt sure he was enabled, with light. That he held the ability to manipulate it. She had to capture her results by other means.

"Look back at that glass. Don't take your eyes off of it." Dale instructed him, in a commanding tone. Christopher did as she requested. "You *are* enabled with light and you *do* hold the ability to manipulate it. Just think what you could do apart from limiting yourself to what you see as trickery and illusion. Think of the power you could hold in your hand. You've never had that, have you? Power. You didn't have any as your dad struck you with his belt."

Christopher broke focus with the glass and turned his head back to address Dale, thinking she was out of line, but she took control of his mind and turned his head and focused back to the empty glass. "See, Chris. You have no power. No wonder your dad disowned you. I'm surprised your best friend never disowned you, seeing you cower every time your parents knocked on the door. Not strong enough to have let them see you with your nails and makeup. Maybe a good belt was exactly what you needed. Maybe your father didn't strike you nearly hard enough." As Dale spoke her cruel, dark and manipulative words, Christopher's eyes swelled. His sight stuck to the empty glass on the corner of the table. The veins in his forehead and neck began to thicken. They pumped. All at the same time as a ray of sunlight beaming its way through the window of the diner and onto the empty glass.

In the thick of the moment, as Dale said the words *your father didn't strike you nearly hard enough,* the empty glass not only melted, but the lino of the table beneath started to bubble and blacken. The family sitting around it screamed as the parents tried to make way for their children to get out. Dale watched as she relinquished her control, to see just how far he just might take it on his own. The bubbling turned to fire and the table began to burn. A little boy sitting behind the flames screamed in terror, too afraid to move. His father jumped in to rescue him as the corner of the diner set off in a small explosion with the windows around it shattering.

Christopher stopped. He let go of his focus. The veins in his head and neck began to flatten back into his skin. The people in the diner ran and fled. The staff had ducked under the counter and were cowering in the kitchen. Dale sat, in admiration of the work she had facilitated. In admiration of what Christopher had carried on to do, of his own accord. It was then that the dark burning flames set into Dale's eyes, as Christopher felt the rush of his first taste of real power. At least, as Dale had set onto his impression of power. He breathed heavily with a sense of accomplishment, but at the same time held a sense of urgency as he stood to run and help the father and son. Dale took back control of his mind and froze him in his place.

"Whoever helped you, Chris?!" Dale shouted. Christopher stood as he watched the two bodies burn, their screams simmering down along with the fire. The father's skin had melted onto his son, wrapped up in his arms.

Dale let go of her control as Christopher stood and started to cry, others now rushing to the aid of the father and son. Christopher stepped back and sat down in the booth with Dale again. He stared her down, powerless, to *her*.

"That was pure fucking cruelty. What *are* you?"

"Liberation. And your salvation." Dale replied.

23 BLANK SPOTS

I emerged from the shallow water with Andrew's hand in mine. Losing balance, we let go of one another as we both fell flat onto our butts, with the water splashing around us. As my vision unfuzzed, I looked ahead to find not one, but two red headed ladies. I squinted my eyes to try and clear my vision. One was of course Precious. The other, not at all the displeased and inconvenienced business woman I'd once first set my eyes upon, in the white nothingness that had gathered the Collective together in one place. It was Audrey, with a rather pleased look on her face. The member of the Collective that had been thrown out into the distance by a purple illuminate glow. She'd clearly survived. With Audrey in sight, Precious where I'd left her and Andrew by my side, I started to feel stronger than ever. What was left of the dark smog was far outweighed by the good around me.

Andrew stood up from the water, offering his hand to help me up.

"Man. That was quite a trip. You okay?" Andrew asked.

"I'm good. Just going to have a sore butt for a while I think!" I replied, accompanied by a small laugh. As I stood up Precious and Audrey approached.

"I found a friend of yours, Michael," said Precious. "Well, more like she found me," she added, as she smiled my way. I stepped out from the water and over the ledge onto the ground to join them. Precious practically leapt as she threw herself around me and kissed my lips. "I'm glad you're back," she whispered.

"It's good to be back," I whispered back to her, then looked over at Audrey.

"Audrey," I said, greeting her with a slight head nod and smile her way. She looked down at Demos and little Lee's bodies, still laying in the water of the portal. "I'm so sorry." I extended my sympathies.

"Don't be. They would have died in honour. They died to have you still standing here. I would have too. It's good to see you're still in this fight."

"The rest. They're all..."

"I know. We all knew, Michael. Demos warned us. He spoke to us. Through his mind, into ours, as Margaret spoke to you. He told us just one would survive. That the one that did, had to ensure they watched over you. I guess I'm that one."

"You all knew?! Why was I the one left in the dark?"

"We had to keep your spirits high. We needed you to fight. We needed you to hold hope."

"Keep my spirit high?! Fight?! Hope?! Audrey, look around you. Look at what I caused. Look at what I let happen. Do you think Demos foresaw all this?!"

"I have to. *We* have to. Demos' thoughts were clouded around you at first. But everything that's happened led to this very moment: bringing us back together; these people being here with you. I have to have faith that what lays ahead was part of his plan. His sight. Not that he told us anything more. I know you'll feel stupid right now but you have to believe we all held our breath for the greater good. For this moment. For what's to come."

"The greater good! Did you look around?! Everyone on earth apart from the enabled has disintegrated. Vanished. Gone. What's left?!" I suddenly didn't feel so strong anymore. I felt faint. My mind fuzzed. Blackness.

*

I opened my eyes to the dark smoggy sky above, as a warm crackling and flickering light came from beside me. I heard laughter. I turned to my side to find I was rugged up beside a fire, with Precious, Audrey and Andrew circled around it.

"Hey, he's up!" Andrew shouted. "My man. My Doc from eight hours in the future." I laughed, missing such banter. Not that he remembered. But I loved that he was just the same as *I* remembered, his soul not twisted by life events, like mine had been.

Precious came and rugged up beside me in her coat. Andrew and Audrey were in theirs.

"I'm sorry about before."

"It's okay. You've been through a lot. Just so you know, I don't believe everyone is gone. Disintegrated, as you put it. When Lenroc bled you - when the boundaries of the underground and earth were broken- as other realms bled into this world, I think Lenroc took hold of the energy of all non-enabled somehow. Managed to isolate a bubble, a force, around those without abilities, sending them to the realm the Collective had created. The banished realm. And resealing it."

"You think?" I asked, excited at the prospect that Pree and Rubis still might be out there.

"My ability might only be in freezing time and space, but I find it is closely connected to space. And I sense something. It's like they're all out there still. Somewhere. In some space. And it's all I've got to go on. That, and the knowledge of what Lenroc managed to harness in the Dark Enabled times."

"Well folks, don't know what all this non-enabled realm talk's about or who this almighty Lenroc is. But I say we rest a while longer, enough for Michael to regain some strength, and then we hit the nearest burger joint to see if we can't make us some food! I'm starved!" Andrew suggested, in his jokester like way.

170

"Sounds like a grand idea; this one and I haven't eaten since we started our little adventure," said Precious, as she rubbed my back. Food did sound good. But Audrey's theory intrigued me.

"So, if you're correct, Lenroc managed to transfer all the energy of the non-enabled to another space. The banished realm. Could it be true that only the enabled remain?" I asked.

"I think so. I think that's the world Lenroc wants to create. It was once to enslave humanity, in the Dark Enabled times. But now, I think it's more than that. I think Lenroc just wants to take over the world."

I looked over at Andrew and then back at Audrey.

"Then, Andrew."

"Yes," Audrey looked at Andrew. "I'd say you're definitely enabled, young man. Whether you have found your ability yet or not. Say, how is it you two know each other?"

"You still don't remember?" I asked. Andrew shook his head.

"Hey, I know nothing about all this enabled whatnot. I can't even dry a dish without breaking it," said Andrew. I looked at Audrey.

"He's my best mate. I think Lenroc's clearing reached him. But it doesn't make sense. There was another who I travelled back to. He knew exactly who I was."

"Well, in terms of being enabled, Andrew, I'm sure we've got time ahead of us yet to see what's lying dormant inside of you. It may be that it's not birthed. I was a late bloomer myself. In terms of the clearing, there would have been reasoning behind it. I'm sure Lenroc picked and chose whom she wanted to recall you at her own device. Who was this other?"

"Well, Michael was actually right in the midst of a story on our way to this place. Did you feel up to finishing that one? Your first day in London, when you first saw the portal?" Precious asked.

"Sure," I said, feeling I had it in me. "I mean, I have to warn you, there are some things I've done that might shock you. Andrew, don't let what

I'm going to speak of frighten you. There are some things I'm not proud of. Things I should be locked up for. But they're part of my story. They were part of my journey here. My encounters with Lenroc. And it's what we do from here that counts, right?" I said, looking back at Precious with a smile. Precious smiled back at me. Audrey nodded. Andrew too.

Audrey made a point of letting me know that I would have been under extreme nurturing and manipulation from Lenroc. That I shouldn't feel too ashamed of anything that happened, Lenroc being the one that let it happen. She guided me straight to whatever I had done. I did feel some truth in that, but deep down inside I knew my own nature. Regardless, I thanked her, and began by trailing back on a little of what I'd told Precious, to explain to Audrey and Andrew that I was brought to London *by* Lenroc. That she had performed the clearing which Andrew must have been part of. I spoke of Primrose Hill and then London's most glamorous bunker, Café De Paris, a place that Precious and I had first started to make our way to. A place that was no longer a destination to me, the people I had hoped to find there being no more. I spoke of how I'd looked down into the crystal water of the portal with Andrew on my mind – although for now I kept that to myself.

I looked at Andrew, and then behind him at the site of destruction where Buckingham Palace once stood, with its part standing staircase.

"Audrey… The Monarch. What part do they play in all this? Do you think they're still here? Do you think they're worth finding?" I asked.

"Think of the royals as our governing board," said Aurdey.

"But isn't the *Collective* the governing board?"

"I prefer to think of the Collective as a sub-committee. The ones that discuss the matters to put to the board. At least, that's how it had been sold to me, when Demos and Margaret recruited me. But yes, the Collective mostly operated of their own accord. The Queen, much like politics, rarely intervened. But if there's anyone with the resources or knowledge of the Dark Enabled times that can help us, it's her. If the Queen is still with us she's in one of two places:

The Tower of London or Windsor Castle. They're the only establishments set up with enabled protection."

"Not Tower Bridge. I awoke there. It's glowing that awful purple. The dark enabled have taken hold of that place."

"Well then, she's either held captive there, or she's at Windsor. Or…"

"Yes, let's not think of that. It seems Windsor is the only destination presenting itself to me."

"What about Buckingham Palace?!" Andrew said proudly. We all looked to its defeat, as Andrew looked behind him.

"Oh."

"Right, well I'm feeling up for this pit-stop for food if you all are. Shall I continue my story over dinner?" I asked.

"Thank God! I could eat a horse!" Precious shouted.

The four of us all stood and left the destruction site of the grounds behind which Buckingham Palace once stood, the bodies of the Collective among it. Audrey looked back at Demos and little Lee one last time, with a look that said *I'm sorry this had to happen – I'm going to make sure it wasn't for nothing.* Precious and I held hands, and we all decided to make our way to Piccadilly Circus, through Green Park. Green Park, also part receiving the growth which St James's Park had. Although the greenery of Green Park tapered down the further we walked. Audrey and Andrew questioned it. I quite proudly announced Precious' ability and what she had done. What *we* had done. Andrew was loving all the talk of abilities and realms. It was a whole new world to him and he was feeding off of it – regardless that it was now saturated with darkness. Audrey was rather impressed. But she warned us to be careful, saying that connecting abilities could lead to extreme power that could become uncontrollable.

As we hit the streets of Piccadilly, we turned right and started to make our way up to the circus, surrounded again by blackened buildings and rubble. Precious and I led, as Andrew and Audrey followed behind us. Audrey was not familiar with London as a New Yorker. Andrew had seemingly never left Western Australia. He jogged up to my side.

"So, we really were best friends, hey?"

"Yeah. You were the best friend anyone could ask for. You always looked out for me. Always looked after me. You don't know how happy I was to see you walk towards me." Audrey called ahead for Precious to join her.

"Let the lads engage in a little catch up!" It was nice to take a moment with Andrew. For him, to take a moment with *me*. Walk and talk about times that had been. Better times. Times that, although he couldn't recall, I remembered fondly. After a few laughs and some stories, he patted my back and gripped onto my shoulder.

"Well, Michael. What's done is done. Something new has begun!"

"That's very true."

"Right. These abilities. How do you find out what you can do? How did *you* find out what you could do?"

It was an unsettling question. Andrew had been by my side the first time I used my ability. Not that I knew at the time. But it was also a rather emotional moment, as he had comforted not just me, but our friend Renae. Comforted us as if we were a pack. When he stood with me at my parents' house, side by side in our suits at the start of the night, he was there in support just before I came out to them. I wondered how Andrew recalled the event – the existence of me having been cleared from his mind.

"Can I ask you a question first?"

"Go for it."

"What do you remember of your High School Ball?"

"My Ball?! Sheesh, that takes me back. I remember I..." Andrew stopped speaking. We walked in silence for a few moments as he seemed to enter deep thought. "You know. It's the weirdest thing. It's like that whole night is a blur."

"I think it's because you were with me..."

"That's a bit spooky, that is."

"How about graduation? You remember any of that?" I asked, knowing again he was with me.

"Blank."

As I walked beside Andrew, my heart broke a little for him, as he realised the blank spots in his mind. The moments that we'd shared which he'd forgotten. The moments that we shared, completely wiped from his mind. Not just me from them. But entire moments of his life were erased, because I'd been in them. It couldn't have been an easy thing to be confronted with.

"I'm sorry."

"Hey, it's not your fault."

"I guess, but I feel somewhat responsible."

"You can't feel responsible for whatever this Lenroc character did to me, mate. I appreciate it. But as I said, something new has begun!"

I admired how Andrew had tried to keep hold of positivity, moving us on from the vulnerable moment he'd just experienced. But I had a feeling it would take its toll at some point. A sad feeling sunk in. Not that I was opposed to it. Sad, as he had always been the one to look out for me. Sad, as *I* just may need to be the one that needed to look out for *him,* sooner or later.

24 UPRISING

Dale took Christopher back to the Uprising Arts Society Headquarters, in his traumatised state, now with the memory of the seared skin of a father and son joined as one. The smell of burned hair in his nostrils. Not speaking one word more after asking Dale what she was; her reply being *liberation and his salvation.* She asked reception for a spare blanket on arrival, wrapping it around him, and she took him up the grand staircase into the deep skeleton of the old mansion that would have once housed a family of fortune. A place of architectural exquisiteness. High ceilings with original Victorian cornicing and restored lighting fixtures. Now, a base for Dale's sinister plans. To house sought out enabled. To build and train her army.

Dale had prepared a room of the most grandeur for her first guest – Christopher. A large, monstrous fireplace took up the majority of one of the walls. Its crackle filled the room with a warm flickering. The sheets on the four-poster bed absorbed its warmth, made from silk that dragged along Christopher's skin like pure pleasure. Now captured in the luxuries, why would the amateur teenage boy have resisted? Although what he'd seen was horrific and, to his mind, immoral, he'd also experienced Dale's power over him. He'd also tasted his own. Beyond the diner in Camden.

The two of them had not come straight back to UAS Headquarters. Dale saw that the taxi she hailed from the diner took the two of them on a detour to Christopher's parents' house. A detour to make him confront his abuser and bystander. Adding to his memory of seared skin, the burning of the place he once called home, with his parents inside of it. Dale fed him words he couldn't argue against, making him question his parents' morals. But not his own. Fuelling him with the hate she was full of. Fuelling him with more.

Now captive to Dale, frightened yet empowered by her, Christopher settled into his new surroundings. His elaborate cage of luxury. Dale worked with him to take control of his ability. She pushed him to new potentials. Potentials he felt unreachable at times. Persistence was key. She also, however, continued her hunt for enabled through applications of more failed applicants. For more vulnerable. More captives. As the years rolled on, Dale worked her way through non-enabled and enabled, giving less and less time to those she quickly realised held no abilities. Providing more and more time with those who did. Pursuing them with her manipulative words. Her mind control. Her ability to lure them into a sense of being too deep. Her status at UAS setting grounds for the young, impressionable and naïve to follow.

Each enabled she brought back to headquarters, taking to the room with the four-poster bed, while the one before them was moved down into dormitories. The headquarters became a place of dark harboured souls from all over the world. The movements of UAS had reached across the globe, exchange programmes and internships set up in every corner of Dale's operation. She had also begun headhunting potential candidates. Trolling the newspaper headlines and looking for stories which led to extraordinary events – linking them to possibilities of enabled impacted events. Freak storms out of nowhere with no data to account for them. Fires which started without explanation. Businessmen who had gotten rich quickly without a trail of records. Five years on from her twenty-first birthday, Dale had achieved an empire of followers. Christopher was by her side as her most loyal subject; he became her in-house trained personal assistant. Dale slowly found ways to dismiss her original staff, to replace them with recruited enabled.

New members were appointed to the board of trustees, as Dale saw that the original formation, appointed by skill, departed one by one. She had no room for non-enabled in her presence, and as her empire grew, so did her hatred for general humanity, even dropping Katrina and Kent like dead flies. Dale herself had harnessed her powers to the point of being able to unlock one's mind and access the matter that enabled a person's ability. She started to absorb the abilities she came face to face with, adding them to her parlour of tricks, becoming more powerful than she had ever imagined.

Dale felt almost ready to push the pedal on her movement. Almost ready to enslave humanity, and kick the dirt in their faces as humanity had done to her. She was ready to stop all the hurt in the world. She wanted the non-enabled of the world to do her bidding. Make them squirm. Have them lick her shoes. She was creating a world for the enabled to live their lives unhidden with humanity cowering before them. Creating a new world, as she promised to her followers. Although there was one more box to tick off the list before she did any of that. As she had been preparing her movement, the young man in black who'd once visited her, Shane, was preparing his. A movement which Dale felt she needed to undermine to be part of. To become the enabled which Shane had been scouting to form council. *The Collective*, as he called them. A group of people to ensure balance was kept as the dark days rumbled ahead.

Over the five years that had gone by, Shane had checked up on Dale annually, to see if she'd done as he'd asked of her: if she had sensed or engaged with any dark activity. Dale kept him on side, feeding him little stories to throw him off her trail. But even so, with each year that went by, Shane felt more and more off about Dale. It was something in her energy that felt off, each year he'd come to see her. This feeling increased when he sought the advice of one of his councillors about his suspicions. A woman who lived in Manhattan. A woman he met with in her favourite coffee shop each year; the very coffee shop in which she had been reading her book as she saw the pages burn and turn to black when Dale was born. A woman who, like Dale, held the gift of sight. A woman named Kerry.

In line with the Manhattaner's advice, Shane also received a tip from another of his fellow Collective whilst visiting a young man in a small polish town called Myslenice. The young man, with the gift of intuition, had grown to channel it to a universal extent, telling Shane that the dark days were not far away. The young man's name was Jakub. Back in London, also now part of the Collective, Shane met with a mother of two in her kitchen, so she could keep an eye on the kids from the counter, sharing with him the pain with which she felt the world was soon to be inflicted, caused by a pre-conceiving empath. Her name was Jenny. The four of them together made up a strong council. A strong Collective: Shane's ability to channel the energy of the world; Jenny's ability to channel the emotions of those within it; Jakub's ability to channel the turning of events ahead; and Kerry's ability to channel glimpses of past, present and future, advising Shane that she saw a woman's blonde bob blowing in the wind from the door to the underworld.

With such information fed his way, Shane felt, if there was ever a time for the figure which gave him his orders to gather this council to intervene, this was it. He sat on the leather stitched seating, in the royal car which had been sent to pick him up, as it drove through the gates of Buckingham Palace. He felt a change of energy in the air around him, as the royal car's wheels hit the gravel set over the grounds. An energy that felt conflicting, but strong. An energy which felt of burden, but importance. An obligatory energy. A powerful energy. As Shane was guided by foot through the historic walls of Buckingham Palace, he felt its energy pulsate through him; the energy of former members of the crown; the energy of politicians and European royalty, which had stepped foot before him. The energy was enabled before him.

Seated in a private drawing room, with lavish antique furnishings and portraits, Shane awaited to greet the Queen. As she entered the room, he stood and bowed his head as he uttered the words 'Your Majesty,' as he was briefed to do so. He was required to address her as Ma'am from then on. Just as he'd been briefed the first time he met with her – the day her majesty had summoned *him*. The day he'd fallen at commuters' feet. The day Dale was born.

The day the royal car fetched him, after Dale's unsettling movement, it had taken him on to Windsor Castle, a much warmer establishment. Wooden panelled walls and scarce furnishings. Buckingham Palace, in comparison, felt intimidating. Shane felt as if perhaps Windsor had been used by means of comforting him on his summoning, whereas Buckingham Palace stood to show the monarch's great importance, on this day, that *he* requested to meet with *her*. The two of them sat down, each in their own elaborate carver-like chair. A table with tea was positioned between them. Her staff poured each of them a cup before making their departure, bowing their heads, and closing the doors.

Although Shane had been the one to call upon the Queen this time around, he still waited to be addressed.

"I thank you for calling this meeting. The time feels right," said the Queen, in a confirming voice of authority, spoken in British royal trained tongue. Spoken as a woman who dealt with many. A woman who was straight to the point. No pleasantries extended.

"No, thank you for seeing me, Ma'am. It's been…"

"Years. Yes. Well. I imagine you've been hard at work considering what you were tasked with. Selecting the perfect balance of council."

"Years it has certainly been. Twenty-five odd, I'd say."

"Twenty-six, Shane. That's how old she is. Into her twenty-seventh."

"I say. You're certain it's a *she* then, Ma'am?"

"A blonde bob in the wind. You've done as you'd agreed. No need to report. I thank you for your service."

"You're very welcome, your majesty."

"Now that you have formed a council, s*he* will want an appointment on it. You must not allow this. She is *not* to be in the same room as the four of you.

I fear she will be your undoing. It is now that I must task you with binding her. Bind her with your energy. Now that you and the council have sourced her as the culprit. You must bring her to the Tower of London where she can be bound and locked in its vaults. Once inside, the energy used to protect the tower will do much the same to keep her imprisoned. Think of good reasoning to see her inside the grounds. On binding her my guards will take care of the rest." The Queen stood from her chair and looked down at Shane as she extended her hand. Shane stood from his chair and shook it.

"I will alert you at once, Ma'am."

"The monarch and the enabled have coexisted and worked side by side for centuries. Together, we've won many battles. This will be no different. Your father was strong. I trust you to be, too."

Shane left Buckingham Palace with a sense of accomplishment – although much was yet to be accomplished. His shake of the Queen's hand had left him with a hard and driven energy. An energy which convinced him that he would get the job done. As such, he asked the royal car to drop him at UAS-HQ. With the knowledge he now had from the Collective and his orders from the Queen, he wasn't going to waste any time, with seemingly little more to waste. His plan was simply to drop in unannounced - as he usually did. Although on this day, rather than just a visit, he would extend an invitation for a nice walk along the River Thames, and see them finishing up at the Tower of London. SImultaneously, Dale had formed a plan on how to approach Shane to be part of his council. Shane stepped out of the royal car and into the grand entrance of UAS-HQ.

Having started the process of absorbing his energy over the last few visits Shane made to Dale, she stood waiting on the staircase for him, as she'd sensed him approaching. Some kind of connection had formed between them with Dale's absorption of his energy. Dale looked down at Shane as he stepped inside, much like she had on their very first meeting. Although this time, Dale felt in control. Shane was thrown off by her pre-empted presence.

"I've been expecting you."

"Have you?"

"To my office." As Dale walked back up the steps, Shane followed up the staircase behind her. What had once been an empty shell was now a thriving hub of artists moving up and down the staircase around them. Each further step inside that Shane took, he felt more and more on alert, each step feeding him with energy that he could only describe as dark.

As Shane walked up the staircase, he stopped on the first landing, sensing an energy that made him feel watched. He looked around to find the busy hub of artists staring at him. Fluttering around him. Putting it down to him being a strange face, he followed Dale along the corridor into her office. As he sat down in the chair in front of her desk, he felt another energy. A great energy. An energy created - unknown to him – by the collection of Dale's enabled. Saturating the building around him. An energy of *dark enabled.*

Dale closed the door to her office. As she walked towards her desk, her heels pierced a sound of unsettlement into Shane's ears drums. With all the heightened energy around him, he was on alert.

"What brings you here today?" Dale asked, as she took her seat. Although she may have held some kind of connection with Shane, his bubble still somehow blocked her from being able to read his mind. "No, sorry. Before you start, I'd like to put something to you."

"Put something to me?"

"Yes. You see, I've been getting stronger each year that's passed, since you first visited me here. I'm sure you've felt that. And I've done as was asked of me. I've kept my eyes and ears to the ground in alert of any disturbances associated with the ones the council and you have felt. I've also reflected greatly on why you would have felt my presence in the world when you did. I have to believe that my presence is destined for greater good, or you wouldn't have come to me. I feel that my loyalty to you over the years, and my new found strength, sees me fit for your council. I'd like to request an appointment." Dale smiled.

Shane sat opposite Dale as she requested an appointment. He had to laugh. He might not have held the gift of sight, but it didn't take a mind reader to know manipulation when it was underway. Especially with his insight from his fellow Collective and the Queen herself. He sat in thought for a moment. He wondered if this would have been the event which led to dark days foretold. Had he no insight, taking on Dale as a new member of his council very well could have been the start of the dark days ahead. He wondered if a binding was even necessary. If standing from his chair and taking his leave could put a stop to it all. Denying her a seat on council which may have led to catastrophic and powerful enabled manipulation. Domination.

Dale looked at Shane with confusion as he laughed.

"I'm sorry, is my appointment to council such a joke to you?" Shane stood from his seat.

"Yes, Dale. It is."

"And what's the joke?!" Dale demanded as she felt her blood boil.

"That if I walk away, it all ends here." Shane formed a belief that his own instinctual conclusions were correct. Truly believing that if he just walked away, the dark days would never come to be. But how wrong he was. If only he had held faith in the days ahead as they were told to him by Kerry, Jakub, Jenny and the Queen. If only he had followed through with his orders to take Dale to the Tower of London and bind her. If only he had fed into the energy he felt around him, when he'd stepped foot into those headquarters. Alas, his misjudgement was what saw the beginning of the dark enabled times, and the birth of a prophecy, which, although was not fulfilled in Dale's first uprising, Shane's misjudgement saw the ripple effect of what was to come.

Starting to make his way back, to let himself out of the office door, Shane suddenly felt an overpowering energy take hold of him. It stopped him in his tracks. Dale had risen from her seat and stood behind her desk, with her arms raised, and the palms of her hands flexed in his direction. A red beam of electrical energy from Dale's palms met a bubble of blue energy pulsating around Shane.

The red slowly encroached on his bubble, as the two colours joined and formed a purple electrical current, which soon took over Shane's bubble, and back towards the palms of Dale's hands. The room filled with a purple glow as the two energies became one. Under Dale's control.

Dale engaged the energy to lock it in place as she let go of its hold. Shane became suspended in the now purple bubble, pulsating around him. Dale walked around to stand in front of the bubble and face him. Her heels hit the floor hard.

"What on earth did you think you were going to stop, Shane? Did your little councilettes tell you I was bad news? Did they send you here to put a stop to the big bad wolf?!"

"My orders were from the Queen! Whatever your intentions, you're no match for the monarch!"

"The Queen?! The Queen now?! Well, that *is* interesting! I get all the good goss from you, Shane. The underworld, the existence of other realms, now the fucking Queen! And just what was your part in all this, sir?"

"My father served the crown his entire life! He started in the military. Made his way in to serve the monarch as a soldier. Found himself as the Queen's Guard around the same time he realised he was enabled. Held the ability to control energy before me. Formed an alliance with the monarch and set up the Tower of London and Windsor Castle's protective barriers to guard the Crown Jewels and residence for retreat. Drew his abilities together with other enabled to form the Commonwealth's portals. He was an honourable -"

"Blah, blah, blah. I don't need to hear how honourable your dad was. You've done yourself a disservice again Shane, taking pride in your dad's endeavours. I didn't know there were portals. Like I said, all the good goss."

"I don't know what you're planning. But I'd suggest using that ability of yours for good. Why pull things down when you can build them up? Protect them!"

"Ha! My ability?! Oh Shane, I've surpassed just *one* ability. You can't imagine the abilities I hold. As for building things up, why would I do that when it sounds like so much fun to kick them down?"

"Dale! You -"

"No!" Dale waved her hand to force an electrical current's hold over his mouth. "I think I've heard quite enough from you. There's so much work to be done, and if you're not going to appoint me onto your little council, well I'll just have to do the work myself. But not alone. Oh no. I've been working with some very inspiring souls, to which, I might add, I'm feeling a little demonstration coming on. This way, Shane!"

Dale swung the door to her office open with the flick of her wrist, then clenched her fingers back towards the purple bubble to pull and push it out towards the corridor, with Shane still suspended inside of it. Dale shot her palms back out in front of her as she pushed the bubble of energy down the corridor and then up and out to mid-air above the grand staircase. Dale held one hand in connection with keeping the bubble afloat, while she flicked the wrist of her other, to seal the front doors shut tight. A purple electrical force pulsated over the doors, as her dark enabled following began to gather around the staircase.

Looking out around her, Dale smirked as her followers looked at Shane entrapped in the purple bubble of energy.

"That's right, my friends! Take a good look at this man! For he is the face of the oppressor! This man! This man wanted to put a stop to our plans! He wanted to save the people who have hurt you! Wanted to protect the people that bullied you! The people that beat you until you were blue! The people who touched you without your consent! This man is the face of our new world! Because this man's face is the first of many to be destroyed!" As Dale called out to her onlooking followers, most of them cheered and clapped, but an odd few looked on in fright, realising just how deep they had gotten. Hoping it was not too late to back away.

Dale looked around at those cheering her on, and caught sight of the people backing away and some who had started to run. "You're either with us or against us! Bring those against us forward!" Dale watched with glee as her followers started to take hold of those running or backing away, pushing them up against the railings of the staircase. "Show me that you're with us! Throw down those against us!" And in commanding so, Dale released Shane from her hold as his body fell onto the hard marble steps, where blood began to leak and form a pool from his cracked open skull. As Dale did, so did her followers. Bodies were thrown down onto the marble steps of the grand staircase of the Uprising Arts Society.

"Take charge! Take hold of your abilities! Use it against them! If they're against us, end them!" Dale called out around her, as the enabled who resisted the dark movement started to fight, outnumbered by the dark enabled around them.

Dale stood on the staircase admiring the carnage around her, by her own doing. The remaining energy from Shane trickled from the blood of his head and up the staircase to Dale. She absorbed it like a sponge. As she did, she felt the flickering of energies Shane had also absorbed. Jenny's empathetic waves. Jakub's intuitive current. Then, Kerry's own sight reflected onto her own, the two creating a mirror-like effect in Dale's own mind. Her name laid out in front of her sight in purple electric energy. From left to right. *Dale Cornel* mirrored as *lenroC elaD*. To which, she blinked and shook off the effect, with the word lenroC imprinted in her mind. She addressed the room, as she used all the energy absorbed inside her, around her and in the room, lifting her from her feet. "I shall lead your liberation into your salvation! You will henceforth address me as your leader! By the name: *Lenroc!*"

Lenroc's message projected out to the world, alongside the images of the battle on the staircase, as she addressed her followers to take their control. The Uprising Arts Society Headquarters, and affiliated establishments in other nations, saw its members spill out onto streets around the globe. The battle that was to be for the ages. Long and lasting with many lives lost. The world's landmarks crumbling to make way for the illuminating towers that gleamed the dark purple, made from Earth's own rock. The Dark Enabled rupturing them from the ground, as beacons of their new world. Towers which held the Dark Enabled's combined harnessed forces, connecting energy from one to the other, acting as an impenetrable force field. And so, with Lenroc's following of lost and tortured souls, the dark enabled times had begun.

25 SPILT MILK

Andrew, Precious, Audrey and I made our way through Piccadilly Circus, a place that once saw you get swept up in the flow of people. Once panicking, as I worked my way to the side of the herd, leaning up against the buildings. Today, we had just strolled right through. Not a person in sight. No traffic to stand at the lights and wait for. Rather walking around them – piled up and toppled around the circus. The tall monument with the angel positioned as though it had already taken fire, still with no arrow held back to its chest, sat on its own. I wondered if, like the iron lions in Trafalgar Square, just maybe the angel protected something here too.

The four of us found our way into a bar and grill. The doors were made from glass that had shattered, allowing us to step inside without hassle. We looked around at the empty booths and tables as we made our way to the kitchen. It was a place that surely in its day would have been filled with tourists, smiling faces, and the fine scent of steaks, fries and burgers. The tables had half eaten food and drinks on them. Andrew picked a half-eaten burger up from one of the tables and bit into it, as he exclaimed *mmmmmmmmm!*

"Andrew!" I shouted disgustedly.

"Yeah, that's cold as fuck. But damn it's good. Let's get cooking!"

The four of us walked into the kitchen and took off our coats, setting out like a pack of wolves hunting for prey. Precious and I were in our fancy attire, which we'd put on for our grand entrance to Café De Paris, while Audrey and Andrew wore more fitting attire for a kitchen. Hunting through the cupboards, we started to call out to each other.

"Found the potato fries!" Andrew called.

"I've got the patties!" I yelled. "Anyone found buns?!"

"Buns?! Boys, I'm looking for steak!" Precious shouted.

"Well, I'm by the fryers!" Audrey shouted. After scavenging through the kitchen, we made our best attempt at cooking up a feast, with the top quality industry appliances.

"Not going to Café De Paris anymore, are we!" Precious said, as I turned to find her throwing a handful of flour at my suit.

"You!" I screamed, trying to get my hand into the bag of flour as she closed it shut and moved away from me. The kitchen's sweet sound of frying and appetising aromas were quickly accompanied by laughs and smiles. Andrew joined in with the play that I'd engaged with Precious. Audrey stood cooking the steaks, while laughing, as she shook her head at us.

The laughs were needed. I was sure of it. If it felt half as good for them as it did for me, to have just let go for a little while, then I was glad. Everyone had suffered such heavy experiences up to this point. Andrew felt like he was the last person on earth alive, as he watched a creature demolish our home city; Audrey blown away, mustering up the strength to return to where the Collective's corpses lay dead; Precious, chased around the streets of London in fear for her life. It was certainly time for a little play and laughter. Having cooked up a storm, we found a booth and got comfortable. Andrew shouted out for our orders, from behind the bar, while he tried to do fancy barman tricks. He smashed two bottles along the way, shrugging when he did.

Andrew brought out our round of drinks and took a seat in the booth with us. We raised our glasses, toasting to our journey on to Windsor, and the monarch being our saviour. We each began to drink and feast, chowing down the food like we hadn't eaten in days. To be fair, although we had no real way of knowing the time that had passed by with the gloomy sky above, it certainly *felt* like it had been days since eating. As we started to slow down on chewing, with our stomachs happily digesting what we had consumed, Precious asked me to finish my tale. Feeling rather positive at this moment, I decided not to get so deep, saying that I would break it down and rattle off the main points.

In doing so, I touched on how I had started to explore the dynamic of polyamory. Getting Andrew and Audrey up to speed. Andrew spitting out his food in shock as he asked, *that's a thing?!* I delved a little into how Pree and Rubis had become two individuals I held dearly. But also, how Lenroc's introduction of a succubus had caused a stir and made me pull away from what could have been real special bonds. That if we managed to re-break the boundaries of earth and the underground, with the monarch on side, then I really hoped to make it work with them. I then looked over at Precious sat beside me and smiled her way with a wink. "And one new addition." Precious blushed and cuddled into me.

I took a moment to reflect and share on the night I walked with Pree to the portal. How I'd fallen in as I spoke and held Victor's cheating face in my mind. But then my mind went blank. I couldn't remember Victor's face. Then suddenly, I found myself asking *who* Victor was. But the moment felt significant. Like when I'd not been able to recall how the portal worked, back when Precious had asked me. Although this time, nothing came back to me.

"It's okay. It doesn't matter. It's in the past," reassured Precious. I felt she held sympathy in knowing my condition, although Andrew and Audrey looked a little concerned. My mind flashed to another memory. One at a pub. One that felt just as significant. Connected maybe. Gathered around a table with Lenroc's group of enabled. I remembered catching eyes with a girl with pig-tails. A flash of her head slamming on the pub table came into my mind. But I couldn't remember how or why it had happened. I pinched my forehead in frustration.

I'd suffered the blackouts. Hell, I'd blacked out for a whole day. But I'd not suffered from memory loss. Not yet. Not until this minute. This didn't feel nice at all.

Precious grabbed my arm and rubbed it. Cuddling in, she assured me it was what I did now that mattered. Andrew stayed silent as Audrey started to reassure me that whatever it was, Lenroc would have lined me up to do it. I smiled and took a breath. I continued with more recent events. How, with the succubus added into the mix, I became an anxious mess. I stopped seeing rationale. Coming home to discover Erin and Dylan at Lenroc's apartment, overhearing things that didn't add up, my uncertainty with everything was off the charts. Leading me to the decision to re-visit the portal. Knowing there was only one group of people who held the answers for me. The Collective.

I explained how I'd launched off from the ground and into the sky, but how I'd blacked out, and awoke in some kind of illuminating purple glow. Dale hovering over me as she asked what I was doing. Her minions Tim, Irene, Ernie and Jade herself, the succubus, gathering by her side. Insuring I didn't make contact with the Collective. Quickly exploding with emotions as they'd tried to manipulate and trick my mind. How I'd shot up out from Lenroc's illuminating hold on me. Running and jumping from the fountain balcony into the portal. Hitting the water as it splashed around me. My mind fuzzing and entering a blackness. Before entering what was a whiteness. Where the answers I'd held laid with the Collective. Where I'd learned of the dark enabled times, the Collective's retreat to the Arctic Ocean and Lenroc's downfall.

Audrey interjected with some of the details as my mind started to glaze over again. I really started to worry. But I tried to keep the worry to myself. Audrey rather quickly took over the talk of the Collective and the Dark Enabled times.

"This all already happened once before? The world destroyed? And our minds were just cleared of it? With this - clearing?" Precious asked.

"Yeah, that's well fucked up," said Andrew.

"You don't understand the jeopardy you would all have been in, had the Collective kept non-enabled in the know," Audrey tried to explain. "The repercussions of publicly having wide-spread knowledge of enabled existence. The world would have become engaged in political warfare."

"But by the sounds of it, you weren't even part of that Collective. What makes you defend their actions?" Andrew asked.

"Yes. But I witnessed the cruelty before the Enable the Enabled campaign. Humanity isn't ready for a lifeforce stronger than it. They'd only tear us down."

"Tear it down? You mean like what Lenroc has done… twice!" Andrew said, raising his voice. "I just saw my damn city fall to pieces by the hand of some fucking big foot. Don't you think if we'd worked together, we might have prevented all this?"

Andrew's tension had clearly risen. Perhaps the result of trying to stay positive for so long. Being on his own for so long. It was now, with others to catch his fall, that he let it all out. A rush of highs from playing and laughter in the kitchen, resulting in a crash of lows. But the tension was quickly broken by the sound of shattering glass from the kitchen. The four of us looked at one another with alertness. At the end of the booth's two ends, Andrew and I stood, cautiously beginning to tip-toe our way over to the kitchen. Precious and Audrey followed behind.

"Stop!" Audrey called out to us at the top of her lungs. Andrew and I looked back at Audrey wide-eyed, wondering why she'd shouted out so loudly. *What the fuck?* I mouthed her way silently.

"It's okay. I've frozen time around us. Isolating the four of us in an exempt bubble. I'll be able to hold it for a few minutes. If there's someone in there they're not going anywhere or jumping out at you. Go! See!"

Andrew and I made our way to the kitchen. We walked inside to find a little girl frozen in fright, looking down at a smashed glass with spilt milk around it. She held a large six-pint container of milk in her little hands. The stream of milk, from the ground up to the container it was coming out of, was frozen solid in the air. Precious pushed her way into the kitchen between Andrew and I.

"The post-box girl!"

"You know this girl?" Andrew asked.

"No. But we spoke for a brief few seconds."

"Before she vanished in front of your eyes," I added, recalling her story of how a little girl had disappeared, sitting by a post-box as the cloaked man with super-strength approached.

Precious crouched down beside the girl and looked at her.

"Do you think she's been following me this whole time?"

"Audrey! It's okay! You can unfreeze time now!" Andrew called.

"Wait! Wait! Wait!" I called. "Don't you think you should hold her arm or something in case she tries to disappear again?" I asked.

"Yeah. That's a good idea," agreed Precious, as she held onto the girl's arm.

"Alright! You can unfreeze time this time!" Andrew called out again.

As the girl unfroze, she dropped the container, and milk came gushing out from it over the kitchen floor. She screamed a high-pitched scream as she looked around at us. Vanishing, again, before our eyes. Precious held onto her arm tight. I could see that she was struggling to keep hold of the girl.

"It's okay! We're not going to hurt you," said Precious. Meanwhile, Andrew had knelt down to pick up the container of what little remained of the milk, having fetched a new glass that he started to pour it into. He offered it to the invisible girl.

"Here you go."

Audrey had made her way into the kitchen beside me, and we each looked as the glass floated out from Andrew's hand. As it started to tilt, the girl reappeared and drank the milk down quickly, soon after, wiping her mouth with the back of her hand.

"Now, if I let go, you're not going to go disappearing on me again are you?" Precious asked.

"No."

"Alright. Well, I'm trusting you here." Precious let go of the little girl, as she walked to the side and got a broom double the size of her, to start sweeping up the smashed glass on the floor. The girl said her name was Daisy and that she thought she must have died with her brother, when they went to the post-box. But rather than hell, she now thought she must have been brought back to be the red haired lady's guardian angel. I looked down at Precious, as she looked up at me, while quietly laughing with each other. The girl finished sweeping, having not gotten rid of the mess, but only by sweeping it under the cupboards. The job was done, and that was good enough for her. I looked around at Audrey and Andrew, as we all laughed.

Daisy brushed her hands together, after putting the broom back where she'd found it. She looked up at us all and asked why we were laughing.

"We just didn't realise we had a guardian angel," said Precious. I laughed again, under my breath.

"It's okay. I never knew about guardian angels either, until I was eight, when my aunt told me I had one. She's clear... clear... clear-voyant. You see."

"Do you mean clairvoyant, sweetie?" Precious asked.

"That's it. She can speak with ghosts and she gets money for it. She said that my guardian angels looked out for me. So, after I died and realised I was yours, I thought I better look out for you. I'm pretty sure I must have brought that man over there to rescue you." Daisy pointed to me.

"You must have indeed. Thank you for that. We're sorry we frightened you."

"It's okay. I don't know how that happened really. Must have been a glitch! As my dad used to say when something went wrong at work."

I could feel the four of us took to little Daisy rather quickly. Taking to the lightness and childlike mind of imagination. She'd certainly defused Andrew's

194

moment of tension, as he knelt down to pour her another glass of milk. Perhaps a child in the mix would do us good. Keep us in line. Keep us kind to one another. Perhaps it was good that such an imaginative creature had found her way to us. Perhaps, we would be as good for her as she would be for us.

I looked around at the four of them interacting. The kitchen filled with smiles again. I thought back to when my mind had glazed over. Trying to recall the girl's name with the pig... *pig what? I still couldn't remember the face of Vic... Vicky? Maybe it wasn't a Vic, maybe it was Vin, Vince?* I couldn't remember either of the names anymore, or why they felt connected. I remembered telling Precious how I'd done some things I wasn't proud of. *Had I hurt them?* Or was I just referring to the drag queens? *The drag queens. What are drag queens?*

I stood in the kitchen, thinking this must have been what Andrew went through, when I questioned him on the events that took place with me by his side. I felt for him. Parts of his memory erased through Lenroc's clearing. But my gut dropped as I realised that it was likely his memory might return. That the monarch might reverse what Lenroc had done to him. Mine, surely wasn't by such means. Not with Lenroc thinking I was dead. Mine was rotten luck. Mine was disintegrated memories caused by a plague on my brain. Mine was unhealable. Irreversible.

26 THE ECHOING WHISPER

The Dark Enabled had taken to the world like fire to a trail of gasoline. The earth itself glowed with illuminating purple. The towers of rock ruptured around the nations of the world like flags which claimed them, connected by the energy of combined harnessed forces of the Dark Enabled. Although, in the Dark Enabled's ignorance, three enabled souls began planning their retaliation. Feeling the energy of Shane vanish from the world, before the Dark Enabled took to it, they sought vengeance.

Jenny, Jakub and Kerry used a connection, which had been setup through Shane to communicate, all at opposite ends of the globe. They brought their own personal connections together, to form a bigger council and a greater Collective, that would see Shane's work carried on in his honour. That would see the downfall of the Dark Enabled, and Lenroc; Jenny, engaging an air enabled that she'd befriended through a secret underground enabled group; Jakub, engaging a member who was teleportation enabled, whom he'd once spotted hopping in the shadows of the ancient streets of Kraków, having confronted the poor guy that had hoped to stay inconspicuous; Kerry, engaging a person who held the ability to manipulate liquid. Someone she reached out to through a personal ad, who used code wording, which stuck out.

Together, through their connected energy, they were able to commune enough for Jakub and his personal connection to hop them from the little town of Myslenice, to Manhattan New York, and then old London Town. They gathered those they came across, enabled with light, along the way. The ones that had gone into hiding. Gathering those that retained a small glimmer of hope, as well as non-enabled with the potential to *be* enabled. They sent the gathered enabled off to join the Dark Enabled army, going forth as scavengers, spies and plants that roamed the land. The Dark Enabled were so consumed by destroying the world and enslaving humanity to do their bidding that their fixation and pleasures became comfort. Comfort and complacency, which ultimately led to their undoing, as the Collective planned ahead for the revolution.

Retreating to the Arctic Ocean, the Collective used Jenny and Kerry's connections to manipulate the air and sea, forcing them into separation around them. It became a place for hiding, but also planning and training. A place of strengthening. Building their own society. Living and working as one among the coral of the Arctic Ocean as the planning and training for the revolution took place.

The Collective worked hard with the non-enabled to release their abilities, as opposed to enslaving and suppressing them, as the Dark Enabled had done. But it was only a matter of time before the newly formed society became full of angst. They wanted to fight and take back their world. Return to some form of normality. The Collective started to carry out hearings by request of their newly formed society. In respect of honouring all representatives of their society, they appointed a young girl by the name of Margaret, the young girl who, in the end, was the last of that Collective left standing. To Margaret, it was simple: the Dark Enabled were to be banished, and the society of the Arctic Ocean agreed.

Although the Dark Enabled had suffered trauma, grief and tragedy of their own, manipulated at Lenroc's hand, they had become the very things they originally stood against. As had Lenroc. Truly lost souls which had become intoxicated with power and started to kill, rape and abuse humanity. Souls which hated the human race. It was the human race that the Collective needed to help them rebuild the world to how it once was, and so the preparations for Margaret's motion of a realm of banishment began. A task which required great focused all-consuming energy and good willed strength. A combining of abilities with encompassing force.

It took every ounce of strength the society had. Months spent sat and gathered holding hands as they joined forces, channelling each enabled's ability to the enabled next to them. Around them. Providing each enabled with each other's strength, and building on that shared strength as one. To create what was one supreme harnessed ability. A tear to a realm which rose above them and the Arctic Ocean in a floating, scintillant distortion. As the tear shone bright above them, joining the one once made before it, dubbed the Northern Lights, the society opened their eyes and stared at the glimmering hope above them. The Collective had used the enabled for all they could. The banishment would be down to the very Collective themselves.

The society began to rebuild their strength. While they did, the Collective started their banishment. To banish the Dark Enabled, the Collective did as their fellow society had. They joined forces to channel each other's abilities, providing one another with each other's strength, and building on that shared strength, within the Collective. Just as Shane had taught them to do, and as they had taught their society. In addition to Jakub's intuition, they were going to need to make use of the new members' abilities of flight, mind control, detection, liquid manipulation, air manipulation and Margaret's ability to space hop. Jenny and Kerry would stay to keep the society safe and assist with the energy it took to keep up the Arctic Ocean walls. Their plan was ambitious. But they felt confident in it.

The Collective completed their harness as one. They were ready. They set off over the Arctic Ocean and flew down to circle the purple illuminating rocky towers, one by one, across the globe. Gathering the Dark Enabled like a sand storm. Country by country. City by city. Town by town. However, although they had managed to feel out the bulk of the army, where they had predominantly joined in forces, the Collective were sure that some still remained. Individuals and clusters left hiding in the shadows. But what they had managed to do was overthrow the Dark Enabled. And so, the society took back to the land as the Arctic Ocean walls came crashing back down, and they joined in on the re-building of civilization. The Collective's fight became one for equality, as civil unrest took hold.

As the ENABLE THE ENABLED campaign took to the world, with a new war on the brink, Margaret led the Collective in her sassy pink power suit, as they burst into a government underground lab to banish Lenroc to the realm created for the Dark Enabled, Lenroc being held captive with a purple illuminating glow around her. The scientists had found a way to use her harnessed energy against her. The Collective formed a circle around her, and held hands, focusing their abilities as one, all while an undercover supervisor named Demos watched in the wings.

They set their minds and focused on the scintillant distortion of a tear, floating above the Arctic Ocean. They closed their eyes as a burst of energy with an illumination filled the room like an atomic bomb had hit the chamber where they stood. Then, they were gone. Lenroc, and the Collective too. All but one. All but Margaret. She opened her eyes, as she felt the hands in hers disappear. It was an energy of protection that Margaret had carried with her, from the Dark Enabled times, which the Collective had secretly formed on merging their abilities, that shielded her from whatever force Lenroc had ensured took The Collective with her. Margaret looked over at Demos. A new Collective was soon to form.

The Collective had certainly connected with the banished realm. Lenroc, however, had connected with *them*, forming a bubble of energy around them, which she used to block her admission to the realm and sending that bubble to the realm in her place. Lenroc, suspended in her own bubble of protection, watched the scintillant distortion of a tear take in the bubble she had placed around the Collective. Right in front of her eyes. Until the bubble became part of the scintillant around it. The Collective, with the exception of Margaret, had been banished at Lenroc's hand.

Lenroc watched as the glittering, glistening tear in space sparkled brighter than the stars around it. She smirked, as she looked back down on the Earth below. The silence was deafening. The stillness was calming. She looked down on Earth in absolute astonishment of what she'd once conquered. In absolute certainty that she would conquer it again. Looking back up at the glittery glistening tear, she heard a faint whisper of words echoing from it. Back down on Earth, in the chamber, Margaret and Demos heard it too. *The dark enabled will break the boundaries of earth and the underworld, by spilled blood of a torn lover.*

27 ON TO WINDSOR

Andrew, Precious, Audrey and I brought little Daisy over to the booth where our half-eaten feast sat unfinished. She started to try bits from each of our plates. A nugget, a few fries, a cheesy bite. It was cute that she thought she was Precious' guardian angel. I hoped it kept her brave, as I looked on at her chomping away at the food in front of her. For I had no doubt that some dark days were ahead. At least she didn't have to run into them alone, certain the brother that Precious had spoken of had vanished with the rest of the world. At least she now had us.

I saw a strong group of people as I looked around at everyone. I felt a kind of family forming. I was glad I was with them. Four strong individuals. I hoped I could stay strong for them, as I worried about the disintegration of my memories. My mind. If not, I hoped that I'd found the kind of people that would catch me if I fell. Rather than let me drop, as Lenroc had.

Andrew and Precious humoured and engaged with Daisy as Audrey looked my way.

"So, I say we finish up here and get a move on," said Audrey.

"Sounds good to me. What's the plan?" I asked.

"You know London better than I," she replied.

"We're headed to Windsor, right?" Precious asked, looking up at us from the booth.

"Yeah," I agreed.

"I mean. That's a fair hike. And I don't want to even think about how to operate a train or what lines go where. But I bet there's some fuelled-up coaches at Victoria Coach Station. I wouldn't want to attempt hopping in a half-fuelled car and needing to walk the rest of the way."

"You know how to drive a coach?" I asked.

"Ah. That would be a no."

"I don't know about a coach, but I've got my truck licence. I could give it a shot!" Andrew replied.

"We could just car hop." I added.

"Car hop?! We're living in the fucking apocalypse. Oops, sorry Daisy. We're living in the apocalypse. If you can't cruise the road in a coach, when else are you going to do it?!" Andrew exclaimed, ever the jokester.

"I don't mean to burst your bubble, people. But I think we've all been very fortunate to avoid any encounters with any of Lenroc's dark enabled army so far. I wouldn't want to tempt fate by driving a large coach on the roads of England. Besides, I'm guessing traffic around a coach station is going to be pretty hefty. Sounds like a lot of vehicles to be frank. I don't know the distance to Windsor myself. But I'm afraid a hike is what it's going to have to be," said Audrey, squashing our excitement.

"I guess you're right. I don't suppose we want that dragon creature catching sight of us and coming down on us," said Precious.

"Okay. Audrey's right. We've been good by keeping low so far. Let's keep at it," I agreed.

"Anyone know the way?" Andrew asked.

"If we make our way to Victoria Coach Station anyway. I've coached it enough times to Ascot to know the way. Many a coach ride spent looking out the window. Should only be about a forty-five minute walk. Down to Wellington Arch. Take the road left. Then right at Victoria Station. But how long from there, I have no idea," explained Precious.

"Shall we make tracks then? You good to go, Daisy?" I asked.

"Yes. My belly is most happy."

Making our way out of the bar and grill we started to hit the road. Daisy walked between Andrew and Precious, holding on to their hands. She'd seemed to warm to them quickly. It warmed my heart. I hadn't felt what a warmed heart felt like in some time. I walked beside Precious, holding her free hand, Audrey beside me, her hands swaying by her sides in the air like the independent New Yorker she was.

"Where do you think all the dark enabled are?" I asked.

"Oh, they're out there. Conquering other parts of the world. Harnessing forces we can't even begin to comprehend. Probably gathered on training grounds. Building their strength. Feeding off every bit of strength they can acquire."

"I just don't get it. What do they hope to do now they're rid of humanity? What's left?" I asked.

"They probably don't even know themselves. So lost and so deep in whatever hatred they held for the world."

"Let's just hope there's better days ahead hey? That the monarch has a plan to take back control. Restore the balance," I added.

We made our way to Wellington Arch and walked down towards Victoria Station, turning right once we reached it and on towards Victoria Coach Station. From there, Precious began to lead the way. We made our way through South Kensington, and then Hammersmith, as the buildings around us began to seem more parted. The roads widened and opened up. We made our way across a six-lane bridge over the national railway tracks with nothing but dark smog ahead, billboards advertising the West End shows sticking out from it.

Ahead was Hammersmith Bridge. Before it, a gas station to our left. Daisy pleaded we go inside to get her a drink. Her little legs had already given up as Andrew piggy backed her on his shoulders. I was rather parched myself.

"I guess we could take a break. Maybe even pack some supplies for the journey ahead?" I suggested.

"Yeah, who knows how few and far between these things are once we pass London's border. I say we find a carry bag or backpack and stock up!" Precious added. Andrew placed Daisy back down on her feet and she took his hand, trying to get him to run with her to the gas station.

"Come on Andrew, come on!" Daisy shouted, the thought of a drink sparking some energy back into her. Andrew looked back at us and shrugged with a smile as he started to run with her between the jagged, jammed cars.

Precious and I cracked a smirk Andrew's way, as he was pulled by Daisy. We started to walk towards the gas station after them. Audrey walked beside us. Ahead, Andrew and Daisy had reached the entrance to the station. Its front door was wide open.

"Come on you slow coaches!" Daisy called out to us and then walked inside with Andrew.

"You don't think…" I started to say.

"Think what?" Precious asked.

"Someone's in there? Let's not take our chances," Audrey said. She ran ahead and waved her hand over the station in front of her, I guess in an attempt to freeze time and again isolate us from it. Precious and I looked at each other and started to run up behind her as we made our way past the cars on the road. We followed as Audrey stepped inside. Andrew and Daisy had started opening up packets of confectionery; a bag of crisps in Andrew's hands and a chocolate bar in Daisy's. They looked at us and laughed, unaware of our urgency. Audrey walked the store aisles and looked down them one by one.

Andrew looked back at Audrey and then to Precious and I.

"What's she looking for then?" Andrew asked.

"We thought maybe there might have been someone inside," I replied.

"Ah. Shite. Didn't even think, you know."

"All clear!" Audrey called out. She waved her hand, releasing whatever freeze or isolation she had applied. The store was small, so it hadn't taken long to check it. We each started strolling it to look for supplies.

"Found backpacks!" Audrey called out.

"Excellent!" I replied. Audrey threw us each one from the corner of the store over its aisles.

"Line your bag with bottled water, then essentials like sandwiches and canned beans, then fill the top with whatever snacks you want."

"Well aren't you savvy," said Precious.

"I'm a New Yorker, honey. Know how to pack my shopping!"

Aseach started to pack their bags, all of a sudden a huge scream came from behind me, as I turned around to find a man who had jumped up on the counter. A spot Audrey had not thought to check. Little Daisy was screaming at his sight. The man held a knife and jumped down by Andrew, who was closest to the counter, putting the knife up to his neck. Audrey waved her hand. The man froze. Andrew looked down at the knife held up to his throat.

"Fuck me! My life just flashed before my eyes!" Andrew slid himself out from between the man and his knife, nicking the edge of his neck on the point of the knife as he did so. He clasped his neck as he winced. Audrey walked towards the man with decisiveness and took the knife from his hand.

"Like I said. New Yorker," she said, as she pushed it up against the man's neck. "Come on boys, each grab one of the guy's arms for Christ's sake. I can't hold him forever."

Andrew and I walked up to the man and held on tight.

"How is this going to work, Audrey?" I asked.

"Right. Well, as soon as I release him you're going to feel instant force and no doubt he's going to be spooked by us all having changed positions in the room. Not to mention appearing around him. So, hold on tight!" As she said, once she had waved her hand he came back with force. Andrew and I backed up towards the counter with him as confectionery dropped all over the joint. The man resisted our hold and pushed and pulled. The three of us fell onto the floor. Audrey walked up and pushed the knife up to his throat. "Unless you want me to push this further I suggest you settle down, son!" He did. Instantly.

Audrey explained that we meant him no harm. That we were just looking to grab supplies and would be out of his way. Little Daisy hid behind one of the aisles and peeked her head out from behind it. The man spat in Audrey's face.

"That was rude," said Audrey, as she wiped the spit from her eyes.

"You lie! You're with them! The purple ones!" The man shouted nonsense, clearly scared out of his mind. Frightened by whatever he had seen before cowering behind the store counter. He started to struggle once more. Then no sooner had he started to struggle, he fell back towards Andrew and I, as his body weight fell onto us. Standing in front of us, Audrey held the knife and it dripped with blood. Audrey dropped it. She held her hands to her face and started to pace backwards. Precious screamed and ran to cover Daisy's eyes.

"I didn't. I didn't. He just... He pushed himself right into it." I saw the look in Audrey's eyes. She was mortified at what she'd done. The man's body slid towards Andrew and he jumped up from the floor away from it. I got up too.

"Andrew, you go look after Daisy with Precious. Audrey and I will sort this out."

"You sure?"

"Go!" I walked up to Audrey. Although I couldn't quite remember why, I felt I knew her motions. This moment held a familiarity to me.

I placed my hand behind Audrey's back and rubbed it. I really did feel her at that moment. Andrew and Precious took Daisy outside as she tried to look back and asked what Audrey had done. I reassured Audrey that she hadn't done anything wrong. She was only protecting herself. All of us really. He'd been the one to push himself into the knife. I'd felt that for sure.

"Thank you, Michael. I can still feel it, you know? The knife. Sliding in." Again, I couldn't recall why, but I somehow knew the feeling.

"How about we get that New Yorker back? We've got a little girl out there and a nice little group who I'm thinking could all use a rest. With this gent out of the picture, it seems like a safer place than any. What do you say?" Audrey agreed. She breathed in deeply and gathered herself. I suggested she go outside with Precious and Daisy to send Andrew back in with me. He and I would sort out the body and clean up the blood. She didn't need to do that with what she'd just gone through. Audrey thanked me.

Shortly after Audrey left, Andrew came back inside and came towards me and the dead man's body. I'd already started to wrap his neck with some plastic bags I found behind the counter to try and stop the bleeding. Andrew stared down.

"Shit. He's really dead. I've never seen someone kill another person before."

"Yeah. We're going to have to clean this blood up. Can you look back there for a cloth or mop or something?"

"Sure," said Andrew, as he shot around the back of the counter. "So, what do you think his ability was? Think he would have used it on us if he knew? Suppose there's a few out there, like me, that don't even know," he said, returning with a mop.

"Put that aside. Let's get him in the fridge." Andrew grabbed the man by his feet, as I took him from under the arms. "I don't know. Just makes me wonder how many people were in the world that I knew, that were enabled."

"Yeah. I still have no idea what the hell I can do." We carried the man's body to the back of the store, where there was a line of glass fridge doors. "Hey, put him down, we're going to have to clear out some products to fit him in."

Andrew and I started shifting out the fridge food and some shelving from the lower compartment. The man's neck leaked blood from out around the plastic bags I'd tried to wrap around it.

"We're going to have to try and find out exactly what it is you can do. Think we're going to need all the strength we can get. That, and I'd hate a little girl to show you up!" I joked. Andrew threw a bag of cold grated cheese at me. We laughed. We looked at each other for a moment. I wondered if Andrew felt any familiarity with me. Knowing he'd laughed like this with me before.

"What about you, mate? I've not seen your magical ability yet. Could be a crock!" He joked back. I smiled.

"Stand back." Andrew and I stood from the ground, having emptied the lower compartment of the fridge, with the doors left open. We both stepped back. I closed my eyes and tried to focus my energy. Channel my ability. I felt it start to surge inside me, coming to me much easier than it had before. I'd felt my strength returning to me, able to harness it on my command. I opened up my eyes and looked down at the dead man's body. I shot my hands out towards it. I noticed the blood dripping from his neck begin to drip upwards as his body shook. The blood started to drip towards the ceiling instead of the floor. I turned my hands with my palms now facing upwards and raised them. The man's body rose with them. I configured my arm and hands to manipulate the body and push it slowly into the emptied lower part of the fridge.

I glanced up and caught Andrew staring in a curious state. Probably conflicted with being wowed by my ability, while not wanting to stare at a dead body being stuffed into a fridge. The guy was big. I looked back at the body, trying to further engage it, as I reached a stuck point. The man's torso had fit but his legs remained floating out from the fridge. I continued to try and engage with the body to push his legs in, as if trying to physically push something into a space that it didn't fit. As I continued to push with my mind, I found myself wondering what I was doing. Why I was pushing. What these legs in front of me were doing out of a fridge. I disengaged. It came back to me quickly, but I'd definitely gone blank for a moment.

28 IN THOUGHT

I stood, watching Michael as he made the fucking dead man's body rise from the ground with his mind. Demonstrating what he could do. *Far out, the guy's a telekinetic.* It was seriously unreal. But he'd hit some kind of block. The corpse was half inside the fridge as its legs dropped to the ground. Michael looked as though he tried to shake it off and he refocused as the corpse's legs began to rise back up from the floor. I asked if he was okay. Michael said he was fine. I didn't quite believe him. He was struggling with *something.* I wanted to help. But I didn't want to get down there and push or my head might end up in the dead dude's crotch by Michael's telekinetic push!

I stood in thought. I didn't know what exactly I could do. Or if I even believed I was enabled like they all seemed to think I was. But something in me wanted to help the guy - wanted to try. A feeling that felt familiar for sure. Maybe I really used to be his best mate. Or maybe I was just overthinking it. I probably just saw another bloke in need of a hand and wanted to lend one. Who knew what I could do? I'd never even tried to find out. But I was going to give whatever it was my best fucking shot. I looked at the legs of the body not knowing what to expect. Maybe they'd burst into flames. Maybe I'd liquify the bloody things. I just wanted to help. I squinted my eyes, wanting to shove those legs into that fridge or see them fucking drop off so we could throw them inside. I felt something inside me begin to activate.

The legs that were floating out from the fridge bent right in half – but the way legs shouldn't fucking bend. Then packed right into the fridge with the rest of the dead guy. My mind felt like it blew. I blinked in a bit of a state. I looked up at Michael. He looked at me.

"Mate. I think I'm fucking telekinetic too."

"You're not wrong. I felt that. It was like you carried some of the load. Took some weight off of me. That was something new altogether. How about that? Two best buds. Shall we try to shut the doors?"

"Gladly."

"In three. Two. One," instructed Michael. We swung our heads to the fridge doors as they both slammed shut. The adrenaline I felt shoot through my body was fucking unreal.

Michael suggested I give it a rest for a bit. Take in what I'd just done. Comprehend it. Take it easy and mop up the blood so we could let the ladies back in. He said he and Audrey had agreed it was best we all spend the night here. I thought that wasn't too bad an idea myself. I think I needed a bit of a rest after that. It wasn't as shocking as perhaps it may have been, given my journey up to this point. But it was still a shock regardless. My legs felt like jelly.

Michael and I cleaned up the place and threw away the bloody mop and fridge food stacked up on the floor. We found some cardboard boxes which we lined the aisles with for sleeping arrangements. To soften to ground. Each with our own aisle for privacy. Some throw blankets we'd found stocked in the back would have to do as sheets.

Michael restacked the food products in a way that the dead man's body couldn't be seen. He called outside for Precious, Audrey and Daisy to come back inside. I stood in thought again. Michael was such a genuine bloke. A guy who operated with his heart. I admired it. It felt as though I'd admired the guy before. The moments we laughed together felt familiar too. I thought back to the blank

210

spots in my mind. The missing pieces of a jigsaw puzzle. It made sense that they were parts where he'd fit. What would the bloke hope to gain from lying to me about such things? The more time that passed, the more I felt myself coming around to the idea that we were in fact best buds.

As Precious, Audrey and Daisy walked back into the store, Michael went about showing them what we'd set up for the night. If it even was night. Who knew what time of day it was, surrounded by this dark smog and empty sky above? We all just needed some time to rest. The timeframe ahead, by foot to Windsor Castle, was unknown. We had to maintain our energy. As Michael showed the ladies around, I walked towards the entrance of the gas station's store. The door which looked to once be sliding glass wasn't so much open as it was stuck in place. I tried to yank it closed, but it wouldn't budge. No wonder the armed man had been hiding behind the counter. Anyone could have walked in at any moment. The bloke was probably just trying to protect his goods. Keep possession of his livelihood once all this came to an end. *If* this was going to come to an end.

The door wouldn't be the best scenario for sleeping arrangements like this. I looked down to find it off of its slider. But the thing felt jammed somehow. I tried to unjam it, laughing at myself as I thought *of course the dead bloke would have done it himself if he could have.* Good thing was, if I did manage to get it back on the slider, it had a lock from the inside. I stood back from the door and squinted my eyes at it as I had done when trying to help Michael. But no such luck. The thing didn't move. It didn't even rattle. I tried again. I released a bit of a grunt and let it go. It wasn't going to happen.

"Michael! Think you might be able to give me a hand?" I called out, and he walked my way.

Michael asked what I was trying to do, and so I explained how if we were staying overnight, we'd probably want a sense of security. But I couldn't move the damn door.

"You try…"

"Yeah. Yeah, I tried that," I answered in defeat.

"Alright. Well, should we try together?" Michael asked. We both looked towards the door and it began to rattle. I laughed, this time being surprisingly pleased. I glanced back at Michael a moment and saw him stare at the door in deep concentration. I went about doing the same myself. I breathed in deeply as I stared at the door, willing it to lift and slide into place. The door lifted, and made its way onto its slider, as it rolled itself shut and even locked itself in place. Michael patted my back.

"You'll get there. If snapping that man's legs really was the first time you've ever connected with your ability, you've probably got a while before you can go about using the stuff of your own accord. It takes time to channel. What's the harm in a bit of support in the meantime?"

"The power of two, hey?"

I agreed with Michael, I'd only just discovered I had an ability. I couldn't expect that I could flick my finger and it would do my bidding straight away. Michael walked to the door and tried to pull it open to ensure it was locked in place. As we all settled down for the night, we each said good night to little Daisy, ensuring she was tucked in cosy and tight. We then took our own spots – myself noticing that Michael and Precious had decided to cosy themselves up in the same aisle. It was endearing to see, I have to say. I was glad they could provide a little extra warmth and comfort for each other.

Audrey decided she would sleep right in front of the entrance by the glass door. That way if anyone tried to break inside, she would hopefully wake to freeze time enough for us to make a getaway. Michael and Precious shacked up together in the next aisle, myself in the one after, with little Daisy in the last, furthest from the door. In thought, I lay on my back and looked up at the old leak-stained ceiling as my vision focused in the dark. I thought of how I'd lived part of a life I couldn't recall. That I held a bond with Michael that I couldn't recollect, but that I felt the bond, in some form or another, remembering it or not.

I closed my eyes and wondered how things might play out. What would actually happen if we made it to Windsor Castle? And what good would four adults and a child even add to an all-powerful established monarch, who was probably already in deep preparation for retaliation? But I had to steer my thoughts to optimism. After all, if not optimistic, what else was there? A broken world overtaken by these so-called Dark Enabled at Lenroc's side. I had to think about a better world than that. In a way, I'd felt lost the last few years. As if part of my soul had left my body. In search of it. In search of a missing piece. In search of some kind of purpose. Perhaps Michael was the piece I'd been searching for. Perhaps, our quest on to Windsor Castle to restore humanity was the purpose I needed. Whether we succeeded or not. Perhaps it was the people that lay in the gas station with me now, that would see me find my way. No longer lost. Even in the dark smog. For I'd felt lost for so long under the blue Australian sky. Perhaps it was just the wrong kind of people that had surrounded me.

As I lay in thought, I heard whispers make their way through the shelves and canned goods towards me. Tuning in, it sounded as though Michael and Precious were having a conversation. I imagined them curled up beside each other exchanging small kisses, Precious probably confiding in Michael about her fears and anxieties. Michael, being the great bloke that I'd found him to be, likely reassuring her they were going to be okay. Their voices soothed me. Their presence soothed me. I couldn't quite make out what the words were, but I listened to the hum of their whispers through the shelves, with a warm smile of comfort on my face.

29 DEAD TO ME

Precious and I lay side by side, underneath the throw blankets, as we faced one another, our hands clasped together between us. Our only comfort was each other, as the cardboard we lay on didn't do the best job of softening the hard floor beneath it. We stared into one another's eyes, as I pulled in towards Precious to kiss her. She kissed me back with an eagerness. Eager to feel something other than the darkness around us perhaps. I'd pulled in to kiss her for much the same reason. Kisses felt good right now.

Letting go of each other's hands, I placed mine around her waist and pulled her towards me as we kissed. Her hands grazed my chest as she clung to my shirt. I pulled away for a moment.

"I really do think you're wonderful, Precious," I whispered to her, and she smiled as she looked at me.

"I think you're wonderful too."

"What's your story? What happened to the girl who used to pick flowers in Ascot? I'm guessing you visit home regularly – knowing your way by memory. But you seemed to give the impression that you'd let that part of your life go."

"You've been pretty vulnerable and honest with me. I think I'm ready to give a little back." I had trouble remembering what I'd shared with her. What

I'd been vulnerable about. What I'd shared. But I felt the bond. Something in me knew that I had. I didn't want to make this moment about me. So, I listened.

Precious explained that as she grew up in Ascot, entering her teenage years, things for her hadn't been so great. Not that they ever had been. She'd gone from a young, neglected girl to an adolescent teen that got all kinds of attention, just not any kind that she invited. Her Pa still took long business trips away, with his return always resulting in arguments. Her ma's special friend still came to visit. But the way he greeted her with scruffs on her head had become seedy stares of desire. Her hate for him, which was once because he'd occupied her ma's attention, turned to loathing and disgust as he tried to engage with her with sexual mannerisms when her Ma wasn't around.

Precious said she was sure her mother knew how her lover's eye had taken to her. Just as she was sure her father knew that her Ma played him while he was away. Just neither of them did anything about it. Neither of them wanted to admit the truth; living in their own pity, not strong enough to face it. Although, with the truths in the back of both their minds, each of Precious' parents let jealousy boil: her pa, for a man he'd never met; her ma, for Precious herself, combined with an envy of her youth.

One night, Precious sat at the dinner table as her Ma stirred a pot of soup in the kitchen, her Ma's lover making eyes at Precious across the table. Precious rolled her eyes with disgust. Her Ma excused herself to go to the bathroom, maybe in an attempt to turn her back on the obvious eyes that were cast. Maybe not. Maybe she just simply needed to piss. But Precious' respect for her Ma had become so low after years of neglect and now jealous envy, that it's exactly where her mind went. She explained how, as her Ma left the room, the guy stood from his seat and walked over to place his arms around her, sitting on the other side of the table. He told her he hoped he knew how much he cared for her Ma and her, as his hands made their way down to her developing breasts, with his thumb brushing the side of them.

Precious explained that this night was a real turning point. How her eyes had started to tear as her body flinched in repulsion. Her pa, rather unexpectedly, walked into the room. He'd returned a few days early from a business trip and caught sight of Precious' discomfort with the guy leaning over her. Her Pa dropped his suitcase and went for him. Laid into him hard. Pounded his fists into his face. Unfortunately, the guy retaliated in defence, even though you might have thought the fucker might have given in, with a fist waking him up to the fact that what he was doing was sick. Alas, he fought back, and their fight pushed its way into the kitchen. Her Ma's lover had pushed Precious' Pa down on the counter, and her Pa grabbed hold of a knife, planting it into the guy's repulsive chest.

Precious described it as all having happened so quickly. Her Ma charging out in streaming tears and screaming at her pa. It was a night that saw her Pa end up in prison, and her Ma blame Precious for *everything* and end up despising her. The passing years saw Precious grow up in a household without love. A household of unspoken words. Living to simply see each day come to an end with little to look forward to. Until one day, Precious had the courage to confront her Ma whilst at the dinner table. Ask her why she never did anything. Never said anything. She accused her Ma of knowing all along. Asked if she was so desperate for attention and affection that she'd turn a blind eye to the creep. Asked her if she would have kept her eye turned if the guy took it further. Asked her Ma where the line was? If there was one.

Her Ma screamed at her, refusing to accept that anything had been going on. Said she had no idea what she was talking about and that she didn't want to hear another word. Precious continued to speak and her Ma pushed herself up from the table to leave. Precious followed, shouting words of truth into her ear. In Precious' fury she grabbed her Ma by the shoulder to turn her. Face her. Hear her. As Precious pulled on her shoulder, her Ma didn't so much turn to face Precious, as she did fall to the floor and slam her head on it. Precious described it again as an event that had happened so fast.

"I just left her there. For a split second I thought of calling an ambulance or trying to revive her. But I just walked back to the table. I finished my dinner, washed my plate and went to bed."

I grabbed hold of Precious' hands and clasped them tightly between us.

Precious went on to tell how, when she'd woken the next morning, she decided to call the ambulance. Pretend that she'd gone to bed early and had woken to find her Ma lying dead on the floor. Only when the ambulance arrived, they shared that her mother wasn't dead. Precious had left her Ma alive on the floor all night, in a comatose state. Thankfully, for Precious' sake, her mother never spoke another word again. She was strapped to a wheelchair for the rest of her days, made quadriplegic by the slam of her head against the hard floor.

Precious described how, with her Pa in prison, she had to share care of her Ma between NHS carers assigned. How, when the carers left the house, Precious would wheel her Ma's chair into the corner of the dining room, facing her to stare into the corner's blank walls, turned away from the room, as she'd spent her entire life anyway. The day Precious' Pa was released, Precious left the house to start anew in London. Closing the door to her Ma and Pa. Leaving her Pa with her Ma, his wife, as he always had done to Precious.

She explained that she had indeed cut her parents away. That they were dead to her. But that she kept up with visits. Not to *see* her parents. But to see their decline. Enjoying her Pa's entrapment. Staying with his wife to care for her as he shovelled mushed resentment down her throat. Knowing that she'd deceived their marriage. Knowing that she'd let the repulsive man that changed their lives into it. But even so, he couldn't seem to leave his wife in such a state. Concerned with how it might look. Destined to live a bitter life of resentment. Precious said she hoped they were banished in whatever realm was above. She hoped they were suffering. She hoped they stayed there. But she felt torn, as at the same time as wishing suffering upon them, she felt bad for wishing so.

I pulled Precious into me and held her as she started to whimper. Holding her. Comforting her.

"As someone once said to me, we all have a history." I told her, recalling the words as she'd spoken them to me, although not letting on I'd forgotten the reasoning why. As Precious settled in my arms, she turned herself onto her side and curled up, as we both drifted to sleep.

As I woke, I looked at the red hair in front of my face, uncertain who it belonged to. I let go of my hold and sat up, confused. I looked down at the red headed girl, standing up as I looked around me at what seemed to be a store, with gas pumps outside the windows ahead. Around them was dark smog. I remembered the dark smog.

30 VOIDED SPACE

I woke to look up and find Michael standing on his feet looking ahead, as if he were lost. As if he had forgotten where we were.

"Are you alright?" I rubbed my eyes and pushed myself off of the ground to stand by his side. He didn't respond. He just stared out the glass front of the gas station. "Sweetie?" I said, trying to prompt a response.

"Who are you?" asked Michael. His question broke my heart. I grabbed hold of his hands and clasped them between us, as he had with me the night before.

"It's me. Precious." He looked at me as blank as he had been looking out the window.

"Is that who *I* am? Michael?"

My heart split right in two. My eyes began to swell at the sight of his, which had begun to tear confusingly. I looked ahead at a young man who had poured his heart out to me, and in turn listened to me when I had listened to him, with no apparent memory of any of it. I tried to keep my face brave as I patted his hands and told him to wait right where he was. I made my way to where Audrey was lying and slowly shook her.

"Audrey. Audrey, I need you." I started to cry, not so brave, hidden behind the aisle Michael in which I was standing.

Audrey followed me, as I walked her to where Michael stood. I'd told her he didn't know who I was. Who *he* was. As Audrey walked up to him, I remembered the story he'd shared with me about his plague of the brain. How he'd been told if he hoped to put off onset dizzy spells, blackouts and the possibility of early onset symptoms of Alzheimer's, he needed to reduce any stress in his life. My guess was, this whole experience had become that bit much, that set off those very early onset symptoms.

As Audrey tried to talk with Michael, he just looked more and more confused. Lost. I looked on at him with the two parts of my heart hanging in suspension. A boy that had gone through so much. Self-admittedly done wrong, but tried to redeem himself. Searching for his loved ones in the dark smog. Bringing others in need of help under his wing. I truly hoped this was a moment that would pass. But as Andrew awoke and joined us in the aisle, it seemed even his historical friend from way back was even unknown to him. My hope that this moment would pass seemed more and more unlikely.

Audrey and Andrew sat Michael down and asked if I would sit with him while they woke Daisy, and prepared for our walk ahead. I held onto Michael with the hope of providing some comfort, as he had to me the night before. Andrew and Audrey gathered our bags, ready to return to the dark smog. Daisy joined us and said good morning as she yawned. From over the aisles, I overheard Andrew telling Audrey how he'd discovered his ability when he was with Michael while Audrey and I had been outside with Daisy. He said he too could move things with his mind. I smiled; of course he discovered it with Michael. I felt Michael brought out the best in people. At least, those he held close.

Little Daisy didn't quite understand what Michael was going through. Nor did I feel it was something I needed to explain to her. She just laughed as she asked him if he could remember certain things, thinking it was hilarious he couldn't remember a sheep. It kept her amused and it didn't seem to bother

Michael. I stood up to stretch my legs, asking Daisy if she would look after Michael for a minute.

"Don't mind lending my guardian angel for a few seconds." I winked at her.

As I stood, I started to walk through the aisles and looked around the store. Something didn't feel quite right. I stopped in my tracks. I looked outside the store in front of the glass.

"Hey! Does anything seem different to you?" I called out to Audrey and Andrew. They both looked around and shook their heads. Maybe it was just me. Maybe I was just fixating on details, trying to distract myself. But the air did feel different. The dark smog seemed darker, or maybe it was lighter. Thicker, or maybe it was thinner.

"You might be a little dazed, Precious. How about you sit back down with Michael and Daisy?" Audrey suggested, as she walked towards me. As she did, I could have sworn I saw her arm pass through the shelving. As if she were a ghost.

"Audrey…"

"What's wrong?"

"Did your arm just pass through that shelf?" Audrey looked at me strangely. She looked back at Andrew.

"Of course not…"

As Audrey insisted her arm hadn't passed through the shelf, she went to lean onto it to demonstrate and fell straight through. I ran to help her up. I could touch her. She wasn't a ghost. Unless we both were. I wasn't sure how that stuff worked. As I helped her up we both looked around us.

"What have you two been doing all this time?" I asked as Andrew walked up to us.

"Sorting through everything we packed yesterday."

"Have you packed anything new?" I asked, hesitant to try and touch the shelf myself.

"No, we packed too much actually. I've been weight distributing between the bags."

I reached out to the shelf Audrey had fallen through. My hand passed through it too. I pulled it back in shock. Andrew walked up and did the same — although his hand lingered in the voided space.

"Is it... Everything?" I asked. Andrew proceeded to walk through the shelf, and through the next as he passed Michael and Daisy, then to the front glass door. He stood, hesitant. Then, he walked through it. He looked back at us through the other side of the glass, then walked back inside.

"The floor. It's not hard like it was when we went to sleep," said Andrew, as he banged his foot against it. Audrey and I proceeded to do the same. It wasn't hard anymore. It felt firm. But not hard. Like dirt. None of this made any sense.

"Well, how far does this go on?" Audrey asked. She too walked through the aisle shelves and out through the glass door. She continued to walk through the gas pumps and then fell as if she bumped into something. Andrew and I ran out to her, passing through everything up to the point Audrey had fallen. I looked around, still feeling like something wasn't right. Audrey's face had been grazed and blood trickled from her nose.

Andrew ran to get his backpack, saying he had packed some medical supplies the day before. I looked out ahead to what seemed like an open road onto Hammersmith Bridge, the bridge we were due to set off on onto Windsor Castle. I slowly walked to where it had looked that Audrey bumped into something. I raised my hand to feel what felt like rock or brick. I placed both my hands upon it. It seemed to be an invisible wall of some kind, not allowing me to take one further step. But why was it there? How had it gotten there?

Rushing over with his backpack, Andrew pulled out some supplies and started to attend to Audrey's wounded face. Michael and Daisy walked out from the gas station's store — both looking as lost as each other.

The dark smog around us started to flicker a purple between its creasing and gathered points. A laugh took to the space around us and a crackling of purple electricity with it. Walking towards us stepped a creature in long draped black robes with a silver staff which shone among the dark smog. Behind it, the monstrous winged creature which Michael and I had seen flying over the bloody River Thames, stretching its neck into the sky as it blew flames of purple into it.

The robed creature looked demonic. It held white bulging skin with large boned cheeks and thick black curling horns, which pierced out from its forehead. Purple pulsing veins ran through its white skin. It shot out its hands, as the silver staff floated in its place, pointing its elongated fingers with thick long back nails to me, Daisy and Michael, its point shooting out some kind of force which threw us each to the ground.

"YOU SHALL BOW IN THE FACE OF ROYALTY!" It shouted. Its shout echoed into the purple crackling dark smog which soon dissolved what had appeared to us to be a gas station, revealing that we were inside the protective barrier walls of what looked like a castle. A castle I knew well. One I'd been inside with my friends, on a tour, and taken with fascination with its history. The Tower of London.

Audrey had indeed bumped into a rocky brick wall – she'd bumped into the tower walls. We all lay on the dirt of the tower's courtyard at this demonic creature's hold. I looked up to find hundreds of other demonic looking creatures and people surrounding us as they appeared all around. They laughed. They cheered. They raised their fists into the air. Above us, some flew. Some were floating independently, while their robes blew in the wind. Others backed onto various sorts of flying winged creatures, like the one stood behind the demonic robed creature in front of me. I knew exactly who this creature was. I pushed myself up from the ground as it looked around at its followers, basking in glory. I spat down at its feet.

The demonic creature turned to me as its robes swung through the air, grabbing its floating silver shining staff. The two of us flew up into the air together, me by their force, as my chin met quickly with the silver staff.

"Hello, Lenroc."

"You dare to address me?! Spit at my feet?!"

"I dare."

"Your *daring* fails you, my darling. Bringing that park back to life is what led me to you and my little prized Michael. Do you really think a spot of newly flourished greenery in central London would have gone unnoticed?!"

"Don't make this any worse for yourself!" Audrey shouted up to me, as she waved her hand, likely trying to freeze time. Lenroc merely waved back down to her, disarming her ability, as we both floated back down from the sky. Lenroc landed steadily on their feet, as they dropped me to the floor, landing on my front. I came to an excruciatingly painful thud. I grabbed my ribs in severe agony, having felt them crack inside of me. Lenroc drifted to Audrey with their robes flowing behind them.

Audrey rose to her feet to stand and face Lenroc.

"Ah. The forgotten one. I should have known you'd come running back!"

"And what trickery is this?! How long have you been on our case?!"

"Oh, you mean our little gas station replica. Trick of the light, my dear. You really can do wondrous things if you delve deep enough into your abilities, young lady. Not that you or your petty Collective would have ever known. Too afraid of your own strength to use it. No. You'd be amazed at the abilities I've acquired over time! Channelled. Harnessed. Mastered. All it took was to wait until you'd all gathered in one place to hop you back here as a group to our little lair. *New Tower!* Like the name? I think it's got quite the ring to it!" Lenroc laughed, as she looked around at her followers who were egging her on.

Audrey looked as though she held no fear. I looked up to her with admiration as she stood up to Lenroc. Daisy cried and cried as Michael held her in comfort. I admired him too. Andrew had rushed to my aid and held me as I started to cough up blood. We had been quite the group. I was so glad that I found them. That Michael found me. I couldn't have imagined better people to have marched the apocalyptic streets of London with.

I quickly found myself in a fit of coughs. I started to struggle to breathe as I gasped for air. It felt as if the air in my lungs had been replaced with a thick gurgling liquid. I took one final cough, as I looked down at my hands, coughing out what looked like a pint of blood. Green grass sprouted up around me and Andrew as he held me. I looked back out at Michael and little Daisy, with my vision beginning to blur, as my head rolled back over Andrew's arm. The last thing I heard was Andrew shout, *no!*

31 NEW WORLD

I looked ahead at Lenroc, with her new demonic appearance, face to face, knowing that she'd absorbed more than just multiple abilities – she'd absorbed the forces of the underworld and all its darkness. She was consumed by it. I turned to look behind me, as I heard Andrew scream, *no!* He held Precious in his arms, surrounded by tall, newly sprouted grass, as blood ran from her mouth. The new grass seemed to be her attempt to cling on to her life, sprouting a form of life around her. But it certainly seemed like a lot of expelled ability for a dying girl.

I looked back at Lenroc in fury.

"The Collective were never afraid of their strength! They just knew it was wrong to abuse it! They knew what abuse leads to! Look around you, Lenroc – is this really a world you want to live in?!" Lenroc stepped forward and pressed her demonic nose up to my human one. She started to laugh once again, stepping back as she swung at me with her silver staff.

I was knocked to the ground with serious force, although I hadn't landed nearly as hard as poor Precious had to her death, softening my fall with my hands. A sharp pain ran from my palms through to my wrists.

"You remember this little thing, Audrey?" Lenroc asked, as she floated her staff around her in a circle. "An enchanted wedding gift. A silver cake knife.

Doesn't it look so much better with a little embellishment? That's all I've done to the world, my darling – embellished it!"

"You call death and destruction embellishment?!"

"I call death and destruction what the world had coming to it, Audrey!" Lenroc snapped back instantly in a raised tone. She started to walk the courtyard of *New Tower* as her robe flowed behind her, her arms stretched out in the open space. "New Tower! The centre of New London! New London, the centre of New World! No more powerless little girls abused by spineless adults! No more..."

"Is that what you were, Lenroc? A powerless little girl? Look at that little girl over there," I said, as I nodded my head Daisy's way, huddled into Michael. "Does she look powerful to you right now?!" Lenroc turned to face me again. She stopped speaking as she walked towards me while staring me down.

"You have no idea what I was. You couldn't even begin to imagine. I know this, because if you had you wouldn't be fighting against us! You'd be fighting with us!"

"What's left, Lenroc?! You've banished all of humanity! Who's left to fight? The remaining enabled you're yet to recruit? Then what? THEN WHAT, LENROC?!" I looked up at her screaming, releasing every bit of strength I had left to try and get through to her. Expelling what little energy I had left, to talk some sense into this truly lost soul.

Part of me felt Lenroc was too far gone and didn't see the point. But part of me had to try. Or else, if I died right here and now, what would it have been for? If I was to die on this very ground, I would lay dead, having stood for what I believed in. I rose from the ground once more, as I dusted off my hands.

"You couldn't even begin to comprehend!"

"Listen to yourself. You don't even know what you're fighting for anymore. You can't even tell me. Say you pull this off. Say you recruit every remaining scrambling enabled hidden in the shadows. It's only a matter of time before the monarch resurges. Takes back control. Then, this will have all been for nothing, just more rubble to tidy while you go into hiding again. Think this through. Think this through!"

Lenroc had been breathing heavily while she listened to me. But her heavy breaths just turned back into laughter as she whacked me back down to the ground with her staff. My head pounded. I held it as I looked back up at her and she crouched down to hold my chin, with her long, cold, narrow fingers, while laughing in my face heartily.

"Bless you. The Collective really were out of their depth, weren't they? Never got it quite right, did they? The monarchy was never enabled, my darling. Your sweet Queen didn't hold any abilities. They were only ever allies. The Queen's reputation as being sight enabled only ever came to be as she'd employed the enabled to serve her. One with the ability of sight and the other with the ability of telepathy. Reading her guests' thoughts and communicating that to her from behind closed doors. Did you really think the monarchy was coming to your rescue?!" Lenroc laughed. "Oh, that is sweet. No darling. Your beloved Queen and the Queen Mother are banished alongside the rest of humanity. The monarchy thought they could govern us – keep control. But they were merely humans. No matter how powerful they'd built themselves up to be. Banished with the rest of them. Not even the Queen's crown and sceptre could save her!"

I couldn't believe my ears. It could have been trickery, that's for sure. Anything to throw me off my game. Take away my confidence. But reflecting on it, although I never did cross paths with former member of the Collective, Shane, I did recall stories of his father forming alliances with the monarch. Moving up in the ranks as a soldier. Perhaps I'd put faith in something that I never should have. Perhaps the Collective, of which *I* was now the last standing, was the only real faith in which anyone could hold. Yet we had held a false faith. Maybe, simply because we needed to. Needing to hold faith in something.

I tried to get back up, but I dropped to my knees in a moment of weakness, not in giving up, but in a lack of faith. I looked over to Michael, as he cradled little Daisy in his arms. If what Lenroc said was true, then just maybe Michael was the only person left I could hold any faith in. Demos had, in the end, after all. I needed him to be strong. I needed his mind returned. I needed the same passionate and driven young man I'd returned to outside the defeated grounds of Buckingham Palace. Not the lost and deteriorating mind of a young man that cowered across from me. I needed to trigger him. Somehow, I needed to set his ability off. Holding faith that, when I did, he would use his ability for the greater good.

I looked on at Lenroc with such pity. She'd really lost her faith in everything in the world. Feeding indulgently from the cheers of the dark enabled around her, reinforcing her with reassurance and validation. However, the cheers had been bought. Some of the followers gathered around her couldn't have been eighteen years old. Teenagers full of angst, and a young naïve rage, against a world they hadn't had time to even begin to understand yet. Lenroc had grabbed hold of their beating hearts and twisted them to her own bidding.

"That may be. But you underestimate those of us that remain. You underestimate the good that this world holds. That it still can. Nothing good is going to come from this *New World* of yours. Nothing."

Lenroc looked down at me as I addressed her on my weakened knees, as she squinted at me. In a sure disappointment that I hadn't been deterred by her news of the monarch. I started to stand again as I rose to look at Lenroc face to face. Lenroc swiped her silver staff between us, sending a force through my body that made me cave back to my knees.

"I don't think so. I think you've said enough. I much prefer you on the ground. Beneath me. Get used to it, for it's where you're going to stay! I don't think you really know what it's like to be held down against your will, do you? Something tells me that your New Yorker front is just that: a front. You've never known any true pain. You've never had to endure pain from another. Not real pain. Your heart and trust has been broken, yes, I can feel that, but that's not the kind of pain I'm speaking of. You haven't endured physical pain from another.

At least not by intention. No. You, Miss Freezer of Time, have held just that your entire life, haven't you? The ability to stop something as it's about to happen. Freeze time in an instant. Mid event. Get away. Put yourself at an advantage. Well, I think it's time you felt just what it is like. I've got just the room inside this castle for you. Oh yes, a room with contraptions they haven't used on people for quite some time. Contraptions which make the tourists of this city gasp at the thought of such vile torture. Well, I don't think it's vile. I think it's justice. Justice that people who live their lives roaming the world unhurt or unharmed get to hold their shoulders back with their head high. While the likes of me, and the dark enabled around us, are made to feel we have to hang our heads in shame. In fear. Prove what harm has come our way, or keep quiet. Made to feel worthless and filthy for it!" Lenroc roared, as a purple illuminated shield of energy covered my mouth and held my wrists and ankles together behind my back.

Lenroc had begun to walk away from me, but then in a defensive fit, quickly returned. "You know, Audrey, and I know you know, as your fellow Collective would have told you, we all make mistakes! But I was never given the chance to redeem myself! After the dark enabled times, I could feel the previous Collective's bounty on my head. With young Margaret. Before this enchanted object drained her of her youth. I knew what they had planned for me. They were going to throw me away like they did with all the others. Banish me to the realm they created to leave me to rot. I had to go into hiding! Live off the fucking land like an animal! Do you know how that felt?! After having worked so hard to make my existence known?! Only to be taken captive by the government and held down against my will. Using my own force of energy against me to keep me bound! Satan knows how they cottoned on to that neat little trick! Experimenting on me like a lab rat, as they sliced and diced and pricked and prodded at me. Do you know what that felt like, Audrey? Do you?! Then Margaret's precious little collective waltzed on in, didn't they, entirely unaware that I'd mastered the harnessing of others' abilities through the energies I'd channelled. Thanks to

Shane. Pushing them into that realm in my place. I had no idea how long I'd been kept in that chamber. All I know is when I came back down to Earth from that realm, everything was as if nothing had ever happened. People walking around, oblivious. Buildings restored. No knowledge among humanity of us enabled. The work I'd put into driving the fear of us all into their veins, thrown aside in the wastebasket! A nice little cover up thanks to the Collective. It took me some time to get my head around that clearing of theirs – but I mastered it in the end! Used it on dear young Michael to ensure the prophecy would come to fruition! Marinated him in my hands!"

Lenroc turned and began to walk towards Michael and Daisy. Her robes dragged on the castle grounds behind her as she stabbed her silver staff into the ground with each step she took, its connection with the ground sending a vibration through it.

"I don't know who you are, but what you're doing is wrong, and it has to stop! You just killed that girl for Christ's sake!" Michael shouted at her, as he held little Daisy, keeping her protected in his arms. Lenroc laughed up towards the sky, lifting her silver staff, before slamming it back down into the ground with full force. It sent sparks of purple, which illuminated a large purple bubble of energy, surrounding the Tower of London.

"I, Michael," said Lenroc, as she looked back down at him. "I am the reason you're still alive. And I can assure you, I've killed many more than your little redhead over there!"

"What do you mean, you're still the reason I'm alive?"

"Ah, you see. Those crusty gashes across your wrists. They could have been a lot worse. I'm sure your friends here would have had you believe I meant to kill you, when you called on me above Tower Bridge. But, no. No, no. I only meant to bleed you, like the prophecy stated. Never kill you. The prophecy never said anything about *killing* you. I just had to give you time to rebuild your strength, you see. To be honest, I thought your first stop would have been to

Primrose Hill, but it seemed your little Pree and Rubis took priority. Putting them before yourself. Isn't that quaint."

"I have no idea what you're talking about!"

"Of course you don't! Because that little plague of the brain has taken effect, hasn't it?!" Lenroc pouted a frown, looking back at me in my purple illuminated restraints, and then looked back at Michael. "Don't know about that either? Oh, you're dying, Michael. You can't remember who you are or where you are, because that brain of yours is shutting down, my darling. No, not even Primrose Hill could fix that. But I can. I've mastered life. I can give that to you. All you have to do is take my hand." Lenroc extended and opened up her demonic palm Michael's way.

32 THE PURPLE CURRENT

I looked up at this demonic creature called Lenroc, as she offered me her demonic hand. Its long, thick and blackened nails pointed down to me, as she stood tall, with her silver staff held beside her. I held a child in my arms. I hadn't the faintest clue who the child was. But they clung to me. I looked around at the strangers scattered around. The boy to my right, with the dead red headed girl in his arms. The woman ahead, bound by some kind of purple illumination. The same kind that had just taken to the castle around us, when Lenroc stabbed their staff into the ground. I had no idea who any of these people were. What was right or wrong. But it *felt* wrong.

Lenroc addressed me again. "Take my hand, and you'll never have to worry about anything ever again. Leave these people. You owe them nothing. I can give you your life back. Bring your memories back. You feel an emptiness inside you, don't you? I can make you whole again!" I sat in thought. I felt an emptiness for sure. I didn't know these people. I didn't know anything. I just saw a hand in front of me with promise. I let go of the girl I had been holding. She quickly clung onto me again. I pushed her back, and she started to cry, as I got up on my feet.

"I don't know who I am. Will you show me who I am?"

"Yes, Michael. Take my hand, and together we will show people who you are! Oh yes, my boy. Your mind may be gone, but your ability remains strong, and with my guidance and leadership you will become more powerful than ever! Take my hand again. This time, the world is *ours*!"

I felt myself enter some kind of trance and took hold of her cold hand. As I took hold, a gust of force entered my body. The silver staff which Lenroc held shot sparks of purple lightning up into the sky. Lenroc cackled, and the sparks crackled. The girl that had clung to me ran to be with the boy. I looked back to Lenroc.

"Who am I?!" I shouted, as the wind picked up around us.

"Michael! You are Michael! The new world will know your name! Take my staff, and with it, end your friends to show your loyalty to the Dark Enabled! End their lives, for yours to begin!"

Lenroc handed me the silver staff. It too felt familiar. Like I'd held it once before. Or maybe, I was confusing familiarity with what was meant to be: *my destiny*. As I took the silver staff from Lenroc's hand, she stepped aside to make way for me, as I walked forward to the woman in a purple illuminated hold.

"What do I do?!" I asked, shouting above the wind that had begun to rise in not just strength, but in volume around us.

"Point it at her! Point it as her and drive it through her heart! Feed your energy through it and feel the strength inside you return!" I looked down at the woman. Tears ran from her eyes, as she locked them with mine, as if she knew me.

To my right, I saw the boy that had held the dead red headed girl in his arms stand and run towards me. He was quickly thrown back in the air as Lenroc shot a purple electrical current at him. I looked back at Lenroc, who was thrown back too, by a mirrored purple electrical current. I ran quickly out of the way, as the purple current became one string of energy between both Lenroc and the boy. Lenroc, rising from where she'd fallen, held her right hand out in front of her to deflect it. The boy, back on his feet, walked towards her, also with his right hand out deflecting the current between them. The two of them began to make their way closer to each other with great difficulty, as the current acted as some kind of force between them, trying to keep them apart.

"Don't you mind this boy! Take that staff to her heart and then join me as we finish him!"

33 MIMIC

I looked on at Michael as Lenroc continued to address him. He looked down at Audrey. Tears ran from her eyes. I knew she was trying to connect with him through her tearing eyes. But Michael was a steering wheel, and Lenroc had taken hold of him. As I watched, I held on to Daisy, but as I looked down I couldn't see her. I extended my hand. I, too, couldn't see *myself*. We had both vanished. Lenroc fixated on Michael, and he on Audrey, and hadn't even taken notice of us disappearing. I supposed that little Daisy's ability had hidden me as well in her fright.

I couldn't let Michael take that staff to Audrey. He wouldn't come back from that. I could sense that was Lenroc's intention. I had to end Lenroc. End Michael's influence. Bring him back to us - before he ended us. I wasn't sure how long Daisy's cloak would work, but I had to make a run for it. Now. Run towards Lenroc and put this ability of mine to some sort of use. I whispered to Daisy that I was going to let go, and when I did, she should stay put. I let go, and ran towards Michael, to see if I might knock him down before I continued on to Lenroc, to save Audrey some time, in the event my attack on Lenroc didn't succeed. But, as I let go of Daisy and started to run, I had reappeared.

I was quickly thrown back in the air as Lenroc shot a purple electrical current at me. As she did, I felt this strange sensation take over my body, filling

236

me. A kind of new energy. I shot up from where I was thrown, and cast back the same purple electrical current from my hand that Lenroc had cast onto me. Lenroc rose from where my current threw her, deflecting the current right back to me. I walked towards her, as if trying to walk against strong waves that wanted to bowl me over. Both of us were connected to the same current, acting as some kind of force between us.

"Don't you mind this, boy! Take that staff to her heart and then join me as we finish him!" Lenroc shouted.

The force between us grew stronger, pushing both Lenroc and I further apart. Michael dropped the silver staff on the ground and walked back towards the rocky brick walls of the castle. He scrunched his hands to his head and through his hair. I looked back at Lenroc who'd tried to hide her surprised disappointment, hiding behind the flashes of illuminating purple electric energy, as we both kept hold of the force between us. As the force became even greater, I brought up my second hand to keep it held, as did Lenroc.

I looked down to find the heels of my feet digging back into the ground, as dirt mounted up around my feet. Looking ahead, Lenroc's robes had started flowing through the air behind her, as her feet lifted from the ground and she suspended herself in mid-air. I looked back down at my feet to find that they too had begun to lift from the ground. I too was now suspended in mid-air. The only thing touching me was the current of purple that made up the strengthening force between Lenroc and I. I hadn't the faintest clue what was happening. I looked back at Michael. Now sat on the ground, he had caved his head into his knees as if he wanted to block everything from his mind. Block the world out. *Why wouldn't he?* I thought. The guy had no idea who he was and just about fell into the hands of the demonic creature I was trying to fight off.

In my suspension, I watched as a follower, from the circle of creatures that surrounded us, ran towards the silver staff dropped on the ground by Michael. They reached for it. But the staff shone a bright beam of blue light which blew them away from it. The force blew through the air. I felt it even while suspended. So much was going on that my mind couldn't compute. I looked ahead, at Lenroc fighting this force, as hard as me. Maybe harder.

"Give it up, Lenroc!" I shouted.

"Not a chance! Your mimic won't last forever young man!" *My mimic*, I thought. Was it that Lenroc was implying what my ability was? What I was enabled with? It all fell into place. I'd moved things with my mind when engaged with Michael. Grass sprouted up around me in Precious' last breath as I'd willed her to live. Just a moment ago, I'd become invisible with little Daisy by my side. I'd shot some kind of electrical current from my hand, just as I'd been hit with one by Lenroc. The ability to *mimic* kicked fucking arse!

The clarification of what I was doing only filled me with confidence and certainty., neither of which I held before in my instinctive and confused suspension in mid-air. I took a deep breath and, in my exhale, I let out a scream as I pushed the force further towards Lenroc. As I did, I looked over to Michael.

"Michael! You're the only one that can end this! You need to pick up that staff and strike Lenroc down!" I shouted, realising while I held this force, which was Lenroc's own, Lenroc too had to hold it. Their own power was surely the only ability with force enough to defeat them. But the staff seemed a force of its own altogether.

"No! Don't listen to him! You need to hand the staff back to me!" Lenroc screamed. I thought back to the blue beam which had shot Lenroc's follower away, to before that, when Lenroc had handed it to Michael.

"Don't, Michael! I don't think she can take it. I think you have to *give* it to her! I don't think anyone can! I think it's yours unless you give *it* to someone!"

As I turned back to look Lenroc's way, her demonic face became enraged, as she stared me down and pushed the force back towards me.

"What are you all doing just standing there?! Attack these enemies!" Lenroc shouted at the circle of followers around her. But it was clear that, in Audrey's confronting of Lenroc, minds had since been swayed. Hesitant. Confronted with the question of what they were fighting for. Lenroc's dark world. New World. It didn't seem so appealing anymore. Nobody jumped to her command of attack. Either that, or they were scared shitless of that silver staff. Instead, the dark enabled started to depart from the circle. However quick as they might have tried to flee the Tower of London, the winged creatures from the sky came swooping down to pick them, tossing them into the castle walls as a battle between them began. The Dark Enabled against the creatures of the underworld.

I looked around me with my hands still holding back the current. Destruction and abilities of all sorts had begun to take to the air around us. Dark Enabled worked together as one to harness their abilities at the creatures around them. The castle walls crumbled as the winged creatures crashed down into them. Fire appeared all around with bursts of explosions. People and creatures alike flew in the air, with bolts of electricity energy thrown from one to the other. A blue haired demon which radiated absolute beauty fell from the sky, disintegrating instantly, as it fell into the current between Lenroc and I. It was fucking unreal. It was like something out of an epic blockbuster battle from a movie. I imagined all of London soon becoming a battlefield as the dark enabled and creatures of the underworld spread out over it.

My imagination was quickly interrupted as I felt a gust of wind come from above. I looked up to find one of the large winged creatures heading straight towards me, a foot with three claws stretched out and down towards me as a beam of blue light shot up at it. I looked to where the beam had come from by my side - and there stood Michael. He held the silver staff in his hands, as he pointed it towards the winged creature, and just like the blue haired demon, it disintegrated.

34 BLACKNESS

I took my hands from my head and raised my face from my knees. I looked out around me as Lenroc commanded her followers to attack us. Nobody flinched. The ones that eventually had, started to throw down their weapons and leave the circle they'd formed. Some began to run, as the winged creatures from the sky soon flew down to catch as they tossed them into the castle walls. I might not have known who I was. Maybe I was never to know - who I had been, who I once was - ever again. But I knew at that moment, who I wanted to be. Who I wanted to fight for. It was not Lenroc.

I looked ahead, at the boy struggling to maintain the force he held between him and Lenroc. Among the destruction, explosions and forces of energy started to take place around me. I looked up as a winged creature headed straight towards the boy holding off Lenroc. I rose from my feet as creatures of all kinds tried to attack me. But it was as if some kind of force was protecting me, as the creatures were blasted away. A force that felt as though it was coming from that staff. I ran to grab it, and held it up towards the winged creature with the boy as its target, blasting it back with a beam of blue light.

"Michael!"

"I don't know what I'm doing!"

"Don't worry! Neither do I!"

I ran up to the bound woman on the ground and tried to use the silver staff to release her from Lenroc's illuminating hold. It goddamn worked. She quickly stood and grabbed me by the shoulders as the little girl appeared beside us.

"Michael! Listen to me! Andrew's mimic enabled! If you both grab hold of that staff and join your forces together while he's still connected to Lenroc, we might fucking win this!"

"I don't know what any of that means. But sure!" I guessed the boy's name was Andrew. I looked around me as time seemed as though it had frozen. Explosions frozen in place, electricity still in the air. I looked back at Lenroc and Andrew frozen in their suspension against one another.

"I can't hold this for long, Michael. Not with this much energy around me. Go. Be ready. As soon as I let go, have Andrew take hold! Blast her, Michael. Blast her from this fucking world once and for all!"

I looked into the eyes of a woman that held absolute faith in me. Even though I didn't know her now, I was certain I once did. I looked down at the little girl, looking up at me. I smiled at her. Should I end this all here? I had at least two people, three including the boy named Andrew, who I felt sure would stay by my side. Help me to remember who I was. Help me to become someone. Someone with good in their heart. Something in me knew that.

I turned around and walked to stand by Andrew's side as I looked around at the frozen battle. In the blink of an eye, the motion of all unfroze around us. I felt the heat of blasts return to the air.

"Andrew! Can you hold that force with one hand?!"

"I'm not sure! I think so! Yeah, maybe for a second!"

"I want you to grab hold of the staff with me! We do this together!" He nodded at me while struggling to hold back the force with one hand, releasing the other, as he shook and grabbed hold of the silver staff.

"NOW, Andrew!" I shouted, feeling I needn't further explain.

"Noooooooooooooooooooooooooooooooooooooooooooooooooooooo!
" Lenroc squealed across the castle grounds, into the dark smoggy sky, piercing through the explosions and electrical crackling around us.

In a flash, a blue beam greater than any it had cast yet saturated the air. The purple energy between Andrew and Lenroc started to separate into red and blue, the red lessening while the blue overtook it, pushing the red entirely from its current as it ran up towards Lenroc's hold. I lost sight of Lenroc in the beam's extreme overexposure of light. It blasted up to the sky as the dark smog was obliviated, overpowered by the beam of light which spread out for what looked like infinity. There was no clear separation of ground and sky. I looked over at Andrew, being the only face I could just make out in the brightness. His eyes looked straight at me.

"Oh, buddy." Andrew said, as if in some kind of realisation. Then, blackness.

35 BEGIN AGAIN

In a flash, a blue beam greater than any the silver staff had cast yet saturated the air, the purple energy between Michael, Andrew and Lenroc separating into red and blue. The red vanished as the blue overtook it. The beam's extreme overexposure of light saw me quickly grab hold of little Daisy's hand, as I lost sight of all around us, and the beam blasted up to the sky. In a matter of seconds, it was as if it was the time Michael had called on the Collective, when we were all gathered in one place. When I'd been unimpressed because I had been pulled from my busy life in New York. Nothing but whiteness. A saturation of whiteness. White nothingness.

The whiteness started to fade. The forceful wind which had been building settled to a stillness. The dark smog was gone. The winged creatures in the sky were gone. The creatures on the grounds that remained of the Tower of London, gone. All that remained were battered and bruised people. Enabled perhaps, but no longer dark enabled, all as shaken as the person that stood next to them. I cast my eyes up to something I hadn't seen in a few days now. Maybe a week. It was a bright blue sky.

"No, no, no, no, no!" Andrew shouted.

I looked down to see Andrew by Michael's side. Michael, collapsed on the ground.

"Come on Daisy!" I said, as we ran to the boys. I knelt down beside them. Daisy clung to my arm. I looked at Andrew as tears streamed from his eyes. He looked up at me.

"I remember. I remember! I remember, I remember, I remember! My best bud. My bestest buddy in the whole wide world!" Michael laid still on the ground with his eyes wide open, facing up to the sky. I bent down beside him, to feel his wrist, hoping that he had caught a glimpse of the blue sky one last time. He held no pulse. Andrew proceeded to start cardiopulmonary resuscitation. I held on to Daisy and rubbed her back as we watched Andrew fight for Michael's life.

"Who's that?" Daisy asked, as she tugged at my clothing.

I hesitantly began to look over to my right, afraid I might find a greater demonic version of Lenroc, that had absorbed everything in existence, rather than the beam that I thought had cleared it all away. Rather, as I looked, I saw a little girl with blonde hair sitting crying within Lenroc's large black robes.

"No." I whispered to myself.

"Can I see if she's okay?" Daisy asked. Before I answered her, I thought for a moment, looking back up to the bright blue sky. It could have been trickery. But I had to hold faith. If I couldn't hold faith under a bright blue sky, when could I?

"Go to her, sweetie."

I looked as Daisy ran over. She sat down with the little blonde girl and stroked her hair. The girl had stopped crying. I looked on at the care little Daisy held for a girl much smaller than herself. Perhaps it was just what the little blonde girl needed. Perhaps it was a lack of care in the girl's life that had led her to the world with darkened smog. The girl took hold of Daisy's hand. Daisy smiled and began to walk back with her. The little thing could barely walk, as she stumbled over her own feet and the bumps on the ground, Daisy bending down to help her balance and steady herself.

I looked back at Andrew who had stopped resuscitation. He looked down at Michael with deep admiration. I grabbed hold of his hand.

"You did good, Andrew. The two of you. Together."

"I'll never be able to thank him for coming back for me. I can't understand why I'm fine."

"Michael was a very unhealthy boy. His days were numbered. But I think you should hold some comfort in the fact that he hung on for you. I don't even think he found *you*. I think you found *him*. Just at the right time."

"Thanks, Audrey."

"You know what I also think? I think Lenroc knew." I looked down at the little blonde girl as Daisy sat her down beside us. "I think Lenroc kept you separated for a reason. Included you in Michael's clearing so you wouldn't seek him. She knew your power. But more so, she knew your bond with Michael. The power you could harness together. Against her. The good influence you had on him."

Andrew looked at me as tears filled his eyes. I squeezed his hand tightly. Then, the sound of a phone rang. Andrew stood, listening out for it. He walked over to where Precious lay dead. He stared down at her, slowly kneeling as he tried to respect her body, then reached inside her jacket pocket. He found the ringing phone. She'd held on to it all this time. Andrew answered it. He looked at me and then turned away as he spoke. I looked back at the two girls sitting beside me. I looked at the once dark enabled, helping each other.

Andrew came back to join us. He explained it had been one of Precious' friends on the phone. They had wondered where she ran off to, under the impression she left them at Leicester Square. They were worried, because social media was exploding with theories that a sleeping agent had been put into the air as the world went under attack. But they explained that apparently there were no leads at this time. I laughed.

"Is that so? Don't suppose they'll get any either. Looks like a lot more wonder is about to take to the world. More wonder, and more healing." All of a sudden a Beefeater came running out of part of the remaining structure of the Tower of London.

"What are you all doing in here?! You can't be here! It's not opening hours until…" He waved his arms about frantically, before catching sight of the damage done to the castle. His jaw dropped, as an emergency vehicle's sirens took to the air. Humanity had returned.

I stood up from my spot and took Daisy's hand. She and the little blonde girl stood beside me. I looked at Andrew.

"How about a walk to Primrose Hill?" I suggested, knowing its healing properties. But also, knowing it held the best damn view of London, as shared with us by Michael.

"Sounds good to me." Andrew looked back down at Michael, and then over at Precious. "What about them?" I looked at each of them. Precious' vibrant red hair. Then, holding the last of my stare down at Michael.

"They served well. They did so honourably. Proudly. Knowingly. They couldn't have died on more honourable grounds. Their bodies will be gathered alongside many others. My friends back up on the grounds of Buckingham Palace, too. We'll light a candle for them. We'll light a candle for all of them."

"What about the…" Andrew paused.

"The what?"

"What about the staff? Where's the staff?"

We all looked around us. On the ground, not far from Michael, I saw the enchanted silver cake knife it once was. I pointed to it.

"What's that?" Andrew asked.

"Your staff. In its original form. In the form it held when it became enchanted. A story for another time. Take it; it's yours. Michael gave it to you. You were right about that - him having to give it to someone. Good intuition there. There may be traits of the Collective in you." I looked up into the sky and smiled. The world now seemingly restored, I wondered if the very Collective, before the one I was appointed, had returned. The ones Lenroc had banished in place of herself.

I looked back down at Precious, and then Michael, one last time. Then, I looked at the two girls by my side and then back to Andrew. I suggested we start to make tracks. Andrew took the knife and placed it in his pocket, then the four of us made our way out from the ruins of the Tower of London. As we stepped out of the entrance onto the castle bridge, we all looked around at a smattering of people that had reappeared. People that looked on at the defeated Tower Bridge, with their hands placed against their faces. People that had gathered by the River Thames, helping others which had seemed to pop up in the water - no longer bloody.

For a time, no words were spoken, as we walked along the River Thames, taking in the beautiful returned blue sky and the prospect of better days ahead. We passed ruins, fallen down buildings and defeated sites. Although there were no creatures of darkness or dark smog surrounding them. No purple crackling in the sky. Just people, helping people. We stretched our legs up to Trafalgar Square, where I told Andrew he had something he needed to do. The enchanted silver knife in his pocket was too powerful to keep on him. Power had a way of corrupting people, I told him. He understood, and threw the knife into the water of the fountain, as it shimmered and disappeared. We looked around at the cracked and crumbled concrete that made up Trafalgar Square. The four iron lions, sitting strong and in place.

"What now?" Andrew asked me.

"It'll be different this time. But we've done this before. We rebuild. Our lives. Society. The world." I paused for a moment. I looked down at each of the two little girls by my side. Then back up at Andrew. "We begin again."

36 WHITENESS

Audrey, Andrew, Daisy and little Dale carried on. They made their way to Primrose Hill, where they each laid down for a while and watched the last of any dark smoke from the City of London evaporate into the air. As they laid, Audrey instructed them to each breathe deeply and concentrate on healing. Little Daisy sparked a memory as her pain began to heal. Little Daisy thought that if all the other people in the world had reappeared, then just maybe her brother Tony had too.

Daisy accepted that she probably was not a guardian angel – referring to the thought as silliness really. It made Audrey and Andrew giggle. On her request, the four of them set back onto the streets of London. Healed and strong. Breathing in the fresh air. They made their way to the hotel where Daisy and her brother had been staying, and up to their very room, where little Daisy knocked on the door. As the door to the room opened, Daisy ran and jumped up to the boy that opened it, with a bright smile painted across her face. The pair were united. They both cried tears filled with joy.

Daisy looked up at her brother as he placed her back on the ground and looked on at Audrey and Andrew, thanking them for bringing his little sister back to him, while tears dispensed from his eyes. Daisy tugged on his trousers and asked if he wanted another little sister. She promised to be the bestest big sister to her and always wash her dishes. Daisy's brother looked at little Dale, stood watching her little hands as she clapped them, between Audrey and Andrew.

"Who is she?" Tony asked.

"Someone in need of a loving home," replied Audrey. Daisy's brother looked down at her as Daisy pleaded.

"Please, please, pleeeeeease," she begged. Tony looked back at little blonde Dale and extended his hand to her.

"Okay. Come on in with us. It's okay."

As Audrey gently pushed little Dale towards Daisy and Tony, Daisy took hold of Dale's little hand, and said she thought they should call her Blondie. Tony smiled at Audrey and Andrew, thanking them again. He offered for them to come in a while, saying that all he had was water. Audrey graciously declined, saying that she and Andrew should be on their way. Daisy's brother thanked them once again and shut the door.

*

Audrey and Andrew walked the streets of London once more, as Audrey led them back towards the portal at the defeated grounds of Buckingham Palace. Caution tape had been cast around the site. Demos, little Lee, and no doubt the bodies of the others, had been taken away.

"So, you've seen London. How do you feel about New York?" Audrey asked. Andrew smiled, and as he once had taken Michael's hand, he now took Audrey's.

*

Earlier that day, a person with pink candy floss hair awoke to a whiteness blaring through their bedroom window. The one and only Pree Possessing. They took off their bed covers and made their way to the window, opening their blinds as they looked out to the fading whiteness, making way for a bright blue sky. However, as bright and blue as the sky was, it held an emptiness to Pree. An emptiness in the world. A man came up behind Pree and placed his hands on their shoulders as he gave them a little massage.

249

"Morning baby," said the man. Pree grabbed his hands, taking them off their shoulders, and placed the arms of the man around themself, wishing they were the arms of a boy named Michael. The boy that had distanced himself. The boy that hadn't been in touch in quite some time. The boy that Pree wasn't sure would be heard from again. The boy that left an emptiness in Pree's world - and heart.

*

Back in central London, a girl with blonde hair, plump red lips and smudged mascara across her eyes, was crouched down in a shadowed alley. Miss Rubis Rouge was the name she went by. It was a name usually lit by the spotlight. Her dress was torn, and had finger markings with bruises around her neck. She flexed her hands out in front of her repeatedly in frustration seemingly trying to do something with no luck. Hidden away from returned humanity, in the shadows of the alley. Another flex saw a crackling of red electricity run over her hands. Rubis looked up to the blue sky, with the sun shining down on the buildings that cast shadow over her face. She cracked a smirk. The red electricity flowed through her and up into the pupils of her eyes. Michael had indeed once hoped that the portal might take him to Pree Possessing and Miss Rubis Rouge. But if only he'd focused on them individually. Each, at one time. For whilst Pree had been banished alongside humanity, Rubis had marched with the Dark Enabled army. If only Michael had managed to make his way to her, still bound to the earth enabled with electrical energy, with the portal not able to separate him between the two that he held in his mind.

*

A few days earlier, further out of London within a room at Windsor Castle, the Queen had been staring out from her window. Bright colours had taken to the sky as a dark and unsettling gloominess spanned across the castle, out across the land from the view of her window, followed by a piercing bright whiteness which sent the Queen falling to the floor. She felt as though she had left time and space. As if she'd been pulled from the universe. She panted slightly, as she pushed herself up off the ground. Not calling for any assistance, the Queen made her way back to the window and looked out at the now blue sky. A dark cloud had begun to form. Sparks of red took to it. The Queen took a deep breath, and exhaled.

Printed by Amazon Italia Logistica S.r.l.
Torrazza Piemonte (TO), Italy

41352169R00150